Buried deep in ~~...~~
peace...and a ~~...~~

Earth faces total domination by an alien force.
The Karanovo Stamp, the only key to freedom,
has been divided and scattered throughout the
ages. Now, a band of heroes, chosen for their
extraordinary gifts, find unexpected, passionate
love while braving dangers far beyond the
present in a desperate race against time....

Follow all four books in this thrilling new series
that continues with *Time Raiders: The Avenger.*

Time Raiders: The Seeker
(August 2009)
Lindsay McKenna

Time Raiders: The Slayer
(September 2009)
Cindy Dees

Time Raiders: The Avenger
(October 2009)
P.C. Cast

Time Raiders: The Protector
(November 2009)
Merline Lovelace

CINDY DEES

started flying airplanes while sitting in her dad's lap at the age of three and got a pilot's license before she got a driver's license. At age fifteen, she dropped out of high school and left the horse farm in Michigan where she grew up to attend the University of Michigan.

After earning a degree in Russian and East European Studies, she joined the U.S. Air Force and became the youngest female pilot in its history. She flew supersonic jets, VIP airlift and the C-5 Galaxy, the world's largest airplane. She also worked part-time gathering intelligence. During her military career, she traveled to forty countries on five continents, was detained by the KGB and East German secret police, got shot at, flew in the first Gulf War, met her husband and amassed a lifetime's worth of war stories.

Her hobbies include professional Middle Eastern dancing, Japanese gardening and medieval reenacting. She started writing on a one dollar bet with her mother and was thrilled to win that bet with the publication of her first book in 2001. She loves to hear from readers and can be contacted at www.cindydees.com.

CINDY DEES

THE
SLAYER
TIME RAIDERS

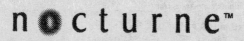

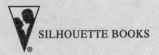

SILHOUETTE BOOKS

ISBN-13: 978-0-373-61818-7

Recycling programs
for this product may
not exist in your area.

TIME RAIDERS: THE SLAYER

Copyright © 2009 by Cynthia M. Dees, Lindsay McKenna and
Merline Lovelace

This is a work of fiction. Names, characters, places and incidents are
either the product of the author's imagination or are used fictitiously, and
any resemblance to actual persons, living or dead, business establishments,
events or locales is entirely coincidental.

This edition published by arrangement with Harlequin Books S.A.

® and TM are trademarks of Harlequin Books S.A., used under license.
Trademarks indicated with ® are registered in the United States Patent
and Trademark Office, the Canadian Trade Marks Office and in other
countries.

www.silhouettenocturne.com

Printed in U.S.A.

Dear Reader,

Every now and then a story comes into an author's life that is so special, so exciting and just so darned much fun that it practically writes itself. This was one of those for me. Of course, it didn't hurt that I got to work with three of my absolutely favorite authors, both as storytellers and as human beings. Then there was the fabulous concept of the Time Raiders to play with. And then there were Tessa and Rustam. From the first time I ever sat down to work on their story, they simply took over and whisked me away.

This book could not have happened without the able leadership of and input from Lindsay McKenna, Merline Lovelace and P.C. Cast. Nor could it have happened without the support and brilliance of Pattie Steele-Perkins, Tara Gavin and Shawna Rice. Lastly, this book could not have happened without the enthusiasm and brainstorming of the entire Rom Vets group—now some seventy female military-veteran authors strong and growing.

And maybe that's why this book is ultimately so special to me. A group of extraordinary women came together in creativity and friendship, applied their experience and professionalism to a joint project, and voilà. Magic happened.

I invite you now to sit back, relax and let the second installment of the Time Raiders' adventures sweep you up into the magic, too.

Happy reading!

Warmly,

Cindy Dees

The Beginning

Fifty thousand years ago, after discovering that human females carried a nascent genetic potential that might one day develop into the ability to star navigate, the Pleiadean Council planted a dozen pieces of a bronze disk, known as the Karanovo stamp, across the Earth, hidden in darkness until mankind advances enough to travel through time and find them.

And then, out of the ashes of the mystery-shrouded Roswell UFO crash in 1947, a secret research project called Anasazi arose. Its improbable goal: learn to use the recovered alien technology for the purposes of time travel. General Beverly Ashton was the last to command this project before a dozen time travelers were inexplicably lost and the project disbanded.

However, the recent discovery of an ancient journal, known as the *Ad Astra,* has given Professor Athena Carswell the information she needs to begin sending modern time travelers back through human history in search of the twelve pieces of the Karanovo Stamp. This stamp, when fully reassembled, will send a signal across the galaxy to the Pleiadean Council, indicating that mankind is ready to be introduced to the rest of the galactic community.

Project Anasazi has secretly been reactivated, and General Ashton, now retired, and Professor Carswell are continuing the project's work. They are carefully recruiting and training a team of military women to make the dangerous time jumps.

But threats loom on the horizon, both from humans who would see the project ended—or worse, steal its work and use it for nefarious ends—and from the Centaurian Federation, which will do anything to stop humans from learning how to navigate the stars....

Chapter 1

Her entire life had come down to this moment. Tessa stepped into the time-travel chamber and closed the booth's curved door. Deep silence surrounded her. The lab staff stood outside, watching her through the clear quartz panels, holding their collective breath as she settled into the comfortable recliner chair. Outside the booth, Dr. Athena Carswell did the same. Tessa watched the professor sink deep into her chair and don the crownlike brain-wave amplifier that would allow her to fling Tessa back in time more than two thousand years.

Calm suffused Tessa. Profound relief. Finally, an end to it all. A goodbye to this life one way or another—either by succeeding and leaping into a far-removed past or by failure of the jump and death. But either way, Tessa Marconi, weird kid turned psychic adult, was done with the mortal coil of the twenty-first century.

The hair on her arms stood up a moment before her skin began to tingle. The sensation built from mildly uncomfortable to an annoying itch to tongues of agony. It might have made a lesser person scream, but she embraced the pain.

She became aware of a subliminal hum—Athena Carswell's breathtaking brain power weaving a psychic bubble around her. The power swirled dizzyingly, and Tessa felt faintly nauseous. *Don't fight it. Ride the wave.* Previous time travelers had reported becoming ill, and it was possible that a few had even died because they'd failed to properly surf the time currents.

Athena herself looked to be an oasis of calm, as relaxed as if she were taking a nap. The only incongruity to the picture was the odd-looking headband she wore. Tessa didn't know the details, but the contraption's twin quartz crystals transformed the professor's thoughts into this crackling pocket of energy.

The lab seemed to waver and shimmer, and Tessa belatedly squeezed her eyes shut tightly. It was important that her brain receive no extraneous input that could anchor her too firmly in this time and place.

Any second now, the bubble would be complete and she would land in the past—twenty-five hundred years ago on a mission so important it might very well help determine the future of mankind. A nimbus of light built around her, bright enough that she had to restrain an impulse to lift her hand to shield her closed eyes. Her body started to feel lighter.

Ready or not, here goes nothing.

Abruptly, a new sound intruded upon Tessa's unnatural detachment—an earsplitting jangle of noise that startled her eyes wide open. Athena lurched in her armchair, jolted out of her trance. Alarm exploded across the scientist's features.

Not good.

The bubble around Tessa abruptly radiated a heat so unbearable she feared she might burst into flame. Frantically, she squeezed her eyes shut again.

Someone screamed, "Noooo!"

And then everything exploded around her.

* * *

Alexandra Patton, psychic medium and soon-to-be time traveler herself, raced across the lab toward Athena, shouting over the earsplitting Klaxon. "What the hell's going on?"

"Fire alarm!" one of the lab techs shouted back.

Alex frowned. "A fire? Here in the lab?"

The tech shook his head. "The computers are fine."

Alex lunged forward to help Professor Carswell struggle weakly to her feet. She steadied the scientist and they both rushed over to the complex panel of monitoring equipment, which was flickering ominously.

"Did you see her go?" the professor bit out.

Alex glanced at the empty transit platform. "No. I was distracted by the alarm. Why? Was something wrong with the jump?"

"I don't know. There was a disturbance in the time flow—"

The lab's door burst open. Alex whirled and snapped to the guard stumbling into the room, "I thought there were supposed to be *no* intrusions in this lab under any circum—"

A cloud of black smoke billowed in, carrying with it a fireman in full gear. He shouted through his Plexiglas face mask, "Clear the building, folks. Immediately."

"How close is the fire?" Alex asked sharply.

The man beckoned urgently with a gloved hand. "Let's go! One of you grab the back of my coat and the rest of you hang on to each other. The smoke's too thick to see through. Hold your breath and stay low. It's not far to the emergency exit."

Alex grabbed on to Athena's lab coat while the professor snatched at something on the way past her armchair, tucking it inside her clothes. They stumbled out into a darkness so thick and oppressive Alex literally couldn't see her hand in front of her face. It smelled awful, a noxious mix of burning wires and sulfuric stink. The smoke made her eyes water furiously, and long before they reached the exit, she was coughing violently. Thank God the guy had told them to hang on to each other. She clutched Professor Carswell's jacket grimly and staggered along behind her boss.

They burst outside, gasping for air. Alex fell to her knees, her eyes watering copiously while she coughed up a lungful of smoke. A half-dozen blurry black shadows sprinted past, heading into the building. Must be more firemen, or maybe they were spirits of the dead. God, she couldn't wait to get back to the peace of the tall-grass prairie, her refuge.

As soon as her lungs and eyes cleared enough to do it, Alex took a head count of the lab's staff. All present and accounted for. Except, of course, Tessa Marconi. She was gone. But where? Or more precisely, *when?*

Tessa slammed into something hard and cold, and lay on her side, gasping for air. *Nobody had warned her the landing would be so violent.* But hey. She felt pain. That meant she was alive, right? Relief washed over her.

Slowly she pushed up onto her hands and knees. And promptly got tangled up in the loosely draped fabric of a long cloak. Thankfully, appropriate clothes had materialized around her during the transit. In addition to flinging operatives all over creation, Athena Carswell was also able to produce period clothing and implant local language and customs in her agents as part of their time jumps. Thank goodness. Showing up here buck naked was the last thing Tessa needed. Wherever *here* was. Or more to the point, *when.*

In theory, time travel was as precise a science as flying a jet halfway around the world and landing on the first brick of a specific runway. But only a handful of people had ever done it, and only a few of them successfully.

Inky blackness swathed her. If she were lucky, that meant nobody had seen her blink into existence. She was in a small chamber of some kind with a stone floor. As her eyes adjusted to the darkness, she made out a faint outline, maybe a doorway.

Using the wall at her back for support, she crawled to her feet. Dizziness washed over her, and she leaned her forehead against the cool stone until the sensation passed. Still a little woozy, but burning with curiosity to find out when and where she was, she pushed away from the wall.

Something scuffed outside and she leaped to one side of the opening, plastering herself against the wall. Her head spun once more and she blinked hard to clear the stars from her eyes as she listened frantically for whoever was out there. What she wouldn't give right now for riot gear and a high-powered flashlight! But the ancient time into which she'd hopefully jumped precluded any modern equipment. Except, of course, a tiny emergency first-aid kit with antibiotics, painkillers, suture gear and a tiny toothbrush and dental floss. Athena had also promised to send Tessa a knife, fire-starting stones, a waterproof pouch and a handful of gold coins. There should be a few other sundries in her bag—a comb, some dried berries and nuts, a length of rope. And then there was her arm cuff, of course. The warm bronze armband clasped her left biceps reassuringly, holding the all-important quartz crystal imprinted with Tessa's unique brain wave pattern. Pressing upon the crystal would signal Athena to bring her back into the twenty-first century. It was Tessa's only ticket home.

Cautiously, she peered outside the tiny chamber. A towering stone column cast a deep shadow over the doorway. She'd seen similar columns in ancient ruins, but this one was intact and didn't show any wear and tear. As her eyes continued to adjust to the dark, she noticed colorful images painted upon its surface.

She'd done it. She'd arrived in some ancient time, and from the looks of that column, near some grand civilization.

Somewhere beyond the magnificent column, a dim flicker of light announced the presence of humans. She stepped through the doorway and stopped, staring in wonder. An entire colonnade of pristine Ionic columns stretched away in both directions. Could it be? Was she really standing in 480 B.C.? A thrill of delight raced through her.

"You there! What are ye about?" a gruff voice challenged from behind her.

She whipped around, her hands coming up into defensive readiness. *A short, thick man. Shaved head. Bare chest. Walnut-colored skin. Dressed in a short affair that was part skirt and part diaper.* But what riveted her attention was the lethal-looking scimitar he held, as if intimately familiar with its use.

"State your business, woman!"

Athena said Tessa had merely to think in modern English, and information implanted in her brain during the jump would make the translation to Persian as the words came out of her mouth. To test her supposed ability to speak the ancient tongue, Tessa spoke cautiously to the guard. "I'm lost."

"Who be ye?"

"I am Tessa of Marconi, a noblewoman in my homeland, but a stranger to this place."

The soldier's eyes narrowed. "Where be thy retainers and slaves if ye be noble?"

The guard definitely understood her. Whatever language she was speaking was appropriate to this place and time. She replied, "There has been an accident. My ship was wrecked upon these shores. I am alone."

He still looked suspicious. Crud. In her army experience, being in charge wasn't always about rank. Sometimes it was purely a function of who stepped up and took charge. She announced with authority, "Take me to whoever receives noble visitors." For good measure, she added firmly, "Immediately."

Apparently well-conditioned to following orders, the guard bent low at the waist in a bow. She followed as he walked briskly down the colonnade. Ahead of them, a buzz of noise gradually resolved itself into laughter, shouting and music, as if a party was in full swing.

Guards dressed like her escort were spaced at regular intervals along the colonnade. Shallow bowls rested on chest-high bronze stands, holding some sort of flaming oil that lit the open-air hall. The gaiety grew louder. The smells of spicy food, rancid wine and sweat assaulted her nose. People spilled out of the feast in pairs and groups, some laughing drunkenly, others singing bawdy songs in various tongues. She recognized snippets of Greek and Egyptian from her studies of ancient languages and heard several dialects she couldn't even begin to guess at.

A few guests indulged in more physical entertainments. She averted her eyes from the graphic sight of a fat, bald fellow partaking of a young man on his hands and knees behind one of the columns. The catamite caught her eye and smiled lewdly at her, licking his lips.

A woman screamed, the sound cut off abruptly as a group of young men closed in around the female in question. Tessa didn't want to know.

Her guide stopped at the entrance arch to an enormous hall and made a sweeping gesture with his arm. "I present to you the imperial court of the king of kings, ruler of the Medes and Achemens, of Ethiopia and India and all between, His Glorious Majesty Emperor Xerxes of Parsa."

Xerxes. Athena had done it. The professor had managed to deliver her to her exact destination—the court of the legendary Persian emperor. If Athena's timing had been as accurate, Xerxes had already marched his massive army across the Hellespont, and around the northern shore of the Aegean Sea. He should be in the final stages of preparation for his assault on Athens.

Tessa stepped up beside the guard. And stared.

The imperial court of His Glorious Majesty Emperor Xerxes of Parsa was currently engaged in a giant, drunken orgy.

"Wait thou here while I find thee a member of the court."

She nodded, unable to tear her gaze away from the decadent

scene. Bright colors assaulted her eyes everywhere she looked in the dim cavern: women bedecked in jewel-toned gauze; elaborate rugs on the marble floors; mosaics and frescoes on the plastered walls and ceiling depicting bloody battles, hunts and lascivious sexual indulgences.

Huge brass braziers emitted flickering light and sweet-smelling smoke that curled, serpentlike, around the pillars and contributed to the thick haze hanging over the room. Slave girls fed reclining men orange slices and red grapes. Young men danced drunkenly to the strains of twangy stringed instruments and nasal-sounding horns.

And bodies. Half-naked or exposed in all their glory, bodies writhed everywhere in a mass of multiethnic humanity that covered every horizontal surface—the floors, the low, cushioned couches around the edges of the room, even the table-tops. In a single glance, Tessa observed more variations upon a sexual theme than she could ever possibly imagine.

Purposeful movement drew her eyes. Her guard was return-ing with a man who was blessedly dressed and walking in a straight enough line that he must not be completely snockered.

This new man stopped in front of her. He gave her dark cloak and hood a once-over while she clutched both more closely about her. "Welcome to the court of Emperor Xerxes, my lady. With whom do I have the honor of conversing?"

Time to put her cover story into action. The historians back at the Project Anasazi lab had worked it out. They'd decided it would be too dangerous for her to come to this time as a female commoner. She would have to pose as at least a minor noble so that no one made her a slave and restricted her movements while she searched for a piece of the medallion.

She replied as regally as she could muster, "I am Lady Tessa of Marconi. I come from lands far to the north and west of this place. A storm has cast my ship upon these shores. I fear I am the sole survivor."

Interest sparked in the retainer's gaze. "What empire holds sway in your country?"

"No empire. The holdings of each local lord are his alone to protect and rule."

"Are these holdings large? Rich? Fertile, perhaps?"

She shrugged under her cloak. "Large, yes. Rich?" She gazed around the hall. "Not by these standards. Fertile? Famine is completely unknown in my home. We have such an abundance of meat and grain that my people sell a huge surplus each harvest." And wouldn't the average American farmer get a kick out of being described that way?

The retainer looked decidedly intrigued now. Almost as if he were calculating the income from seizing her lands. "Have you supped, Lady Tessa?"

"I have not."

"Come. Let us break bread together."

Something tickled the back of her mind about the significance of breaking bread with someone—must be some local custom that Athena had implanted. Tessa frowned. Better safe than sorry. "Forgive me, kind sir, but I do not hunger. Perhaps I may warm myself by a fire for a few minutes and then seek my rest?"

The retainer frowned, but replied courteously enough, "As you wish. Come with me."

She picked her way gingerly across the room, dodging some of the more…athletic endeavors of the guests. Her host deposited her by a fireplace so large she'd need to stand on a chair to touch its mantel. A roaring blaze poured out heat. She was already warm under her sturdy cloak but wasn't about to take off the garment and risk rape in this assembly of debauched drunks.

Not to mention that the professor could very well have dressed her like a freaking harem girl under this cloak. Tessa had already registered a complete lack of undergarments, and a suspicious breeze had wafted up her skirts as she'd followed the guard earlier.

If time of day translated during time travel, it should be barely 9:00 p.m., but this party looked to be well advanced. She was hungry and hot and more than half tempted to leave. But academic curiosity got the best of her. Was Xerxes here tonight, in the flesh? The name of the fabled Persian emperor still echoed down through history. He'd assembled the largest army in the history of mankind for the purpose of invading Greece, but ultimately failed. Tessa had studied the histories of the invasion in detail. She probably knew the names of many of the lesser kings and generals in this very room.

She scanned the hundreds of men in the hall, seeking some indication of which one might be the mighty emperor. Many wore jeweled circlets and a few wore the crowns of kings who served the Persian emperor. The variety of race and dress was impressive. But then, the Persian Empire spanned North Africa, Eastern Europe, all of the Middle East, and stretched well into Central Asia.

Which of these were General Masistes, Xerxes's brother, and General Mardonius, ill-fated commander of the doomed invasion of Greece? Was Artaxerxes, heir to the throne, here? Maybe even Xerxes's Jewish Empress, Esther, of Old Testament fame? Despite the perspiration plastering Tessa's dress to her skin, the thought of standing in the presence of these giants of history made chills race across the back of her neck.

Unfortunately, historic celebrity spotting wasn't her purpose for being here. Finding a piece of the Karanovo stamp was. The stamp was an incredibly important bronze medallion, decorated with depictions of the constellations of the zodiac. When all twelve pieces of it were assembled, it was supposed to signal some faraway council that mankind was ready to enter the ranks of star-traveling races. Tessa's job was to find and retrieve a piece of the medallion.

To that end, she cast her mental awareness outward, seeking the distinctive sine-wave signature of the bronze wedge. *Hmm.*

Not in the room, but definitely in the vicinity. Off to the east. She zeroed in on it more tightly. A clear pinprick of energy tickled her second sight. It was not buried; rather it was out in the open in some way. She sensed wood near it. Moving toward water. The signature was unmistakable, just like the other Karanovo piece she'd handled.

Outstanding. This mission was going to be a piece of cake. She'd make a graceful exit out of this den of iniquity, find the segment of the medallion, then activate her cuff and let Athena bring her home.

If anything, faint disappointment filled her at how easy this was turning out to be. She'd hoped to spend a little time here. But if all went well, she might be in this era for only a few minutes. Bummer.

A raucous cheer went up twenty or thirty feet away from her, making her jump. A stunning brunette had stepped up onto a raised dais at one side of the room. Her high-waisted red gown was elaborately embroidered—and transparent. The diaphanous silk barely clung to her breasts, in open defiance of gravity. A gaudy necklace dripping with what looked like pigeon's-blood rubies encircled the woman's long neck. She raised graceful arms, swathed in jeweled bangles.

Her voice was huskier than Tessa expected, earthy and dripping in sex, when she called out over the din, "Do you wish to see my sorcerer perform?"

A roar went up. Many of the otherwise occupied guests disengaged, to make their way toward the woman. With an excellent sense of theatrical timing, the brunette waited until the noise died down and the musicians had been waved to silence.

When every eye in the place was firmly fixed on her, she called with grand dramatic flair, "Bring forth my magician! I, Queen Artemesia, present to you the shape-shifter of Halicarnassus!"

Artemesia! Tessa stood up eagerly to get a better look at the legendary woman who'd ruled the seafaring kingdom of Halicarnassus single-handedly and with great success. How incredible to have read about this Persian noble in Herodotus's histories and now to be standing before her in the flesh. Delia McCowan, a colleague back in Arizona and a time-travel veteran, had warned her of how strange it could be finding oneself in the midst of living history. But this…this was beyond amazing.

Artemesia was speaking again. Something about a man who could become a beast before their very eyes. Tessa raised a skeptical brow. She didn't for a moment doubt the existence of psychic skills—hers were formidable—but *shape-shifting?* This she had to see. She looked across the crowd at the heavy curtain behind Artemesia. One of the advantages of being five foot seven in ancient Persia was that in this assemblage, she was taller than all of the women and many of the men.

The curtain behind Artemesia swept open.

A tall man stepped forward—tall even by modern standards. Such was the arrogance of his demeanor that, had he not already been identified otherwise, Tessa would have pegged him as Xerxes. His skin was bronze, but more as if tanned than genetic. Dark brown hair flowed in a mane about his shoulders. His eyes were blacker than any depravity this room could hold, snapping with disdain for the mere mortals at his feet. No wonder folks in this time period believed in gods, if men like this walked among them!

His features were classic—strong jaw, high cheekbones, smooth brow. His nose was as arrogant as he was. A slave ran up and unlatched the man's cloak, whisking away the scarlet wool with a flourish.

A sigh went up from the assemblage. The sorcerer was naked above the waist, his lower body draped in little more than a linen towel held in place around his hips with a jeweled belt. And what a body. It was as perfect as his face. His shoulders were broad and powerful, his arms wreathed in corded muscles.

Artemesia stepped close to him and ran her hand possessively across his belly. The sorcerer's stomach muscles contracted into a six-pack a bodybuilder would envy. The queen's long fingernails left four red trails across his skin. Tessa's gut tightened, as well. There was something…primal about this man. Almost animal. Raw and sexual.

Artemesia looked toward the far end of the room and called out, "Majesty, perhaps you would honor us by choosing a beast for this display!"

Tessa craned her head to see who the woman addressed, but a large cluster of guards crowded around whoever answered. A male voice shouted back, "Let us have an elephant!"

A cheer went up and all eyes fastened on the sorcerer.

Tessa watched with interest as the magician raised his hands chest high, his palms facing outward toward the crowd. He closed his eyes and released a slow breath. Several women screamed. People in the first few rows of the audience cringed back in terror. A collective gasp rose around her. Tessa glanced around, startled. Everyone stared at the sorcerer. Quickly, she glanced back at him. *What was going on?* He looked fine to her, just standing there with his hands out.

His contemptuous gaze raked across the crowd, passed over her, then jerked back. Across the heads of the assemblage, the two of them locked gazes. His black eyes drilled into hers with an intelligence, a razor sharpness, that stripped her bare. And she had plenty to hide. As the stare stretched out, it was as if he willed her to come to him and submit to him. But she was no wilting lily to be so easily intimidated. She was a military officer, a combat veteran who'd braved the mostly male ranks of the U.S. Army and earned the grudging respect of men determined to despise her. At least until they'd discovered her little secret. It turned out that the army rank and file weren't quite ready for psychics to command them.

The sorcerer was staring at her as if he already knew about

her gift—or curse, as it were. His hands fell heedlessly to his sides, his gaze still locked on hers. Another gasp went up from the crowd, and then cheers and wild applause erupted, along with shouts to do it again.

Still he stared at her.

Okay, he was starting to creep her out, here.

"A monster! A monster!" the crowd shouted. "Make yourself into a monster!"

Tessa took a step back, then another. An intense need to get away from this man and his sledgehammer charisma overwhelmed her.

He took an aggressive step forward, but Artemesia grabbed him by the arm and pulled. Impatiently, he shook off the queen's hand, still staring at Tessa. Thankfully, he didn't pursue her as she backed away from the fireplace. From him.

Clearly irritated, he glanced down at his queen, who was saying something inaudible to him. Tessa seized upon his momentary distraction. Turned. And fled like a big dog from the Sorcerer of Halicarnassus.

Chapter 2

Great galaxies above. Who was that woman?

Rustam shook off Artemesia like a pesky fly, while across the room the stranger's aura crackled, practically violet around her. Only a psychic of extraordinary power could gather so much energy to herself and not implode. Other thoughts, desperately hopeful thoughts, crowded in. Had someone come for him? Was he finally rescued?

"Make yourself into a monster," Artemesia hissed.

"Not now," he snapped back.

"Do it or I will have you whipped."

He might be her slave, but even she knew not to cross certain lines with him. He was fortunate that she was the sexual predator she was—and that he could sate her appetites as few men could. Otherwise, his lot in life here would have been much worse. Even without the sex, though, he held a measure of power because of his psychic abilities that even she could not deny.

"Touch me with the rod and you will die where you stand, woman."

Artemesia jerked back. "Mind your tongue," she muttered.

He looked up to where the glowing stranger stood by the fire. Curses! She was gone. Who *was* she?

Irritably, he turned his attention to the rabble at his feet. Ignorant and superstitious, their minds were child's play to manipulate. Sending an image of himself as some creature or another barely required conscious thought, let alone tapped his true mental power. Maybe because he was angry that the stranger had slipped away, or maybe to teach Artemesia a lesson, he sent them all an image of the most gruesome creature he could imagine.

The crowd screamed in horror. *There. Let that be the stuff of legends for centuries to come.* He projected the image long enough to give everyone nightmares tonight. Then, in disgust, he dropped the sending and leaped easily from the stage, leaving Artemesia to make her own way. A pair of eunuchs jumped forward to lift her down.

He strode across the room in search of that globe of violet energy and the woman it hovered around. The entire room was still suffused with a faint afterglow of the stranger's aura. Incredible. He pretended not to hear Artemesia calling out to him in that demanding whine of hers, which set his teeth on edge. But then a pair of Immortals, Xerxes's personal guards, grabbed him by each arm. He could've fought them, and likely defeated them, but a dozen more guards would replace them. The idea was to stay alive long enough to escape this godforsaken court and get back home.

He stopped, chagrined.

Artemesia's arms wrapped around him from behind and she purred in his ear. When *would* the woman learn that he was not fond of things feline?

"Does not the feast put you in the mood for pleasure, Rustam?" she murmured seductively.

The woman was attractive enough, her sexual appetites sufficiently depraved to keep even him mildly entertained. But he wasn't in the mood tonight. Apparently, she wasn't going to take no for an answer, however. Meanwhile, the residue of the strange woman nipped at Rustam's skin and frayed his mind until he was so edgy he could hardly contain his own power.

He looked around urgently for a convenient male. Someone of sufficient rank and political influence for Artemesia to deem worthy of her attention. Someone young and strong enough to pleasure her long into the night. *There.* The distinctive toga of a visiting Greek. Rustam recalled hearing that some general was newly arrived, Hippoclides of Dardanus. He'd supposedly come to negotiate an eleventh-hour peace with Xerxes before the Persian emperor annihilated Athens and conquered all of Greece.

The Greek's back was turned, but from the massive musculature of his bare shoulders he was a bull of a man, fit and in his prime. Impatiently, Rustam reached out with his mind and dragged the Greek away from a goblet of wine and to his feet. A group of drunk Persian nobles stumbled past, staggering intentionally by accident into the Greek with shouts of laughter.

Rustam took a quick step, placing himself directly behind the general. Planting his hand between the man's shoulder blades, he physically shoved Hippoclides at Artemesia.

As the Greek bumped into the Persian queen and grabbed her to steady her with an exclamation of apology, Rustam mentally blasted them both with a full broadside of lust. Sparks practically jumped off the couple as they gazed into each other's eyes. The queen grabbed the Greek's hand without a word and dragged him off toward her chambers. There. That ought to keep Artemesia occupied for a while.

The residue of his mind blast sent the entire hall into a renewed frenzy of sexual activity. Tonight he'd have no trouble collecting a bedful of beautiful women eager to experience the legendary sexual prowess of the Sorcerer of Halicarnassus. Only one woman was on his mind, however. A shadowed form in a dark cloak and bathed in power.

He roamed the hall in tense frustration. No sign of her anywhere! He accosted several court servitors, and none of them knew where the tall, fair, newly arrived woman might be. Swearing under his breath, he slipped out of the orgy into a servant's tunnel that led to the kitchens. He ducked into a dark niche, tucking his tall form into the low arch. He closed his eyes and reached out cautiously with his mind.

Ever so gently, he mentally searched the palace, seeking out that enormous bubble of power. The trick was to locate her without her becoming aware of his probing. The task took concentration he hadn't bothered to muster in months. *Damn.* He was getting lazy in his accidental captivity. He must get back into the habit of exercising his mind powers.

There. In the south pavilion of one of the lesser palaces: a burst of energy that made the fine, dark hairs on his forearms stand up. He opened his eyes and moved swiftly down the tunnel.

Cautiously, he approached a small chamber, the kind allotted to minor nobles of little political importance. Odd. No guard stood at the door. What noblewoman would dare to travel alone? He eased up the iron latch and pushed her door open. No sword dropped across the opening to bar his entry. He sniffed the air experimentally. No one stood immediately on the other side of the wooden panel. He slipped silently into the unlit chamber.

Moonlight shone through the open window, falling across the floor between his feet and a low bed against the far wall. Gauze curtains were pulled around it, hiding the bed's occupant. He eased forward, skirting the blue-white shaft of light. He pulled his own power inward as much as he could, minimizing his aura so as not to give warning to the stranger.

He drew near the bed. A lone figure lay upon it, not under the covers. Expecting trouble? Gentle curves and long legs announced her to be a woman, and tall, the same one he'd seen earlier. Her violet aura was not so strong now that she was at rest, but a faint lavender glow suffused the room. In its dim illumination, he made out exquisite, exotic features.

He started. This woman was *not* of Persian descent. In fact, she didn't look as if she came from anywhere in this part of the world. What in heaven's name was she doing here? His people would have sent a man after him to bring him home, not some woman. So who was she? What other heretofore unknown society possessed the same psychic power that his did?

He must find out.

He gathered himself, bunching his muscles, and sprang forward, straddling the woman's hips with his knees, clamping one hand on her neck and the other over her mouth. She lurched in surprise, but, interestingly enough, did not attempt to scream. Her body was slender, but strong, beneath him. She fought just long enough to test her restraints, and then subsided. Her eyes didn't reflect the sort of panic they should have. Oh, she looked scared enough, but she also looked determined. No, she was by no means done resisting him. She was merely biding her time.

She reached up fast and gave his thumb a good yank. With a man of average strength, she'd have ripped it nearly off his hand. As it was, he merely tightened his grip and grunted in annoyance. But then her knee jerked up sharply, connecting solidly between his legs. Agony exploded in him, and his grip loosened. The woman wrenched free of his grasp, scrambling clear of his thighs to the far side of the bed, against the wall.

She dared attack him? Rage, white-hot and pure, consumed him. Were he not exceedingly curious as to who this woman was, she'd be dead where she cowered this very instant. He gritted his teeth, rode the waves of pain and managed—barely—to hang on to his temper.

"Who are you? What do you want?" she demanded.

Lying on his side, curled in a ball, he ground out, "I might ask the same of you." As the worst of the agony receded, reluctant admiration for her fierce self-defense tickled at the edges of his awareness. She would make a worthy mate. And the sons they could breed—

"You're the one who barged into my room and accosted me," she retorted tersely. "Identify yourself."

No woman of this place would dare be so blunt with a man like him, particularly not one in her bedroom, alone with her. She ought to be screaming for her life. Definitely a traveler from a distant land. But where?

He looked up, wincing. The woman actually looked ready to fly at him! Self-defense he could forgive. But a female attacking a male outright? Fury, still lurking just below the surface of his mind, bubbled up. She had no right to challenge him! He gathered power to blast her, but restrained himself at the last moment. He wanted answers before he turned her brain to mush.

He surged up onto his knees, towering over her, clearly a great deal stronger and more physically dominant than she. He felt better. The woman's aggressive posture wilted. She crossed her arms defensively now. Apparently, she knew not to tangle with a sorcerer in his prime. But she still had the temerity to glare at him.

She said nothing, so he waited her out for several seconds. He'd never met a female who could keep her mouth shut to save her life—except for this one, apparently. The silence stretched out. How odd. He'd need to proceed carefully with her.

Jaw clenched, he said, "I am called Rustam. How shall I call you?"

"Tessa."

"What sort of name is that?"

"My name. And that's enough."

He snorted. "Don't announce that around here. It sounds like a shortened form of Tessalonia, a common Greek name. People have been killed for less."

"Actually, it's French."

He was not familiar with the term. He probed her mind to see if she was thinking of a location, but hit a blank—an entirely disconcerting wall. Startled, he demanded, "How did you come to be here, Tessa?"

"I thought you said I shouldn't use that name."

"We're alone." He would have to be more subtle to get past her barriers. He sent her a faint mental thread of trust. Relaxation. Eagerness to talk. "You didn't answer my question. How did you come here?"

She shrugged. And said nothing. That, too, was strange. His mental suggestion hadn't worked. He amped up the sending of desire to talk to him.

If anything, she frowned and seemed to draw further into herself. Which reminded him...

He blurted, "What did you see when I shape-shifted into the elephant?"

"Nothing."

"Nothing?" he exclaimed. Was she *immune* to his mind powers? It couldn't be! Were *her* powers actually more powerful than his? His mind raced with the possibilities of that prospect—none of them good for his kind. He had to get back home and warn his leaders! And while he was at it, he'd love to take this woman along as his hostage to prove his point. But first he had to find a way to subdue her.

"I saw nothing," she repeated. "You just stood there with your hands up while everyone acted like you'd grown a second head."

"Not a second head," he replied drily. "I merely turned the one I have into an elephant's."

"I never saw a thing."

Fascinating. Experimentally, he sent her a forceful command to tell him what she was doing here. And got back a slight frown. He asked, "Would you mind if I held your hand?"

"Yes, I'd mind!"

He sighed. "I vow not to hurt you. 'Tis but a small experiment."

"What sort of experiment?"

"Trust me. I only want to hold your hand."

"I think not."

He moved forward, close enough to see her individual eyelashes in the moonlight. Still she didn't cringe. A brave soul, indeed. Even Artemesia would be shrinking away from him by now. He looked down at this woman in the dark. And unleashed the full power of his mind until their auras mingled, the crackling arcs of his blue and her violet twining about them in a sensuous dance.

Her energy field bit into his skin everywhere it touched, like the tentacles of a jellyfish, leaving a sharp tingling in its wake. *Gods, the power of this woman!* Did his energy field do the same to her, or was she entirely immune to it? She shifted restlessly before him. Apparently, she felt it at least a little, at any rate.

Very slowly, he lifted a hand toward her. Treating her like a newborn foal shy of its first touch by man, he moved his fingertips until they were a bare whisper away from her cheek. Her power danced across his palm, sending his nerves into a riot of nearly forgotten sensation. Carefully, slowly, he aligned his vibrational frequency to hers until the pain of her nearness subsided.

Synced up with his, her aura slammed into him in an entirely new wave of sensation, as alluring as the former had been uncomfortable. She was all light and heat and warm breath across his skin, sending a bolt of intense desire through him. By comparison, the local women might as well have been made of mud.

He'd *forgotten*. It had been so long since he'd been with one of his own kind, he'd forgotten what a psychic link did to the sex act.

He couldn't resist. His fingertips grazed her cheek. Ahh. Soft. Alive. She inhaled sharply, and he withdrew his touch immediately. But the damage was done. She'd loosed a terrible craving in him. For *more*. More of her velvet softness. More of that sizzling electricity between them.

"Who *are* you?" she whispered.

He intoned in a deep voice from someplace subconscious within him, "I am your destiny."

Tessa stared up at the intruder for a moment in complete disbelief. These Persian alpha males were awfully darn sure of themselves. She couldn't help it; she laughed. "That's the dumbest line I've ever heard," she chuckled.

Thunder gathered on the big man's brow.

Whoops. She wasn't a modern woman anymore. This was the ancient world, where women were treated little better than cattle, and valued less. She reined in her mirth and did her best to assume a contrite tone. "My apologies. But I do not know you at all. It's hard to credit such a declaration from a complete stranger."

His brow smoothed out, but lightning continued to flash in his black gaze.

"What do you want from me?" she asked.

"How is it you did not see my trick?"

Ahh. The shape-shifting thing. "I have no idea. I just…didn't see it. Maybe I'm too skeptical for such things to work on me."

"I don't believe it."

"Honestly, I have no explanation. I actually would have liked to have seen what the others saw. They seemed tremendously impressed."

He appeared slightly mollified by that confession. They stared at each other in silence for several seconds.

"In case you hadn't noticed, this is my bedchamber," she said gently, "and you're in it. I was trying to sleep when you barged in."

"Are you throwing me out?"

Was that amusement or disbelief in his voice?

"I'm afraid so."

"You still haven't answered my question. What brings you here?"

She shrugged. "I have been shipwrecked. I am far from home."

"Far indeed," he echoed significantly.

Tessa lurched. It almost sounded as if he knew…. Impossible! Even the idea of time travel would be too far-fetched for the ancient mind to conceive of, let alone believe in.

"We enter into the game, then," he murmured.

Alarm exploded within her. She asked quickly, "What game?"

He cocked an eyebrow. "The dance between a man and woman as they circle closer to one another…." His voice was husky and low, sandpaper on her skin, sending shivers through her. "Letting the suspense build until they give in to mutual attraction and indulge in their forbidden desires and fantasies with one another."

Forbidden desires and—

Whoa.

Military mission. Seek lost medallion piece. Bring it back to Arizona. Save the world…. Nope, nowhere in her mission briefing was there any mention of falling into the sack with the hunky Persian guy. Damn.

He moved even closer, managing to make walking on his knees on a soft mattress graceful. He invaded her personal space until she backed away from him and felt cool stone at her back.

"That's far enough, Tonto," she warned.

"Who is Tonto? Is he a lover I must kill to have you?"

She stared. This guy sounded serious! Lord, he was big. Overwhelmingly so. Sleek. And very, very male. The way these ancient guys embraced being macho was surprisingly attractive.

"Not to worry. Tonto is merely a character from a well-known story in my land."

He planted a hand on the wall beside her head, his voice dropping to a half whisper that made her belly go liquid. "Tell me this story."

"Tomorrow. I'll tell you tomorrow. But in case you hadn't noticed, it's the middle of the night."

"'Tis early still. The feasting will go on for hours yet."

Feasting. Right. Was that what he called that mad orgy? He planted his free hand on the other side of her head, effectively trapping her. No way could she take this guy out by brute force. He'd completely ignored a thumb lock that would have put most men on the ground in agony.

He leaned in close enough so his warm breath caressed her temple. "We have all night, you and I."

All night? Abruptly, images of the two of them naked in a tangle of sheets, making love until she was too sated to move, roared through her brain. Her breath hitched in a way no man had ever made it hitch before.

"Ahh," he whispered. "You do see it, after all."

Befuddled by the haze of lust in her brain, she looked up into his eyes. "See what?" she mumbled, as more images of crawling all over that big, muscular body of his danced before her mind's eye.

He lurched, pulling back far enough to stare down at her. "You sent to *me*? How did you do that?" he demanded.

"Do what?"

"You sent that image to my mind!"

"I…what?" Color her confused, here.

He closed in on her so fast she barely saw him coming, let alone had time to mount any sort of defense. His hands grasped her upper arms, pulling her like a rag doll against his chest, which was as solid as the stone wall behind her—only burning with heat and pounding with lust.

"I *saw* that," he said through gritted teeth. "Don't toy with me, daughter of French—I'll chew you up and spit you out. Tell me how you sent that to my mind."

She didn't know why she did it. Maybe the driving desire pressing in on her from all sides just became too much for her. Maybe it was frustration at finding this Neanderthal so damned attractive. Or maybe she was just stupid enough to rise to the guy's bait. But she tipped her chin up fast, too fast to stop and think it over. And kissed him.

Chapter 3

They stood in the wreckage of the lab, soot-blackened and dripping wet. Alex looked around in disgust. Dooming mankind or not, Project Anasazi had just taken a kick in the butt. So, just what the hell would happen if the time travelers of Project Anasazi didn't find the twelve pieces of the Karanovo Stamp and put it back together? Would invaders from the Centaurian Federation come here and destroy every woman on the planet? It was probably true, even if it sounded like sci-fi bullshit.

Alex snorted. And if someone had told her a year ago that such a thought would enter her mind and not cause her to think she'd gone crazy, she'd have never believed them. But then, she heard dead people talk and wasn't crazy, either.

And Carswell wanted her to jump next? Alex had two words for the professor: *hell no*.

She picked her way over to where Professor Carswell was staring down at a ruined computer console.

"Project Anasazi is over, isn't it?" Alex asked quietly.

Athena looked up, startled. "Of course not. I've still got the headband, and the programming to amplify its sine waves is a fairly straightforward algorithm. I even have backup copies of the software. I can be up and running again in a matter of hours. It may take a few days to repair the booth, but it's not a difficult job. And of course, the *Ad Astra* notebook is safely tucked away."

"Well, that's good. And I hope Tessa is okay, but you don't look so great, Professor. What's really going on?"

Athena's penetrating gaze pinned her in place. "There's not a scorch mark anywhere in the room. Not one."

Alex looked around with fresh eyes. The professor was right.

Athena continued, "Explain to me why, then, if the blaze never reached this lab, the firemen ransacked every desk and filing cabinet, and smashed every computer in this room to smithereens?"

Alex didn't say anything. She decided at that moment that she would wish Project Anasazi all the best, but there was no damn way she was going to follow Tessa in this suicide mission.

The instant their lips touched, their auras blended into an indigo vortex of such intensity Rustam could hardly look at it. The power writhed around them, sinuous and seeking, forcing them inevitably together. Her mouth opened beneath his in a gasp of surprise—and desire such as he'd never felt raged up in him. She tasted of mint. And her pheromones shouted of sex. His arms swept around her and he all but inhaled her.

It was too much. His mind lost control of it all, and the power around them leaped and spun wildly. A frisson of alarm skittered down his spine. Uncontrolled power of this magnitude was incredibly dangerous. It could destroy them both.

Tessa's arms crept around his neck and the colored strands

flew even faster, whirling crazily about them. Their energy fields merged into a burning sphere so bright he was forced to close his eyes against its blinding glare. It built and built until it went supernova, exploding around them in a display of fireworks that buffeted his mind so violently he barely managed to remain conscious.

Tessa collapsed against him with a cry, her body limp in his arms. Had she fainted? Dizzy himself, he held her close while she slowly roused. A familiar, but stronger than normal, thumping sound startled him. And then he recognized it. Their hearts. Beating as one in perfect simpatico.

And he was lost.

Out of the sudden blackness around them, completely devoid of blue or violet, came a new sensation: her lips moving against his neck, soft and warm. He tucked his chin down to gaze at her, and she lifted her face. Kissed him again, pulling him into her effortlessly. He had no will left to resist. Down, down he fell, into an endless, dark tunnel of need so overpowering he could barely form thoughts, let alone resist it. He was helpless in the face of her feminine allure. If she was the weapon of a new breed of magicians, then his people were well and truly lost. Not only was he incapable of fighting her, he had no desire to fight *this*. None. Even if it led him to his doom. He was mesmerized. Entranced. The great sorcerer ensorcelled.

"Tessa," he groaned, "what have you done to me?"

They fell onto the bed together. Her slender body moved sensuously across his and he could only fling his arms wide and surrender, to let her have her way with him. Her thigh rubbed across his arousal, her lush breasts pressing through thin fabric against his bare chest. Her nails lightly raked his neck and shoulders, sending frissons of pleasure shuddering across his skin. Her hair fell in a white-gold curtain about them, glistening in the moonlight.

"What have *you* done to *me?*" she muttered.

He mustered the strength to spear his hands into her hair. To force her to look into his eyes. "Nay, 'tis most assuredly you who have beguiled me. What magic did you use?"

She stared down at him in the moonlight, her eyes wide, and so mesmerizing he could lose himself in their silver depths forever.

Gathering all his remaining strength, he reversed their positions, his right forearm holding her shoulders down, his weight squashing any thought of movement on her part. His thigh forced her legs apart, and she sprawled wantonly, his for the taking, beneath him. He'd searched for a woman like this ever since he'd reluctantly accepted that he might be stuck in this place forever. And to think she'd just walked into his life out of the clear blue. What were the odds…?

And then the rage came—his old friend. His wellspring. The storm within from whence came all his power. *What were the odds, indeed?* Grateful for his fury's return, he welcomed its maelstrom. A need to dominate this woman consumed him. To take her by force and brand her with the mark of him for all time…

Caution of who and what she was slammed into him. She'd already let slip a small demonstration of her mental powers when she forced a sexual image into his brain, past his formidable mental defenses. He stared down at her, trembling beneath him, appearing completely at his mercy. Surely Tessa wasn't as helpless as all this. She was going to tempt him to rape her, and then, in his moment of climax, when all his mental defenses were down, she would destroy him.

He flung himself away from her, springing off the bed furiously. "I will not fall for your tricks!" he snarled.

She sat up, looking small and forlorn. A fine actress, Lady Tessa of Marconi.

"I am no green boy you can bewitch. I am a—" he broke off. *He must never utter those words aloud in this place.* "I am a mighty warrior and a great sorcerer. No woman will get the best of me."

Tessa's eyes glittered in irritation. "From the way you're ranting and raving, I'd say I've already gotten the best of you."

He took an aggressive step toward the bed. Still, she didn't flinch. And yet again he was struck by her audacity. Was she simply dense, or really so brave—and foolish? Even Artemesia had the good sense not to bait him when he was in a towering temper like this.

"Get. Out." Her voice was clear. Calm. Forceful. Her words fell like crystals, shattering upon his eardrums.

She dared to toss him out? Him? Off balance, he knew not whether to roar with rage or howl with laughter. Time. He needed some time to regain his equilibrium. To think about the presence of this woman and what it meant.

"This is not over, my fair-haired seductress. Not by a long shot." And with that, he stormed out of the room.

Bright sunlight woke Tessa the next morning. That and the oddest noise. It was loud. Vaguely human. A rumbling roar of sound all around her. What in the world? Perplexed, she arose and threw back the slatted wood shutters.

And stared.

Stretching away on the plain lay a vast tent city, extending as far as the eye could see. The sound was coming from soldiers. Training in sweeping formations, tending equipment, lounging at rest. Tens of thousands of them.

Professor Carswell had dropped her smack-dab in the middle of the Persian army!

As part of her military training, Tessa had studied great battles through history, picked apart the tactics, and here she stood in the midst one of history's greatest armies. A shiver rippled through her. Of thrill or trepidation, she wasn't sure. Maybe both.

How far along was the invasion of Greece, anyway? Had the legendary battle of Thermopylae and the heroic stand of the Spartans happened yet? Had Athens fallen? The great naval battle of Salamis taken place?

How was she supposed to find a bronze wedge, small enough to fit in the palm of her hand, in the middle of all this? She cast her mind outward, seeking the prize. Only a muddled tingle that might be its distinctive signature reached her. The number of triangular bits of bronze out there with all those soldiers and their equipment had to number in the millions. She might have found needles in haystacks before, but this was ridiculous. She had a remarkable talent for finding lost things, but *this* remarkable…

If she spent a year in this place, she couldn't search a hundredth of that massive gathering of humanity in front of her. Now what?

The plan was to retrieve the bronze wedge ASAP, then return home with all due haste. And, she amended mentally, to stay far, far away from the Sorcerer of Halicarnassus in the meantime. She didn't know what had come over her last night when he'd barged into her room and her bed, but in the bright light of day, their spectacular kiss couldn't be attributed to anything other than temporary insanity. She was on an ultrasecret military mission, for goodness sake. The last thing she needed to do was get entangled with some local man, particularly a very distracting one.

No help for it. She had to take a deep breath and start searching for the section of the medallion. And hope she got lucky.

After availing herself of the chamber pot, she pulled on the high-waisted, loose-weave, white linen dress Athena had conjured for her. The embroidered decoration was unobtrusive, but exquisitely done. Not so gaudy as to draw attention to herself, but finely enough made to declare her high status in society. She tucked her all-important bronze-and-quartz cuff safely under the left sleeve, where it clasped her arm a couple of inches above the elbow.

Time to find herself a hunk of bronze.

This search was supposed be a breeze. After all, she'd seen and handled the mate to her missing medallion, and had a precise sense of the vibrational energy it put out. She'd try again to locate it, concentrating fully this time.

Tessa sat down cross-legged in the middle of the bed and closed her eyes. Her consciousness expanded to take in the entire room, then the rooms around her, and before long, the entire palace.

For as long as she could remember, she had simply to know what object was missing—to see a picture of it or even get a good description of it—to be able to find it. Buried objects could be a little tricky, as well as dismembered ones. She'd been worried when Professor Carswell asked her to find a piece of a missing disk, but when she found out it was bronze, she was much more confident. Metal and certain kinds of crystals gave out powerful energy fields that were a snap to sense.

The familiar trance settled over her, her "search mode." When she was little, she didn't know any better and hadn't hidden her talent. But by the time her parents had moved her to her sixth new school district, she'd gotten the idea, and managed to grow up relatively normally, if somewhat isolated from ordinary people. As an adult she'd successfully hidden her strange ability until the incident in Iraq. A squad of her men had gone missing in a sandstorm, and she'd set out into the blinding dust after them, alone. She'd walked right to them, and then turned around and led them unerringly back to base. And the jig was up. Rumors had circulated through the army of the oddball officer who could find lost things. Any lost thing. Anywhere. And in short order, the folks at Project Anasazi had found her.

And here she was. In the middle of ancient Greece looking for part of a lost bronze medallion. A far cry from finding misplaced inventory on an army post.

Where are you, little fella?

Hmm. She was getting only a faint buzz of energy at the moment. Athena Carswell had told Tessa she'd be close to the medallion when she blinked into Persia but had warned her she might not be right on top of the bronze piece. The code that was given on the last piece found could have been slightly misinterpreted. Or worse, the medallion piece could have been moved from its original location.

The aliens who'd hidden the pieces of the disk fifty thousand years ago had apparently done their best to place the medallions in ways that would ensure their remaining undisturbed. But unfortunately, humans liked shiny things and had a tendency to pick them up and carry them off.

Tessa opened her mind up fully, seeking what direction she should go to draw nearer to that which she sought.

She waited.

And waited.

Her brow crinkled in confusion.

She was getting nothing. Absolutely nothing. She *never* got nothing!

Panic jumped in her gut. Had Professor Carswell and company gone to enormous effort and expense to train her and send her here, only to have her fail? She was the supposed expert at this. She'd passed with flying colors every test they'd thrown at her when they'd checked out her bold claim that she could find anything.

What had gone wrong? Was she in the wrong time frame? The entirely wrong place? Professor Carswell had been specific. Somewhere near wherever Tessa blinked in, the second fragment of the medallion could be found.

She'd gotten that reading on it so clearly when she'd first arrived last night. Why wasn't she sensing the damned thing now? Surely it hadn't been moved so far overnight that it was now out of her range!

She crawled off the bed, deciding to try again outside. But as she took a step toward the wooden door, a knock sounded upon it.

Her pulse jumped. For a hopeful second, she wondered if it was Rustam. *Oh, come on.* He was some half-drunk man who'd come on to her soon after she'd been bombarded with images of her first—and hopefully last—orgy. The kiss had been a complete anomaly. She was a military officer, for God's sake. On a vital mission.

Okay, and wearing a filmy dress and no underwear.

Still. Their encounter had been a one-shot deal.

"Your ladyship. Be thee awake?" a female voice whispered.

Startled, Tessa unlatched the door and flung it open. A pretty young Persian woman stood there. She looked frightened.

"What can I do for you?" Tessa asked kindly.

The servant blinked. "Nothing. 'Tis I who serve you. Her Highness, Queen Artemesia, sent me to attend you."

Tessa thought fast. Why would someone with as high a rank as Artemesia even be aware of her existence, let alone take enough interest to send a servant to her? Did it have something to do with Rustam's visit to her room last night? This couldn't be good. The idea was to stay as invisible as possible on this mission. Just slide in, find the medallion, and slide out. Tessa asked, "What's your name?"

"Malah."

"Nice to meet you, Malah."

The girl ducked her head, embarrassed, and commenced straightening up the room, which took approximately thirty seconds. Nervously, she asked, "Shall I bring food to break thy fast?"

"That would be great."

In a few minutes, the girl returned with a pottery dish and a small clay jug. The former contained dates, olives, flat bread and a sharp white cheese. The jug held a milky, beige-colored water that tasted faintly of mud. But hey. It was wet. Not to mention she'd taken every inoculation known to mankind before she came on this little junket, and was loaded up on so many antibiotics that no germ stood a chance in her system for weeks to come.

Malah waited expectantly while Tessa nibbled at the meal. All in all, it wasn't half-bad. The fruit and bread were fresh, and the strong goat cheese grew on her. When she pushed the food away, the servant stepped forward with a small, damp towel and washed Tessa's hands, which was a little weird. But when in Rome—or when in Persia, as the case might be...

"My lady queen bids me invite thee to her chambers when thou hast broken fast and completed thy toilet."

Tessa blinked, startled. The girl was talking about her toilette—getting dressed and putting on makeup and otherwise primping. Did she look that bad? She'd already combed her hair and washed her face this morning, and Athena hadn't sent any makeup with her.

"I'm afraid my toilet is already done," Tessa replied regretfully. "Am I not presentable enough for Her Highness?"

A fleeting smile crossed the girl's face. "You are most beautiful. And exotic."

"Exotic? Me?" Tessa exclaimed.

"I have never seen a person of your coloring. Your hair is like spun gold and your eyes like silver. Your skin is as white as snow."

She wasn't *that* pale. But in comparison to the olive complexions of the locals, she wouldn't argue. "When have you seen snow, Malah?"

"Back at Persepolis, baskets of it are brought down from the mountains to cool the emperor's drink in times of hot weather."

"Speaking of location, what place is this?" Tessa asked curiously.

"'Tis the city of Trachis, recently seized from the Greeks."

"Where is it near?" The servant gave her a strange look, so Tessa explained. "I was shipwrecked and do not know where exactly I am."

Malah nodded in comprehension. "We lie at the foot of Mount Oeta, a few days' march north of the pass at Thermopylae, a short ride inland from the Gulf of Euboea. The emperor makes final preparations for his attack on Athens—" The girl broke off. Then added hastily, "Or so I have heard."

"Don't worry. I won't tell anyone about the emperor's not-too-secret secret plans. It's rather hard to disguise the movements of an army this size."

Malah smiled in relief. "If thou wilt come with me, my lady?"

"I'm not your lady, but yes, I'll come along."

The girl mumbled under her breath, "Would that thou were."

Hmm. Artemesia was a harsh mistress, eh? No surprise. Apparently, the queen was in the know about Xerxes's military matters, however, which *was* a surprise. And servants like Malah overheard snippets of the planning meetings.

In daylight, the palace turned out to be a complex of many separate buildings that must've comprised most of the city center of Trachis. Tessa followed the servant across rough cobblestone streets that made her grateful for her flat leather sandals.

Rustam jolted awake, disoriented. In his dream, he'd been back on his ship, commanding his crew as he navigated vast crossings. But when he opened his eyes, his ship was nowhere to be seen. Gauze curtains obscured a stone ceiling overhead. *Damn. Still stuck in Greece.*

A wave of energy crackled painfully across his skin, pricking him with ten thousand tiny needles from head to toe. It must have been this sharp discomfort that had awakened him. A stronger wave of outright pain washed over him and he lurched upright, looking around quickly. Thank the heavens. He was alone. As a sorcerer he could probably get away with glowing in his sleep, but he'd rather not have to explain the phenomenon to these superstitious locals.

He looked down. Odd. He was still glowing.

The energy danced across his body randomly, like heat lightning, not in the usual orderly whirl of his gathered power. The needles became knives, stabbing with a thousand assassin's blows. What the—?

He lashed out with his mind, slapping the force field away from his skin. That lessened the pain to a bearable level, but the indigo zigzagging rays still tingled sharply.

Tessa.

What was she up to? Was this an attack of some kind? Testing his power against hers when he was unconscious and his defenses were lowered? The little witch.

He surged out of bed, ignoring his discomfort, and threw on a pair of loose trousers. He grabbed a length of linen and tossed it over one shoulder, too irritated to bother draping and belting it properly. Slamming his feet into sandals, he stormed out of his quarters.

He burst into her room without bothering to knock. Empty! Where in the halls of hell was she? He cast his thoughts outward. And got back a buzz of disjointed energy. Oh, she was out there, all right. He just couldn't sense where.

Fury, and a faint frisson of fear, lashed through him. He spun and strode from her room, on the hunt. When he found Tessa of Marconi, the two of them were going to have a little conversation about her powers.

Soldiers hustled along the streets, jostling Tessa carelessly. But when a gilt litter came by, borne on the shoulders of four African slaves and carrying a heavily veiled woman, the warriors parted respectfully.

"Artemil," Malah murmured to Tessa, "the emperor's concubine."

"I thought he was married to Esther by now."

"Begging thy pardon?" the girl asked in surprise.

"Who is the Persian empress?" Tessa enquired quickly.

"Esther, Jewess of Susa and Babylon."

"And she shares Xerxes with concubines?"

Malah grinned. "'Tis said she holds all of his attention. But Artemil is the mother of Xerxes's firstborn son, therefore she retains her title and status as concubine. But it is also said she comes no more to his bed."

"Why in the world would she come along on this campaign?"

The maid smiled slyly. "Isn't it obvious? She wants back into Xerxes's bed."

Ahh. Bedroom politics. Artemil's procession passed by, and Tessa and Malah continued on their way. As they walked, Tessa asked, "Is Esther here? I should very much like to see her. She is renowned even in my land as a great queen."

"Nay. She stays at Susa and administers the empire with her uncle, Mordecai."

Malah stopped at the steps of a large building bordered by double rows of tall stone columns in the classic Greek tradition. "Here we are."

"This looks like a temple."

"It was. Xerxes expelled the Greek gods from this place and installed the greatest Persian god, Ahura Mazda, in their stead. The emperor and his closest advisors stay here now."

Gutsy guy, tossing gods out of their homes. Tessa mounted the stairs eagerly, drinking in the gloriously carved friezes, the perfect symmetry and balance of the building's design. But when they reached the doorway to Artemesia's chambers, she hesitated. As eager as she was to meet the great warrior queen, she couldn't afford to screw up this interview. *Be unimportant. Uninteresting. Just some foreigner passing through.*

Malah held back a painted leather curtain and Tessa stepped

into a giant bedroom dominated by a raised bed that could hold a half-dozen people comfortably. Oh, God. A brawny, naked man sprawled across it, asleep. As far as Tessa knew, Artemesia was a widow. Her lover, then.

Secretly relieved it wasn't Rustam in the queen's bed, Tessa averted her eyes from the man and spotted the striking brunette from last night, sitting on an upholstered bench in the far corner, getting dressed. Or rather, being dressed. One serving woman brushed her nearly floor-length hair, while another slipped sandals upon her feet and tied the thongs about her ankles.

"You may approach, white woman."

Tessa's steps faltered. She hadn't intended to stop and wait for permission to approach. Good thing the queen had granted it before Tessa insulted her.

Now what was she supposed to do? She did *not* want to commit a serious etiquette faux pas with this woman.

Artemesia gestured to a low bench beside her. "Sit here."

Grateful for the instruction, Tessa sank down onto the hard surface, which placed her in a position of having to look up at the queen. Close up, the woman was even more beautiful. Her dark eyes were large and faintly up-slanted, her mouth sensuously full, her skin golden and flawless.

"What is your name?"

"Tessa of Marconi, Your Highness."

"From whence do you come?"

"My home is a year's journey or more to the north and west of here, far into the unconquered lands of the barbarians."

"And how is it you speak our tongue, then?"

She obviously couldn't tell the queen that, in setting up a time jump, Professor Carson managed to infuse the process with what she called "Intent," resulting in the time traveler absorbing details of the location, including language, customs and culture, even knowledge of common plants and animals.

She looked up. Artemisia had turned away from the mirror a servant held up for her, and was staring at her expectantly. Tessa answered hastily, "Is not the Persian Empire the greatest in all the world? Even in the untamed lands, we have heard of you and study your ways."

Artemesia nodded, as if the fact was self-evident. She turned to one of her maids and snapped, "Where is my pearl brooch? If you lost it, you clumsy girl, I shall have you whipped."

The servant paled, trembling. Tessa closed her eyes quickly. *Pearls. A brooch. Warm emanations of water, with a bit of metal undertone.* It ought to be immediately evident where the piece was. Yet, she had to struggle to get even the fuzziest of readings on it. What in the world was going on with her powers?

"Ten lashes—"

Tessa interrupted the queen quickly. "Perhaps if she looks under those cushions in the corner, your maid will find the brooch."

Artemesia's brows flew together thunderously. But she waved a hand, gesturing for the maid to do as Tessa had suggested. Quickly, the panicked girl fell upon the pile of pillows, digging through it frantically. "Here it is!" she cried, holding up a large, round pin encrusted with pearls of various colors, creating a flower motif.

"How did you do that?" Artemesia demanded of Tessa.

Crap. Crap, crap, crap. "Just a lucky guess," she replied meekly.

The queen eyed her entirely too speculatively for Tessa's taste. "Why are you here? Do you seek to capture the eye of the emperor?"

"Heavens, no!" she exclaimed.

Artemesia looked her up and down. "Properly garbed and appointed, you could catch his eye, mayhap. You are certainly strange and beautiful enough. Yet you answered without hesitation that you seek this not. So I ask again. Why *are* you here?"

Because a group of scientists from twenty-five hundred years in the future is trying to find the pieces of a puzzle that will earn mankind entry into the galactic community and gain us protection against the Centaurian Federation, which is apparently deeply unfriendly to Earth. "I am lost, Your Highness. Shipwrecked by a great storm."

"The same storm that sank so many of our ships, no doubt," Artemesia said bitterly. "I told them to build vessels that were less top-heavy, but would they listen to me, the fools? Not one of my own ships sank."

"You are wise, Your Highness."

"'Tis no feat to appear brilliant when you are surrounded by idiots."

"Or by men," Tessa quipped without thinking.

Artemesia glanced over at her, startled. Then toward the man snoring in her bed. And then burst out laughing, loudly enough to make him stir in his sleep. "Walk with me." The queen rose, her bearing regal.

Tessa berated herself fiercely. She *had* to corral her tongue and think before she spoke, or she was going to get herself into serious trouble! Relieved to have dodged disaster so far, she followed Artemesia out into a garden. The sound of the army was louder here, but the sweet scent of jasmine hung thick in the air and a breeze cooled them under the shade trees.

They walked for nearly an hour, while servitors read letters to the queen and passed along various requests and problems for her to deal with. A new sail was needed for one of her ships. Drunken soldiers from Halicarnassus had gotten into a fight with some other satrap's soldiers and were duly fined. Lengths of cloth had arrived from a merchant in Jerusalem and were in need of distribution to various servitors. Offerings for a temple had to be chosen. And tax income was reported. Lots of that.

Artemesia handled it all with careless efficiency. Her management style was rather more autocratic than Tessa's, but two millenia and the democratic form of government separated them. The queen completely ignored her while conducting her business. Tessa wasn't quite sure why she was out here trekking around and around the walled garden in the woman's wake, but had no idea how to take her leave without offending the queen.

"How do you plan to proceed from here?" Artemesia asked her suddenly.

Tessa started. She'd been absently watching a bee fly from blossom to blossom on a vine while she tried with no luck to sense the medallion. "I suppose I shall seek a caravan headed toward my home."

"No caravans pass by here. All who can flee before the army of Xerxes do so, for it is worse than any swarm of locusts, stripping everything in its path bare to feed itself."

Tessa shrugged. "I will find something. A trader's ship, perhaps."

Artemesia tapped a front tooth with a long, buffed fingernail. "Xerxes upon occasion sends envoys to far-flung places. Mayhap you could arrange passage in the retinue of one."

Tessa nodded. "An excellent suggestion, Your Majesty." Was this all an elaborate ploy to get a potential rival out of the court?

"Artemesia!" a male voice called out. The baritone was compelling as it vibrated deep in Tessa's gut. A hypnotic sound of pure machismo.

The queen's eyes went limpid, then seductive, then calculating in the blink of any eye. "Hippoclides," she breathed.

Forgetting Tessa instantly and entirely, the queen whirled and hurried back toward her bedchamber, almost as if mesmerized. Wow. That guy must rock in the sack. Tessa turned to take a peak at a man who held an imperious queen at his beck and call.

He stood on the steps, a powerful-looking man with a toga draped carelessly around his large frame. Artemesia rushed up to him and the two embraced, kissing with a fire that would burn a lesser building down around them. The man clasped Artemesia's behind, hauling her up against him while she tore his toga off his shoulder. They were half-naked before they reached the doorway.

Tessa looked around the walled garden in dismay. How was she supposed to get out of here? The only exit was through the queen's bedroom.

Malah appeared from out of nowhere. "Come with me, my lady. Your interview is over."

Is that what that was? An interview? Bemused, Tessa followed the servant, *oh, joy,* back into the bedchamber. Artemesia and her lover were going at it like a pair possessed, and Tessa averted her gaze. But the slap of flesh on flesh, Artemesia's cries of ecstasy and the man's grunts were self-explanatory.

Tessa breathed a heartfelt sigh of relief as she slipped, unnoticed, out of the chamber.

And ran straight into an immovable wall of muscle.

A thoroughly annoyed voice muttered, "There you are. I've been looking all over for you. We need to *talk.*"

She closed her eyes in chagrin. *Rustam.*

Chapter 4

"What in the high god's name were you doing with Artemesia?" Rustam demanded under his breath, taking her none too gently by the arm. He waved off Malah with his free hand, and Tessa was dismayed to see the servant scuttle away.

She shook off his grip, or at least tried to. Unsuccessfully. "I have business to take care of, Rustam. Let me go. I'm not your plaything to drag around."

"I will make you my plaything if I wish," he muttered direly as he hauled her outside the temple and into the street.

The promise in his voice stole her breath away. "Where are we going?" she demanded.

"Some place private. To talk."

"Is there any privacy in the middle of a million-man army?"

"'Tis closer to three hundred thousand. Maybe five hundred thousand if you count servants, artisans and other hangers-on."

Well. That answered one of history's great questions. Historians had debated forever whether Herodotus's report of the million-man army was a gross exaggeration or not. Too bad Tessa would never be able to tell modern military historians the true figure. She half ran to keep up with Rustam as he propelled her through the streets of the Greek city and out into the sea of tents. It was a matter of pride not to ask him to slow down. Besides, she was in good enough shape to keep up. The U.S. Army saw to that.

The men swarming around her looked rough. Mean. Eyed her in a way that made her want to crowd close against Rustam's side. Wow. These steely, scarred men made the highly competent soldiers she served with back home seem like pampered sissies. Of course, these warriors had already survived a grueling march all the way from Central Asia and several major battles.

She and Rustam walked for more than a mile before the tents gave way to long rows of paddocks filled with elephants, then camels, and finally, horses. Rustam held his free hand out, and horses lined up by the dozens along the fences to nuzzle at his palm. He made small sounds under his breath, and the animals arched their necks and nickered back. He was good with equines. Great with them, in fact. It was probably a required skill for macho warriors of this time period.

A rocky outcropping rose in front of them, while Mount Oeta loomed, blue and forbidding, in the distance. Rustam's pace never slowed as he stormed up a narrow, winding path, apparently assuming she would follow along like an obedient dog.

Finally, she groused, "Slow down, already. I've got flimsy sandals on.

He glanced down at her feet, which were dusty and scratched, then bent quickly and picked her up, tossing her over his shoulder.

"Hey! Put me down!" She beat on his back to no avail. The man was a *rock*. A big, muscular, overwhelmingly male rock.

Something in her gut went hot and liquid. *Oh, for crying out loud.* She did *not* melt around macho jerks.

The macho jerk in question stopped all of a sudden and dumped her in an unceremonious heap on the ground. "Ouch!" She glared up at him. "You are such a… I could really learn to dislike you."

"You lie," he replied smoothly.

"I do not—"

He cut her off. "You want me. I can smell it."

"Smell…? Excuse me?"

"Desire hangs on your skin like the flower petals you crushed in your fingers this morning."

Whoa. He had a great sense of smell. "Okay, Tarzan. You dragged me up here on top of this rock to talk. So talk."

"Tarzan?" His eyebrows drew together.

"Another character out of a story from my home."

"You know too many stories."

"And you're still a…never mind."

He held a hand down to her. Were she not hopelessly entangled in her skirts, she'd have ignored it. But given the circumstances, she reluctantly grasped it and let him lift her easily to her feet. He didn't release her hand when she was vertical, though. He pulled her uncomfortably close to his chest and glared down at her. "You still want me."

She didn't deign to reply. She tugged at her hand, and he let it go. When he said nothing, she snapped, "What do you want?"

"You."

She gulped. Managed to say glibly, "Since *that's* not happening anytime soon, what else do you want?"

"What do you seek in this place?"

Interesting—and alarming—that he assumed she was looking for something. "I merely seek a way home."

"Don't we all?" he muttered with surprising bitterness. He glanced at her again. "Give me your hand."

"You just had it. And besides, it's mine."

"Woman, you are as prickly as yon cactus. And more contrary, I vow." He gestured toward a prickly pear clinging to the poor soil.

She shrugged. "You're the one who hauled me up here."

He turned away to gaze at the distant mountains. "Two days' march from here lies the road to Athens. And the pass at Thermopylae. It is a highly defensible position, and with every hour the Greeks can delay Xerxes there, the more time they will have to prepare Athens for his assault. Know you what will happen when Xerxes's army comes to the pass?"

Of course she knew. Three hundred Spartans, led by their king, Leonidas, and helped by a handful of Thebans and Thespians, would make a heroic and ultimately suicidal stand in the pass. They'd die to the last man, but they'd buy the populace of Athens enough time to evacuate the city and avoid wholesale slaughter, thereby saving the Greek civilization and ensuring its influence on mankind for millennia to come. The battle and the Spartans' stand still resonated through history as one of the greatest acts of heroism ever accomplished.

"I'm no soldier," she replied, "I have no idea what will happen at Thermoplylae."

He glanced down at her, perplexed. "Why do I hear untruth in your voice? Surely in your home women are not warriors?"

She forced a laugh. "The weaker sex? Why, we can barely lift a sword or shield, let alone wield both in battle." How in the heck had he heard untruth in her voice? If he was so perceptive, she might as well stop talking to him altogether. No way was she going to get through a conversation of any length in this place without lies, and lots of them.

"Thermopylae is a good place for the Greeks to make a stand. They will cost Xerxes many men and rob his army of its swagger."

He sounded as if he already knew the outcome of the battle.

He must be well versed in military strategy. "Will you fight in the battle?" she asked.

He shook his head. "Artemesia will not hear of it. I am her personal sorcerer."

"She would keep an able-bodied warrior out of the fight to do parlor tricks at parties?" The military officer in Tessa was offended at the idea.

He laughed gently. "'Tis for the best. I have no wish to write history."

She knew the feeling. "How soon will Xerxes march for Thermopylae?"

He shrugged. "A few days. A week, maybe. His men are almost whipped up to a sufficient pitch of battle fever."

The sun was beating down mercilessly and Tessa feared for her fair skin. "Unless you wish to see me turn as red as a…pomegranate…I need to get out of this sun."

He reached out to rub the pad of his thumb lightly across her cheekbone. "Indeed, you are a creature of snow and ice, far too fair for this clime."

She really wished her breath would quit going all wobbly like that every time he touched her.

He continued in a husky murmur, "Is your heart likewise carved of ice?" He moved nearer, his dark eyes ablaze. "Nay. I think not. I think you but hide from the fire within. You fear it."

"I fear nothing," she retorted.

His mouth curved up almost cruelly and his eyes went as black as sin. "Maybe you should."

His hand slipped behind her neck, under her hair, and slowly drew her toward him. He was too big and strong to bother fighting with. He'd just toss her over his shoulder or pin her with a wrestling move. But by way of passive resistance, she kept her eyes open, staring up at him. Disconcertingly, he stared back as their mouths drew close. Sparks flew between them—of challenge, of friction, of incendiary attraction.

She commented drily, "Let me guess. This is the part where you kiss me senseless and I'm supposed to swoon with desire for you and give in to whatever you want."

His lips curved in a sinful smile. "Yes," he murmured. "It is."

Okay, so give the man brownie points for honesty...and for making her knees go weak, dammit.

He closed the last few inches between them. Their lips touched.

He groaned under his breath, and her knees nearly buckled under her. It was all there again. The driving need, the over-whelming pull between them, the tingling electricity racing across her skin. Out of the corner of her eye, she actually thought she saw colored lights dancing around them. Last night *hadn't* been an anomaly.

She was in serious trouble, here.

Surprisingly, it was Rustam who broke away first, panting like a racehorse, a fine sheen of perspiration glistening across his bronze skin. "You seduce me as easily as a courtesan giving a green lad his first kiss."

Her heartbeat pounded in her ears, an irregular flutter that was totally unlike her. "I think you've got that backward," she managed to retort. Their gazes locked, startled. Mutually alarmed, even. She had all kinds of logical reasons to avoid this man. But darned if she didn't want more of that electricity zinging between them.

"We need to talk," he rasped.

"About what?" she asked reluctantly.

"The court. You are as a lamb to slaughter within it."

Okay. Not where she thought he'd been going. "How so?"

"'Tis a serpent's nest of treachery and plots. You must proceed with utmost caution. Drawing the attention of Arteme-sia and her ilk can only lead to disaster."

Tessa couldn't agree more. But she was perplexed as to why he felt compelled to warn her. "Why are you telling me this?"

"Just have a care, all right?"

"All right."

"Beware in particular of Artemesia. She is highly intelligent and schemes to advance her own cause by climbing upon the shoulders—or corpses—of any who stand in her way."

"That's the impression I got of her."

"Tread lightly with her. Never insult her. Never appear more beautiful. And never, ever, demonstrate more intelligence than she."

"An alpha female, huh?"

He nodded soberly. "Territorial. And vicious when crossed. Don't get me wrong. She's loyal to friends and can be grandly generous. But she's ambitious."

"Thanks for the warning."

He nodded.

Silence fell between them, as close to companionable as they'd managed so far. She took the opportunity to cast her mind out across the valley at her feet, seeking any hint of the elusive bronze medallion piece. The signature—if it actually was the correct one—was incredibly faint. Which meant it was distant.

Odd. She should've time-jumped very near to it. She tried to sense what direction to travel to reach it. But every line of energy she sensed led directly to the man next to her.

Not helpful.

Thanks to his sorcery performance last night in little more than a towel, she knew he wore no jewelry, no armor, no pouch that might contain a bronze trinket. He couldn't possibly have the medallion on him. So why was he all she was sensing? She glanced over at him, frowning.

He was frowning back at her.

"What?" she asked a trifle irritably.

"What are you doing?"

"Nothing. Looking at the valley. The entire Persian army arrayed at my feet is an impressive sight."

***

Rustam snorted. *Ha. She was doing something, all right.* Energy was surging around her like a roiling thundercloud. He reached out with his mind to sense her thoughts. That was strange; he was getting nothing. Not even a general sense of her mood. He always could read people. They displayed their thoughts and feelings like open books. He must be tired. He'd tossed and turned, hot and aroused in his lonely bed, for most of the night.

The prickling sensation was back, racing across his skin until he felt an urge to scratch all over. "Stop that!"

Tessa jumped. "Stop what?"

"Whatever you're doing."

"What *are* you talking about?" She looked distinctly alarmed now.

He stepped close, grabbing her by both shoulders when she made to turn away. He hauled her up against him and glared down at her. "Tell me why every time I'm around you, the hairs on my arms stand up. Why I see colored lights at the back of my eyes until I get a headache. Why you drive me mad with want of you. What magic spell do you cast upon me, witch woman?"

"I'm not a witch, I haven't cast any magic spells on you, and I don't have the slightest idea what you're talking about."

"You lie. I don't even have to hear it in your voice. Your eyes slide away from mine and you vibrate with guilt in my hands. Who are you?"

"I told you. I'm Tessa of Marconi. I come from far away."

He dragged her up higher until she stood on her tiptoes, pressed against him from shoulder to ankles. "Yes, yes. And you were shipwrecked. I know all that. But who are you? Why *are* you here? Who are your people?"

Frustration glittered in her otherworldly, silver-blue eyes. He damn well knew the feeling. Stubbornly, she remained silent, denying him the answers he needed.

He hurled his mind against hers. "Answer me!"

She moaned in distress. He didn't care. He slammed her with more power, strangely chaotic and unfocused for him. It zinged back and forth between them, and he absorbed the pain heedlessly, too angry to care about any injury he might cause himself.

"Rustam, stop!" she cried out.

"Answer my question. Who. Are. You?"

"I am…a traveler. I come…from far away."

Her mental defenses were astounding. He felt his own power beginning to drain. Was she actually sucking energy out of him? How was she doing *that?*

Supremely frustrated, he lifted her entirely off the ground by her upper arms. And kissed her angrily.

And every bit of energy he'd poured into her slammed back into him in a single blast. He reeled with the force of it. Stumbled backward, setting her on her feet and gripping her as much to keep his own balance as to restrain her.

She came to him of her own accord then, sliding her arms around his neck. "I don't know what it is about you," she mumbled, sounding as frustrated as him. "But I can't keep my hands off of you. Lord knows, I ought to."

And then *she* kissed *him.* In an instant, his heartbeat sped up to match hers. Today, both their pulses and auras aligned without conscious effort on his part. The indigo haze wrapped around them in a blanket of power that magnified their desire tenfold. He plundered her mouth with his, and their tongues danced a ballet in perfect unison. Where his body was hard, hers was soft. Where his was angular, hers was curved. Where he pulled her close, she yielded. And where she drew his spirit into hers, he went. Willingly. Completely. Helplessly.

He'd heard of this sort of bonding before. But it was mostly the stuff of ancient legends and children's bedtime stories among his people. Soul bonding they called it. But she wasn't even remotely of his clan or even his nation. And yet the dizzying whirl of their combined energy built even more quickly and violently than last night, exploding in a burst of light as bright as a new-formed sun.

How they ended up on the ground, with him leaning back against a boulder and her curled in his lap, he had no idea. He stroked her golden hair absently and she snuggled in closer against his chest, apparently asleep. Did he actually pass out? The thought was shocking, yet he was too calm, too damned indolent all of a sudden, to care. More shocking was the fact that his anger was gone. *All of it.* Even the deep, dark well-spring from which his power emerged.

What had this woman done to him?

Chapter 5

The leader of Alpha Team stood in front of his employer's desk, wincing.

"What do you mean, you couldn't find the document? It had to be in the lab! I had solid intelligence that the professor keeps it there!"

"There wasn't time, sir. The smoke bombs started to wear off and we had to get out. We did succeed in locating the safe and identifying the type of locks on it. The thumbprint system will be easy enough to circumvent, but the retinal scanner and the digital lock itself will be a bitch. We could just blow the whole thing up. Everything inside would be destroyed and your professor would be out of business."

"That's no good. She's no doubt got a copy squirreled away somewhere. Besides, I want to read that book."

"Then why aren't we trying to track down the copy instead?"

His employer studied him speculatively across his burlwood executive desk. "I don't know where to begin looking for it."

"With all due respect, that's what we're for, sir."

He answered with a slow nod and a dawning smile. "Make it so, then. But hurry."

"What time frame are we looking at for retrieval?"

The client's gaze clouded. "I don't know exactly. My contact wasn't specific. He just said I needed to be in possession of the information in that notebook soon."

"Or else what, sir?"

"I've been told that whoever possesses the data will be in a position to take over the world. If I don't get my hands on it, I won't be that person."

The Alpha Team leader stared. *Ooh-kay, then.* Note to self: the boss man was a whacko megalomaniac head case. Oh, he and the boys would keep working and taking the guy's lavish money. But any need to die for the client had just dropped off the bottom of the scale.

His employer was speaking. "Can't emphasize enough the importance of what you're doing. Time is of the essence. That journal is critical. Everything depends on it."

Tessa roused slowly from…sleep? A faint? A konk on the head? She wasn't quite sure. She hugged Rustam a little more closely, enjoying the shelter of his unbelievably strong arms. Whoa. *Rewind.* Rustam's arms? She jerked upright, startled and furious with him and her for getting into this situation. She had no business sitting in anybody's lap, dammit! She had important work to do and this was a huge distraction.

"I gather by the look of horror on your face that you are awake and ready for another battle of wits?" he said wrily.

Irritation slitted her eyes. "Don't get sarcastic with me. You're the one who dragged me out here and then kissed me. Women in this part of the world may swoon at the slightest flex of your perfect biceps or one sultry look from those sexy eyes of yours, but I'm not that gullible."

He grinned lazily and drawled, "Perfect biceps? Thanks. Say something else nice about me."

She tried to leap out of his lap, but a casual tightening of said biceps held her firmly in place. "Oooh! You're infuriating! I hate men like you!"

"Temper, temper." He tsked. "And as for this swooning business. Seems to me that's exactly what you just did for me…" He laughed mellowly, sounding as lazy as a summer day. Since when was he Mr. Easygoing? She frowned. For that matter, when was she ever this cranky? Rage bubbled up from deep inside her for no apparent reason, like lava spilling out of a volcano. An urge to do violence, to hurt someone, all but overcame her. Thankfully, Rustam released her just then—before she lost control and scratched his eyes out.

She leaped to her feet and whirled to glare down at him. As quickly as he turned her loose her anger dissipated, leaving her drained, but calm once more. He gazed pleasantly up at her for a moment, then his dark eyebrows slammed together. He jumped to his feet with such agility and speed she barely saw him move.

He snarled, "Do that again and I will kill you."

"Rustam, I am a patient person. But if you do not cease making wild accusations and talking in riddles, I *am* going to lose my temper."

"And then what?" he threatened silkily.

"I don't make threats," she replied evenly. "I just do what the situation calls for."

His fists clenched, and for a startled moment she thought he might actually strike her. But instead he spun away, cursing violently. She released her breath slowly. She got the distinct feeling she'd just played with fire and somehow managed to escape unscathed. Obviously, she and this man were oil and water. They needed to stay away from each other, lest they drive each other completely crazy.

"I'm going back to the palace," she announced quietly.

Without waiting for him to follow, she turned and started down the mountainside.

Out of reflex more than conscious thought, she cast her awareness outward to see if she could pick up the direction of the medallion again. Before Rustam had kissed her senseless, or whatever the heck that had been up there, she'd gotten the vague impression that the bronze piece was well east of her current position and possibly moving south.

No surprise. Now she was getting nothing but chaos. That man seriously messed with her head. Not to mention her talent—

Her random thoughts screeched to an abrupt halt. Rustam messed with her psychic ability. She'd been able to sense the medallion last night until he'd come into the room. When he'd climbed on her bed, she'd briefly sensed it again, and then she'd kissed his lights out and lost her connection to the piece again. Today, she'd had it briefly up on top of that mountain, and then he'd kissed her, and poof! No more medallion.

Clearly it was time for her to leave the exalted presence of Biceps Boy and go after that bronze wedge by herself, far, far away from his corrupting influence.

Even if he did kiss like a god.

She might not have kissed all that many guys in her day, but there was no doubt in her mind this man was in a class by himself when it came to kissing. Even now, she craved more of him and his magical mouth. And she was *not* a craving kind of girl.

When she reached the army encampment, she experienced a moment of real trepidation. She had to make her way across a good chunk of the camp, alone. In provocative clothing designed to make her look like a courtesan.

She would feel much safer with Rustam's towering strength at her side as she hesitated on the shore of the sea of men. *I'm an army officer, dammit! I know how to walk among the rank and file and not get messed with.* Of course, the rank and file she strolled past back home were eminently more civilized than this bunch.

No help for it. She squared her shoulders, put on a don't-mess-with-me expression and waded into the jumble of tents.

She was abjectly relieved to reach the palace complex in one piece. That was *not* a route she would attempt alone at night, nor one, frankly, she'd like to try again in broad daylight. She felt as if she'd just walked through the worst of crime-ridden neighborhoods and survived by sheer, dumb luck.

She had to leave this place and head east and south if she was going to accomplish her mission. It was early afternoon now. By the time she procured supplies for the journey, it would probably be too late to leave today—especially with Xerxes's army to get around. First thing in the morning, then.

Thankfully, the gold coins Athena had sent with her went a long way in the city's main marketplace. With a mobile army all around her, finding a horse, saddle, bedroll, water skins and a sack of dried food posed no great difficulty.

Hauling her new gear back to her room garnered her no end of strange looks, however. Apparently, ladies of her rank didn't usually fetch and carry. But she'd be damned if she'd force Malah or some other slave to do manual labor for her when she was plenty strong and fit enough to do it for herself. Let them think her an oddball foreigner. She could live with that, and she'd be gone soon enough.

When Tessa arrived at her room, she stowed her supplies beneath her bed. It worried her not to be able to lock her room. She didn't want to be robbed while she attended tonight's feast. That morning, Artemesia had ordered her to do so, and Tessa hadn't a clue what might happen if she turned the imperious queen down. Instead, she'd meekly consented to come to the feast. If she was lucky, maybe Rustam wouldn't show up. She could eat a little supper, pay her polite respects to Artemesia, and then slip away and get a good night's sleep before she set out.

But when Malah arrived at sunset, carrying a pale blue gown over her arm, so sheer the girl's skin was visible through several layers of the fabric, Tessa had serious second thoughts about the whole venture.

"I can't wear that!" she exclaimed as Malah shook out the gown for her.

"You have no choice, my lady. Artemesia sent it for you. You will give her grave insult do you not wear it."

"But...it's see-through!"

Malah frowned. "'Tis the fashion, ma'am. And you've a nice enough figure for your height."

Tessa grimaced at the backhanded compliment. "I refuse to parade around at an orgy dressed in that thing. I'd be asking to be jumped by every male in the room!"

The servant's mouth twitched. "I believe that is precisely the idea, my lady."

She rolled her eyes. Now what? She dared not offend Artemesia. Especially not after Rustam's earlier warning about those who crossed the queen ending up dead. But Tessa couldn't possibly go out in that...negligee!

"Can we put my white shift under it?" she asked.

Malah considered. "We would have to add a belt.... I could probably borrow one from Artemesia's wardrobe. I can ask her chief dresser if you like...."

"Just don't make it too nice a belt. I'm told she doesn't like to be outshone."

Malah made a face. "Aye, that is true enough." The maid eyed her speculatively. "Something simple, I should think. Delicate. A piece to compliment your beauty and not overpower it."

Tessa sighed. "Just make me as ugly as you possibly can without making Artemesia angry."

The maid frowned, obviously judging her temporary mistress more than a little mad but too aware of her place to comment upon it. Malah showed her to a communal bath a little while later, where Tessa briskly shampooed her hair and scrubbed off the grime of the day's hike. Thankfully, the place was not crowded. She gathered from the bath mistress that most of the nobles had bathed earlier and were already deep into their preparations for tonight's celebration.

The attendant, who turned out to be the gossipy sort, also hinted that tonight's feast was rumored to be special. Apparently, Xerxes had been closeted with his kings and priests all day, and some sort of an announcement was expected.

Tessa winced. She prayed the emperor wasn't going to launch his army against Thermopylae tonight. She needed to get out of here and well away from the Persian army before the fighting commenced. The last thing she needed was to get trapped in the middle of a war!

She put up with Malah's fussing and fluffing and pleating and draping as patiently as she could. She'd never been a primp-happy female in the twenty-first century, and she wasn't one now, either. Finally, the maid pronounced her ready for the feast. Tessa had no mirror in which to examine herself, so she'd have to take Malah's word for it.

Because the gown was sleeveless, she slipped her all-important bronze-and-quartz arm cuff into her small pouch and tied it to her belt. She reached for her dagger, but Malah gasped in alarm.

"Oh, no, m'lady! 'Tis forbidden to carry arms within the emperor's presence! If you were discovered with that you would be put to death on the spot!"

Tessa jerked her hand away from the dagger. Yikes. The true extent of the danger a time traveler faced struck her yet again. Athena might be able to implant the language and culture of a time period, but not even the professor could cover every detail. Were it not for Malah, she'd have committed a grave crime without even knowing it to be one.

After a murmured word of thanks to the servant for her

help, Tessa took a deep breath and stepped out into the hallway. The feast wasn't hard to find. She just followed the stream of gaudily clad nobles streaming toward the celebration. The bath mistress hadn't been wrong. Wind was in the air of something big tonight, and it didn't take psychic powers to sense the assemblage buzzing with anticipation.

Thankfully, Tessa was seated in an obscure corner of the gigantic hall, as befitted her status as a minor noble. Still, she stood out like a sore thumb, a pale blue icicle in the midst of a thousand bright butterflies. Her table companions turned out to be two married couples and a Persian army officer of some kind. Thankfully, the officer was much more interested in ogling the male servants in the room than in looking down her dress.

She'd have loved to talk tactics and strategy with her peer from ancient times but dared not go there. And anyway, he got drunk so quickly she wouldn't have garnered much useful information from him.

Emperor Xerxes's grand entrance was a spectacle she would never forget. Slave girls threw flower petals at his feet. Horns blared. A hundred guards lined the emperor's path, forming an arch of scimitars with a precision that would have made a modern drill team sigh with envy. And then came two dozen kings and queens, promenading down the archway and taking their places just beyond, kneeling on cushions and bowing down until their foreheads touched the floor. Finally, the great one himself arrived. Tessa got a good look at him before she bowed, along with everyone else in the room. He was a handsome man, actually, with dark curls, a hawk nose and intelligent eyes. He wasn't Greek-coin beautiful, but wore imperial power with regal ease.

As she took her seat to await the meal, Tessa pondered the difference between his power and Rustam's. Xerxes's was the charisma of a supremely confident political and military leader.

Rustam's energy, on the other hand, swirled around him like a living thing—of him and yet not of him—an essence he controlled but did not entirely own. Even though his power originated within him, it was larger than him, in the same way that a child could spring from its parents' loins, and yet eventually surpass its parents.

Rustam's personal charisma was every bit as aggressive and confident as Xerxes's was; he just contained it more carefully. It was if he didn't want the world at large to notice it. She'd only gotten a full grasp of it herself when he'd kissed her.

How was it that a sorcerer-slave from what she knew as modern-day Turkey could match the force of personality of one of the most powerful men in history?

As if her thoughts conjured him into existence, she suddenly caught sight of Rustam across the hall. He wore yet another skimpy towel low on his hips, held in place with an elaborately jeweled belt. Tessa knew now that the brief skirt was the garment of a slave, yet somehow he wore his with all the panache of a prince.

A veritable army of servants marched out of a half-dozen tunnels around the room, loaded down with massive platters of food. Although the slave attending her table looked at her as if she was crazy when she asked how recently the ox and lambs had been slaughtered, she wasn't about to risk a serious case of food poisoning on spoiled meat right before her journey.

She was relieved to find out the animals had been butchered last night and roasted throughout the day. Although the spices on the meat were somewhat strong for her taste, all in all, the meal was very tasty. A theme of honey and fruit and savory spices like cinnamon and saffron dominated.

She only sipped at her wine, particularly after her army officer escort mentioned casually that "herbs" were mixed into it to increase its intoxicating effects. She did not need to get wasted tonight of all nights! Goblets were hoisted all over the room, emptied, and refilled steadily.

In short order, the party was on.

Music started up, wine flowed and dancing girls and boys performed. Clothes came loose, people started to pair up—or group up, as the case might be—and the tone of the feast went from PG to X-rated in no time flat.

The guests had seriously let their hair down and were well into whatever state of revelry they preferred when Xerxes stood up across the room. Someone bellowed for quiet and then a deafening fanfare of horns—more nasal and reedy than trumpets, but easily as loud—blasted the room into silence.

He announced, loudly enough for his voice to penetrate every corner of the hall, "I have consulted with my generals and my priests. The army is ready and the omens are ripe. Tomorrow we march on Athens!"

This announcement was greeted with a loud and protracted outburst of crazed cheering. It felt strange to Tessa to sit there, knowing the disappointments and ultimate failures that lay before this wildly enthusiastic assemblage. She was witnessing the last great moment of the Persian Empire before the beginning of its centuries-long decline. A chill chattered across her skin.

She felt his gaze upon her without even having to look up. But she did, anyway. Rustam nodded soberly at her across the heads of the screaming crowd. He looked as if he, too, had an inkling of what lay ahead. Not surprising. He was extremely intelligent, and probably knew as well as anyone that the Greeks would not go down without a desperate fight. He'd said as much earlier when they'd been up on that mountain.

The room finally settled enough for Xerxes to continue. "We will crush these upstart Greeks and their ridiculous notions, and I shall finally fulfill the vow I made to my father to conquer the Peloponnese. May the might and glory of my empire shine over all the world, that the one god, the great god

Ahura Mazda, shall know my name and honor me in his sacred halls."

Tessa swore under her breath. She'd run out of time. She had to get out of here—and soon—if she was going to avoid getting trapped on this side of the Thermopylae Pass for who knew how long. Every day she spent in this time was another day she risked a slip-up, or discovery as a fraud. The faster she found that and got her happy self back home, the better.

A male servant startled her just then, hesitantly touching the hem of her gown. She looked down, silently appalled at how slaves were expected to grovel.

"My lady?" he murmured. "Her Majesty, Queen Artemesia, orders you to attend her."

Disaster, thy name is Artemesia. Tessa sighed. "Lead on, MacDuff."

"Mac—who?"

"Never mind. Just take me to her most spectacular and munificent majesty."

For just an instant, the man's eyes glinted with humor. And then he scuttled off with her in tow, her feet dragging toward she knew not what. But her gut told her this would *not* be fun.

Chapter 6

There was nothing quite like having to step over a naked couple having grunting, sweaty sex to get where you were going, Tessa observed wryly. Of course, the sight that greeted her when she got to Artemesia's table was eminently worse. A young man was barely visible under the table, his head buried between the queen's widespread legs, while Rustam stood behind her chair, fondling her uncovered breasts. At least he had the good grace to looked bored out of his mind.

Artemesia's eyes were more arrogant than usual, swimming with lust and, oddly enough, power. A vague haze of red seemed to cling to the woman. Or maybe it was just the brilliant scarlet of the queen's dress playing tricks on Tessa's eyes. Except it looked as if Rustam's hands were manipulating the shimmering haze, swirling it across Artemesia's skin. And every time one of those eddies erupted, the woman arched into his hands and moaned.

Weird.

An unwilling, but undeniably visceral, response vibrated low in Tessa's core. She didn't think of herself as a voyeur, but it was really hard to be surrounded by all this sex and not react to it a little. Okay, a lot. She wished Rustam's hands were playing across her skin like that, and she was the one moaning in response. *Sheesh. Stop that!*

"Ahh, our naive little foreigner," Artemesia purred. "Do you disapprove of our…entertainments?"

"Certainly not," Tessa answered smoothly. Please let Artemesia believe her! "I particularly like your notion of what constitutes a pair. Where I come from, one plus one usually equals two."

Artemesia chuckled. "Why stop at one lover if two is better? Or three? Or ten?"

Ten? Tessa couldn't help but gape.

Artemesia's laughter turned into a wavering moan of orgasm as the young man did something under the table that Tessa really didn't want to know about.

She glanced up at Rustam. "Will you be finished here soon?" she asked lightly.

His eyes went as black and hard as obsidian. He shook his head a single time. Whether he was furious with her or with the woman writhing under his hands, Tessa had no idea.

She looked down at Artemesia, who seemed all but unconscious in the throes of a major orgasm. Breezily, Tessa said, "Well, Your Majesty, I hate to interrupt your multiple orgasms. You go on and have fun now. And thanks so much for the invitation to the party. This has been most…educational."

The queen didn't look to be in any condition to prevent anyone from leaving her royal presence at the moment. Frankly, Tessa doubted the keening woman remembered her own name at the moment.

Rustam opened his mouth as if to say something as Tessa turned to leave. She paused momentarily, one eyebrow raised in question. But then he shook his head again and gestured with a jerk of his chin toward the door. Right. As if he was in any position to order her around!

And on that wry note, she turned to leave what she sincerely hoped would be her last orgy at the imperial court of the king of kings, ruler of the Medes and Achemens, of Ethiopia and India and all between, His Glorious Majesty, Emperor Xerxes of Parsa.

As she neared an exit, a pair of jostling, laughing young men closed in on her.

"Aww, you're not leaving are you, Lady of Snow?"

"We have yet to even learn your name, fair one! Do not so callously abandon us without satisfying our curiosity."

"I'm afraid your parties wear me out. I don't have the stamina for this sort of thing."

The youths laughed. "It takes practice. Lots and lots of practice."

She grinned and rolled her eyes. "I'll leave you to it, then. I really am tired. Maybe tomorrow night I'll last a little longer."

A shadow passed across the taller one's face and he retorted sourly, "No feast tomorrow. The emperor says it's not seemly to celebrate while our foot soldiers are fighting for the glory of the empire."

She had to go with Xerxes on this one. The idea of partying hearty at the officers' club while her troops put their lives on the line was blasphemous to her.

"Let us give you safe escort back to your quarters, fair princess."

She glanced over her shoulder, seeking a glimpse of Rustam. If anyone was going to escort her back to her room, she'd assumed it would've been him. After all, he was crazily possessive of her and didn't seem to want to share her. But at the moment, his dark head was buried in Artemesia's neck. That woman was still going at it? Dang. It almost made a modern girl feel a wee bit inadequate.

Tessa turned her attention back to the eager puppies beside her. "If you want to walk me back to my room, that's fine. Just so long as you understand there'll be no invitation to come in, and no hanky-panky."

"What's this *hanky-panky?*" the short one asked. "It sounds fun."

Tessa swept her hand wide to encompass the hall. "*This* is hanky-panky."

The youths laughed and she sighed in relief as they stepped out into a colonnaded hall. It wasn't just the quiet that was welcome; it was the cessation of sensory overload. Even her skin felt relief from the buzzing, heavily sexual vibrations that had jangled across it in the feasting hall.

"This way, my lady."

"But my room's that way."

"This is a shortcut. Trust me."

In her military career, she'd learned two incontrovertible truths. One was that shortcuts were never short. And two, if someone told you to trust them, you never, ever should.

She stopped dead in her tracks. "I'm tired and just want to go to my room and sleep. Go back to the party. I'm done for the night."

"I don't think so," one of them said, abruptly unfriendly. The two young men grabbed her by her elbows.

Two on one, she'd have eaten these guys for lunch, but out of nowhere, six more young men materialized, surrounding her like a pack of dogs. She looked over their heads for the nearest guard.

"Guard!" she called. "I need you to escort me back to my quarters. Now."

The man started to take a step forward, but then his eyes widened. He took a look at the group surrounding her, and pointedly turned his back to face the other way, his spine rigid.

Dammit.

Gotta get them talking. Distract them. Buy time. Maybe someone else would come out and interrupt the ugly direction this was going.

"Who are you, anyway?" she asked conversationally. "I gather you all know each other."

The youths seemed startled that she showed no fear, but actually stopped hustling her off toward the shadows behind a pillar to introduce themselves. From what she gathered, they were young princes for the most part, sons of Xerxes's top advisors and military commanders. No wonder the guard had turned his back.

The youths laughed. But it wasn't a pleasant sound of amusement.

She had to get her back to a wall. As close to the banquet hall as she could manage. Maybe someone would hear her cry for help and come out to investigate. Or maybe not. She recalled the young woman who'd screamed right after Tessa arrived. No one had rushed out to help her.... Apparently gang-raping slave girls was socially acceptable around here. *Slave girls...*

As several hands grabbed at her, she drew herself up to her full height and said sharply, "Unhand me. I am a princess and you have no right to touch me. I'll have you up on charges before Xerxes for this. And when the emperor loses the trade and food imports he's going to get from my country, he'll be furious. After all, he's got an army to feed. He'll string every last one of you up by your thumbs and flay you alive."

That gave a few of the least drunk of them pause, but unfortunately, didn't faze the rest. Why, oh, why had she left her dagger in her room?

Her shoulder blades bumped into uneven stone. A column. Not ideal for protecting her back, but better than nothing. She tried one last time. "Gentlemen, I'm going to tell you this once and once only. I am not some helpless female you can bully around and intimidate. I am giving you fair warning that I will do whatever it takes to defend myself. Don't do this. Go find yourself some woman who's willing. Leave me alone."

Apparently, that served as an unspoken signal for the young men to rush her. Cursing under her breath, she whipped her foot out in a knee-high sweep. The move was illegal in martial arts tournaments precisely because of the damage it could cause. She clocked the closest guy on the outside of his knee, and he went down, swearing vilely.

The other youths checked, startled. But then a feral gleam entered their collective gazes. "Ahh. A fighter," one of them crowed. "I like 'em with spirit. More fun when you break 'em to be ridden."

Panic climbed the back of her throat. This was not going down well. Not well at all. She was way outnumbered, and nobody was coming to help her. Grim realization that she might lose, and that these men might rape her, washed over her.

Her cuff. She needed to get out of here. Except her mission would be a failure, and someone else would have to come right back and pick up where she'd left off—without the benefit of her psychic skill at locating objects. Given that the medallion piece seemed to be on the move and no longer at court, her ability was vital to this mission's success. But rape? That was emphatically *not* part of the job description.

What if she blinked out of existence before the very eyes of this group? What stories would that cause? What superstitions would she start? Would she damage this culture—or more to the point, leave a modern fingerprint upon it?

Normally, Tessa didn't hesitate in making a decision, but she truly didn't know what to do. On one hand, she really, really didn't want to be attacked. On the other hand, the future of mankind might rest upon her sticking with this mission. She needed to get away from these assailants for just a second or two before she used the cuff. They were drunk enough that she ought to be able to duck around the column and activate it before they realized what had happened.

Hands grabbed at her, too many to swat away this time, buzzing around her as persistent as angry wasps. Dammit, she hated to fail. Rising fear at the back of her throat reminded her that this was no joke, though. She could *die*. But then, she'd known all along that she could die on this mission. She fingered the pouch at her waist. Should she go ahead and use the cuff now?

Unbidden, a vision of Athena Carswell and Beverly Ashton flashed through her head. Both were formidable women, and both were counting on her. They believed she could handle whatever came at her on this mission. It was why she'd been hand-selected and intensively trained for this.

So be it. She'd confront these drunks and figure out a way to get away from them before she had to use the cuff.

Meanwhile, these ancient twerps wanted a fight? Then a fight they would get. More than they bargained for. Without warning, she sucker punched the nearest guy as hard as she could, right in the nose. Blood spouted, and he doubled over swearing.

"Bitch!" someone shouted.

And then they jumped her. It all turned into a flailing jumble of arms and legs and flying fists and painful yanks at her hair. Her gauzy blue dress ripped—frankly, she wouldn't mind if they tore it off of her, as it kept wrapping inconveniently around her legs. Someone punched her solidly in the right eye, nearly knocking her down. *Must stay on her feet.* Once she went down, she'd be lost.

A blow landed in her gut, momentarily doubling her over as the air whooshed out of her. She took a deep breath and came up swinging, continuing to throw kicks and punches and elbows. She didn't actually have to aim. Everywhere she struck, there was flesh and bone to meet her blows. At one point, someone got a hand over her mouth. She bit the palm until she tasted blood, and somebody yelped.

And then inspiration struck her. She yelled, "Fire!" at the top of her lungs. Never mind that she was in an almost entirely stone structure with nary a stick of wood to fuel a fire. If she could cause a stampede out of the feasting hall, or at least get a bunch of people to come investigate—

"Shut her up!" someone hissed. The youths surged forward in a rugby-style scrum. They outweighed her by hundreds of pounds, and new urgency fueled their attack. From her years of tactical training, she knew that in hand-to-hand combat, superior numbers will overwhelm superior skill every time. When all eight youths rushed her in a concerted attack, she was done. Time to leave.

Except as she reached for her pouch, she went down beneath them. Hands grabbed roughly at her then, shredding her dress and grasping her arms and legs with intent to pin them. Desperation coursed through her as the reality of this attack began to sink in. It was one thing to understand intellectually what might happen. It was another entirely to experience it.

Must reach the cuff. Vague awareness of her stupidity in waiting this long to bail out crossed her mind. But she didn't have time to berate herself for her mistake just now. She fought with all her remaining strength to reach her pouch, to press the quartz crystal that would signal Athena to get her out of here—now!

But in short order, the gang sat on her arms and legs. Still, she struggled to free her hand. Escape was so close, and yet so far away. She continued to squirm and heave, throwing off the guy who appeared to be their leader as he tried to mount her.

"Hold her still or knock her out," the enraged young man growled.

Something hard slammed into her left temple. Bright light exploded in her head, and she saw thousands of little pinpricks of light behind her eyelids, but fought grimly to hang on. *Think.* There had to be something she could do. But what?

As rough hands yanked her knees up and shoved them apart, she had just enough consciousness left to form a single thought.

Rustam! Help!

Fingers pushed and groped painfully between her legs, and she vaguely heard someone comment, "Hey, she's blond down there, too!"

She felt as if she were separating from her body, drifting up and away from the person on whom this outrage was being perpetrated. She was starting to retreat to some other place, a calm space of white light and quiet, where no weights held her down and no hands grabbed or poked at her, where she was blessedly alone.

The nightmare swirled around that other person, too awful to be real. Leering faces grinned down at that woman like lustful demons in flickering torchlight, the sweet smoke of the braziers making somebody—her, but not her—violently nauseous. *So. This is what hell looks like.*

Something blunt and smooth pushed at her inner thigh, and she gave one last, futile heave. Spittle sprayed on her face as a spate of swearing erupted over her. "Hold her still, dammit!"

A powerful hand closed around her throat and squeezed, cutting off all her air. In a matter of seconds, the scene began to go gray, tunneling down to a narrow field of vision. Damn. She'd been hoping none of them knew a move like that.

She closed her eyes, happy to sink into that other, peaceful oblivion and miss entirely what came next.

And then the weight between her knees abruptly disappeared and something heavy thudded nearby. The hand around her throat loosened. Despite her resolve to pass out, instinct took over and she gulped in air frantically, choking and coughing. Suddenly, all the weights lifted off of her. Her vision began to return, and she gaped at the sight that greeted her blurry eyes.

Rustam, magnificent in his fury, stood before a half-dozen

of the young men, his teeth bared in a snarl of towering rage. He sneered, "Why don't you try picking on someone your own size, boys?"

The word *boys* was pitched just right to irritate the living crap out of her assailants. Sluggishly, the realization that he was drawing their attack intentionally broke across her brain. The youths yelled and rushed him.

As Tessa struggled to sit up, Rustam went into action. She was happy to see that he fared much better eight-on-one than she had. But then, he outweighed her by a good hundred pounds of solid muscle.

Someone landed a punch on Rustam's jaw as she dragged herself up the column to her feet. He spat out blood and kept on fighting. A few more deep breaths and she was definitely starting to feel like herself again. And then she saw something that made her blood run cold. Knives had appeared in several of the young men's hands.

She didn't stop to think; just registered that the youths' backs were all turned to her and that Rustam was in trouble. She charged. Targeting a different attacker with each hand, she slammed her fists into the bases of their skulls. They both went down, probably with no idea what had hit them. She carried her momentum into a spinning roundhouse kick that caught another target squarely in the kidney. He dropped, screaming in pain.

As the youths turned in surprise to face this new threat, she shouted to Rustam, "Knife!"

He nodded grimly, wrapped the ends of his shoulder drape around both forearms and plowed into the mass of now-confused young men. Truth be told, Rustam did most of the rest of the dropping of drunk princes, but Tessa provided just enough mayhem factor to make his job easier.

A few minutes later, Rustam stood panting, a trickle of blood running down the side of his face from a cut over his left eyebrow. Arrayed around him on the floor were the unconscious heaps of all eight of her attackers.

"You all right?" he asked, looking at her across the sprawled bodies.

She nodded, too winded to answer him. And then Rustam startled her by vaulting over the bodies separating them and sweeping her into his arms all in one explosive movement. He crushed her in his powerful embrace, and she didn't mind one bit. He smelled of musky fear and the sweat of exertion, and she'd never smelled anything better in her entire life.

To hell with being a macho army officer. She buried her face against his chest and sobbed in relief.

He held her until the worst of it subsided, and then muttered in her hair, "Better?"

She nodded and mumbled against the warm security of his body, "Thank God you came."

It occurred to her to wonder how he'd known she needed him. Maybe he'd seen the youths follow her from the room. Or maybe Tessa and he truly had some sort of psychic link. Either way, the important thing was that he had come. In time, no less.

He leaned back to look down at her, his eyes black with banked fury. "Did they hurt you?" he asked grimly.

"They roughed me up, but you got here before they managed to rape me."

She glanced down as someone groaned at her feet. Rustam growled, "In that case, I shall kill them quickly and painlessly."

She looked up at him, shocked. "You can't kill them!"

"Why not?"

Why not, indeed? It wasn't as if she expected the Persian criminal justice system to do anything to them. Not only was she bloody well not sticking around here to press charges, she wasn't even sure that what the youths had tried to do was illegal. If they outranked her enough, they might have been perfectly within their rights to demand sex from her. For all she knew, she might be the one who ended up being sentenced to lashes or slavery or whatever they punished women with around here.

The problem was, if Rustam killed them, Xerxes would be forced to act. He'd have to appease a whole bunch of angry combat leaders on the eve of battle. For all she knew, Xerxes would delay marching on Thermopylae to deal with eight murdered princes.

A nightmarish scenario flashed through her head. What if the Greeks had a few more days to bring reinforcements to the pass? What if they *stopped* the Persians at Thermopylae? Would the Spartans get credit for crushing the Persians and rise to preeminence—shifting the development of Greece into a warlike, autocratic state instead of the scrappy but isolationist Athenian democracy it became?

No matter how justified she might feel if Rustam killed the jerks sprawled at her feet, she dared not tamper with history that way.

She just needed to get out of Xerxes's court. To slip away with the least possible fuss and go get that hunk of the medallion. The guards, still standing with their backs stubbornly turned to the scene, had seen her and could readily identify her. They no doubt knew Rustam on sight, too.

She reasoned with frantic calm, "You're a slave, Rustam. These guys are high-ranking nobles. You'll be killed yourself if you slay them."

His jaw tight, he mumbled, "Thank you for your concern. But I'd happily die, taking these whoresons down for what they tried to do to you."

Mutely, she shook her head in denial, terrified of the consequences of such a scenario, but completely unable to explain it to him. At all costs, she must not reveal that she was a time traveler.

He snapped, "Then what do you suggest we do with them? If we leave them like this, they'll come to in a few minutes. You and I will be arrested and crucified for laying hands on them. And with the cuts and bruises we gave them, there won't be much question but that we assaulted them, and not the other way around. It'll be their word against ours. And as you said, they outrank us."

She blinked up at Rustam. *Crucified?* For hitting back when someone tried to rape her? Outrage simmered in her blood at the unfairness of that. So much for the romance and adventure of this time period. The stark reality of women's and slaves' places in this society, substantially below that of a good milk cow, slammed home.

She sighed. "Let's just get out of here. If we're lucky, they'll be too embarrassed to admit that a slave and a girl beat the snot out of them, and they won't tell anyone about it."

To that end, she turned to flee for her room. But a familiar touch on her arm stopped her.

Rustam murmured, "A moment. There is something I can do...." He knelt beside the nearest figure and touched the youth's temple with two of his fingers. Rustam's eyes closed as he concentrated intently on whatever he was about. In turn, he knelt beside all of them, repeating the performance, putting his fingers on each youth's temple for about fifteen seconds apiece.

Tessa looked on, perplexed. If she wasn't mistaken, the air around Rustam and each young man shimmered faintly. If she hung around with him much longer, she was actually going to start believing in magic.

He stood up briskly after his Vulcan mind meld with the last attacker. "Let's go." He grabbed her hand and took off, walking briskly.

"My quarters," she muttered. "I've got gear. Provisions. We can leave tonight."

He veered toward her room. As she trotted along beside him to keep up with his long strides, she huffed, "What did you do to those guys back there?"

"I, uh, planted a suggestion that they wake up believing they got into a brawl with each other over a game of dice."

She screeched to a halt in the middle of the dim hallway. "You planted a—" She stared in shock. "You can *do* that? Who in the name of heaven *are* you? *What* are you?"

"Long story," he muttered.

"I've got time."

"Not now, you don't." He took off, all but running down the hall.

They reached her room, and she quickly pulled her bags out from under her bed. Rustam swept them up easily. She reached for her belt pouch—

And didn't feel it. She groped quickly among the tattered folds of her skirt. *Where was it?* Alarmed, she fished at her waist urgently. Her cuff was in that pouch! Her only ticket home!

She must've lost it in the fight. "We have to go back there. I lost something."

Rustam lurched. "Are you crazy? We can't. Those idiots will have regained consciousness by now. They've probably staggered back into the feast and are already hitting on some other poor girl. But if they see us...let's just say all my mind powers will have been for naught. Seeing us will make them remember everything."

"You don't understand," she cried raggedly. "I *have* to go back! I dropped something that I absolutely, positively can't lose!"

"What?"

"Long story." She repeated his words wryly. "But we *have* to go get it."

"We'll die if we go searching for this thing."

"I'll die without it."

His eyebrows shot up. "What is this item that holds your life in the balance?"

Damn. In her panic, she'd revealed far too much. She backpedaled hard. "It means the world to me. It's the last thing I have of my home...after the shipwreck and all. Its sentimental value is beyond price."

"Ahh."

Dammit, he didn't sound convinced. "C'mon. Let's go. You'll just have to do some more of that black magic of yours and make us invisible or something."

"I don't do black magic, and this is madness."

"Then call me insane. But let's *go*."

Chapter 7

Rustam frowned. He heard true panic in Tessa's voice. Whatever she'd lost was of utmost importance to her—enough to risk her life to recover it. It would be tremendously dangerous for them to approach the feasting hall again, but apparently, that was exactly what they were going to do.

He sighed. "What did you lose?"

"My belt pouch."

"Oh. That. I picked it up when I was adjusting one of those randy pups' memories." He pushed aside the fold of his short skirt and pulled her leather pouch off of his belt. A wave of enormous power passed through him, literally staggering him. *What the—?*

He hadn't felt anything like that since the last time he was on his ship!

Left. Right. Left. Right. Left. Right... An image of extraordinary clarity washed over him, as if he was seeing it in person. *Marching soldiers. Coming this way. With purpose. Focused on Tessa...and him.* He swore under his breath.

"Ohmigod. Thank you!" Tessa cried, startling him badly, jerking him back into the present. She lunged at the pouch, clutching it close to her chest like a long lost treasure.

What manner of talisman did she carry in there that so magnified his abilities? Rustam had never felt the like from any Persian artifact. "We've got to go," he bit out, grabbing Tessa's saddlebags and tossing them over his shoulder. "Soldiers are coming for us."

She didn't question his assertion nor did she need any further encouragement to grab her last bag and bolt for the door.

"Which way?" she asked as they stepped out into the dark hallway.

He'd sensed the soldiers coming from his left. The fading residue of that single moment of sharp vision didn't tell him more. "Right," he stated.

She fell in beside him as he took off at a ground-eating run. *Please the gods, may she be as good a runner as she was a fighter.* He'd been stunned when she'd waded into the melee with his attackers and proceeded to take out several of them with well-placed blows. He'd heard of warrior cultures far to the north where the women fought as ferociously as men. After seeing Tessa in action, he fervently hoped never to find himself at war with such a people.

A voice shouted from well behind them. He couldn't make out what the man said, but it might have been something to the effect that he and Tessa should halt. Rustam put on an extra burst of speed as she raced beside him.

"This way," he hissed. His unusual status as both slave and playmate of the Persian elite gave him access to every corner of the palace. He used that knowledge now to duck into a narrow servants' hall, winding his way through a rabbit warren of passages that led to the palace laundry and sewage disposal area. He suspected the guards behind them wouldn't be nearly so familiar as he with this portion of the complex.

"Good grief, what's that smell?" Tessa panted.

The stench *was* overwhelming. Apparently, the winds tonight were blowing back up the offal shafts. He grunted, "Chamber pots are emptied here. Breathe through your mouth."

"Egad," she muttered in a muffled voice.

He ducked back out into a main hallway as soon as possible, traveling at a right angle to their earlier flight. Several expensively clothed figures rounded a corner ahead of them, and he yanked Tessa into a dark shadow. Not enough space here to hide entirely, though.

He swept her into his arms, burying his face against her neck and pulling her head down to his shoulder. As the laughing nobles drew near, he ran his hands through her hair to obscure her face—and swore. Her fair hair would mark her identity more surely than the sight of her face would. Wrapping his arms tightly around her, he did a quick one-eighty, placing his back to the colonnade and shielding her with his body. To be safe, he pulled the corner of his shoulder drape across her head.

The laughter retreated behind them.

"Hello. I'm suffocating in here."

"Sorry." He unwrapped her quickly. "I was afraid they'd see your hair."

"Ahh. Sorry I'm so exotic. I assumed there would be at least a few blondes in this place."

That was an odd thing to say. He looked at her quizzically, but she added hastily, "Shouldn't we be going?"

He shook himself. "Right." After checking the hall, he took off running again. He spotted a small, unmarked door a minute later. Perfect. It led to a series of chambers Artemesia used for…discreet assignations. Which was to say, when she wanted to seduce a man whose wife might object, she arranged for trysts in these little-used guest quarters. Best yet, the suites opened onto avenues passing the far side of the palace.

But when they got to the street, the night was far from quiet, as a gigantic army prepared to move in the morn. "We've got to cover your hair," Rustam murmured.

Tessa thought for a second, then said, "I've got just the thing." She dug into one of her bags, pulled out a shawl of dark-colored cloth and draped it over her head.

He reached out to tuck in a strand of loose hair for her. Her fair features glowed like the moon overhead, pale and perfect. No statue had ever been so beautifully carved. But unlike marble, her skin was warm and soft beneath his fingertips, vibrating with life force so strong it danced all the way up his arm. He swayed toward her, drawn to her glorious energy like a moth to flame.

Her lips parted slightly as she gazed up at him. He knew she would taste like honey and spices. Her lips would be warm and yielding beneath his, her teeth smooth and even. Her tongue would dart kittenlike around his, driving him out of his mind—

They had to go. Soon. Before word reached the stables to seize them. He growled, "Stay close behind me."

She nodded briskly. He liked that about her. She was no weak and fussy female who fluttered her hands helplessly and feared to do anything new. She just nodded her head and dived in, all business, to do what had to be done. He stepped forward onto the wide, paved avenue. These Greeks certainly built good roads.

He walked confidently but not so quickly as to draw attention. A group of soldiers rounded a corner well behind them, and Rustam melted into the next alley. He sprinted down it flat out, half lifting, half dragging Tessa beside him. He plastered himself against the wall and she did the same beside him. He peeked cautiously into the next street. All clear. He slipped around the corner and took off walking again. Tessa breathed deeply beside him but didn't sound overly winded. Thank the gods. They might make it out of this mess yet.

"Where is your horse?" he asked under his breath.

"The royal stable. The small barn."

Small being a relative term. The barn she referred to housed at least three hundred horses—the personal mounts of Xerxes's officers.

Rustam murmured, "Perfect. Mine is there, as well."

He dodged into another dark, twisting street. This one was narrow and lined with brothels. Usually the resident females flocked to their doors to call out lewd offers to him. But tonight, he was lucky. They were all otherwise occupied, which, now that he thought about it, was predictable the night before a great campaign commenced. He and Tessa made it all the way to the far end of the lane without seeing a soul.

They emerged into a large, hard-packed dirt square. The south practice yard of the royal stables. Tonight, the space flickered with plentiful torches. Farriers trimmed horses' hooves while smiths checked and repaired various pieces of equine armor.

"Try to look like my servant," he instructed Tessa. "Stay a pace behind me."

She nodded and promptly cast her gaze to the ground.

"Slump your shoulders. Look more downtrodden. And try to think the thoughts of an unattractive woman."

That occasioned a quick glance up at him, her eyes dancing with humor, but then she did as he ordered. He turned and started across the square. With each step, he expected someone to shout at him, to order him to halt and surrender himself.

This was madness, of course, to flee on the eve of a battle. Even if the drunk princes never recovered their memory of events to accuse him and Tessa of assault, the two of them could not help but be suspected of spying for the Greeks. Why else would they flee in the middle of the night, hours before Xerxes moved on Thermopylae?

Rustam sighed. After being stranded in Persia, he'd spent nearly two years in Halicarnassus, and then Susa, with Artemesia. He'd established himself as an intelligent, educated man. A wise advisor. An innovative thinker who was an asset not only to his queen but also to Xerxes himself. Now he was going to throw all of that away. And for what? A blond stranger with a violet aura and eyes he could lose himself in forever.

Stupid, stupid, stupid.

He didn't live to chase women. They pined after *him*. When one caught his fancy, or he needed to slake simple lust, there was always an eager female about. But here he was, chasing after Tessa like a randy colt.

The sprawling stables before him were a beehive of activity. Soldiers and grooms were hard at work, making sure all was in readiness for tomorrow's march. Rustam was well known among these men for his extraordinary skill when it came to handling the most difficult animals. They often called upon him to help train problem mounts. Thankfully, none of his acquaintances raised an alarm upon spotting him. Word hadn't reached here yet to stop them, then.

"Where's your horse?" he murmured.

Tessa took the lead, moving quickly to the stall of a big, gray desert-bred mare. "I bought her this afternoon."

As Tessa backed her out of the tie stall, he looked the horse over quickly. Not heavy-boned enough for a warhorse but deep-chested and sturdy. This mare would go all day without faltering. Tessa had chosen well.

He asked quietly, his gaze fixed on the mare's intelligent brown eyes, "What's her name?"

"Uh, I don't know. The guy I bought her from didn't tell me."

Rustam reached out with that wordless part of himself he reserved for communicating with horses. "She looks like a Cygna to me."

"Cygna it is."

The mare nodded her head several times, as if to approve the choice. He smiled knowingly at her. He ran his hands over Cygna's legs, checked her teeth and felt the strength of her heartbeat. A fine mare, indeed. In another time, another place, she might even be worthy of his personal band of horseflesh.

"How did you pay for such a fine animal?" he asked Tessa.

"I had some gold in my pouch when the ship wrecked. I figured that if my life was going to depend on my horse, I'd better invest in a good one."

"You did well. She's a noble beast. Now go get your saddle. And hurry."

Tessa returned soon, carrying saddle and bridle. Between the two of them, they had the mare ready for travel in no time.

Tessa glanced across Cygna's back at him as he tied down the last saddlebag. She abruptly looked uncomfortable. "Uh, you go on ahead and get your horse. I'll meet you outside."

"We shouldn't be apart."

"Yeah, well, I need to change into riding clothes, and I'm not exactly crazy about stripping in front of you. It's bad enough that I'll have to do it with all those men milling around out there."

He realized belatedly that his nose was all but pressed against a *man's* saddle. For riding astride. And she was currently wearing a long dress. "Ahh. I'll meet you outside in five minutes. No more."

She nodded, and he strode down the aisle to where his mighty black stallion, Polaris, was stabled. He had turned down a king's ransom for the beast more than once. Quickly, he saddled the horse and led him outside.

True to her word, Tessa was waiting beside the barn, already seated astride the mare, who in the midst of the chaos, was rock steady. Rustam grinned as he took note of her riding breeches and tunic. She had great legs. Long and lean, but well-muscled.

Grinning, he commented, "You look like a boy."

"Well then, I guess I'm about to wreck your reputation for being a ladies' man."

"I'm afraid my preference for females is rather well documented," he replied drily.

As she rolled her eyes, he urged Polaris forward. Cygna fell in beside them. He glanced down at Tessa. "You've heard of my reputation, have you? Tell me more about it."

"How can you joke at a time like this?" she retorted under her breath.

"Because if we don't smile and talk and look relaxed, we'll draw far too much attention to ourselves. We haven't a care in the world, you and I. We're off on some small, but urgent, errand before the morrow, and nothing more. Now smile."

She looked faintly startled but did as he instructed. For a contrary woman, she'd thankfully chosen to listen to him at all the right moments this evening.

He guided his horse around the edge of the main camp, which was quieter than usual. Whether the common soldiers had already drunk themselves into a stupor or merely retired early, he couldn't tell.

Polaris's hooves thudded quietly on the dirt as they headed for the far side of the camp.

"How are we going to get by the sentries?" Tessa asked as they passed the elephant enclosure. "Surely Xerxes has some posted."

He snorted. "He is nothing if not a competent military commander. He was trained by Greeks, after all. Actually, I was thinking in terms not of passing the sentries but rather going around them."

"How do you plan to do that?"

"Not far from where we walked earlier, there is a cliff. It is not guarded, for it is impassable."

She stared at him doubtfully, waiting for him to explain further.

"A small goat trail winds up the cliff face. Your mare is sure-footed enough to do it, and Polaris has done it before."

"In the dark?" she asked.

"Well, no. But Polaris is a fine beast."

"And you're willing to trust your life to him?"

He answered quickly and without hesitation. "Absolutely. And your Cygna is also an excellent horse. They will look out for us."

"Forgive me if I don't share your optimism."

He replied confidently. "You'll see."

They walked quietly until a stone outcropping loomed just ahead of them. True to his word, no sentries or lookouts were posted nearby. Tessa stared up skeptically. He set Polaris's feet on the first rise of the narrow path, and then turned him completely loose, to choose his steps as he willed.

"Loosen your reins and give the mare her head. She will navigate the path more safely than you ever could."

"You're sure about this?" Tessa muttered, following his example and dropping her reins all the way to the knot tying their ends together.

He nodded firmly. "I am."

"No. I mean about going with me."

He glanced over his shoulder in surprise. She gazed back soberly. "If you want to return to the palace now, you still can. You can tell them I forced you to come with me but that you escaped. You can blame the attack of the eight ass—uh, princes—on me. Artemesia thinks highly of you. She'll believe you and back you up with Xerxes. You don't have to throw away your life like this for me. After all, you're probably not meant to do that anyway."

He frowned. *Meant to...* That was a strange thing to say. "I am the master of my fate. I do not wait upon the pleasure of the gods to dictate my course."

"Of course," she replied hastily. "Ignore me. I'm just babbling. But I'm worried about you going with me. I can manage on my own from here."

"The same way you managed against those boys back at the palace?"

"That's different. That was eight to one."

"And who's to say you won't end up facing the same odds or worse out here?"

"The idea is to avoid bumping into anyone out here."

"And how, exactly, do you propose to do that? You're fleeing before three hundred thousand soldiers, and racing right into the jaws of the entire Greek army. This peninsula is narrow and mountainous. You have limited choices in where to go." He glanced back at her and caught the frown wrinkling her brow. "You need me. Therefore, I stay."

"Doesn't Artemesia need you? What about Xerxes?"

He shrugged. "My place is not with them."

Her frown deepened, but she did not reply to that. He turned his attention forward as the trail grew steeper and narrower. He continued to leave Polaris completely to his own devices to find the best path up the broken, rocky slope. But he reached out with his mind to strengthen the bond between his horse and Tessa's, so the mare would unhesitatingly follow the big stallion's lead.

Rustam needn't have bothered. The mare was as in tune with his horse as her rider was with him. Odd. How had that happened? Or had Tessa's extraordinary aura already affected her horse, as well?

All of a sudden, the tumbling of loose stone broke the silence, and Tessa cried out behind him.

Chapter 8

"Report," the man sitting behind the desk snapped at his hired guns. These guys were supposed to be the best, but it was taking them an infuriatingly long time to get a lead on Athena Carswell's research notes, or whatever the hell was in that special notebook of hers.

The leader replied briskly, "We got ahold of the blueprints for the professor's house. Turns out a safe was built into the foundation. We believe that may be where she's storing the copy of the journal."

"Excellent. How soon can you break in and get it for me?"

"Tomorrow morning, sir."

"Why not tonight?"

"The safe is located under her bed. Unless you want us to take out the professor—which will cost you more—we propose to wait until she goes to work. Then we'll have all day to get into the vault."

He hated to wait even another minute. But if he could get

his hands on that notebook in the next twenty-four hours, that ought to satisfy his insistent visitor. The guy had stopped by his office again this morning, suggesting time was running out before something huge happened—something that would sort out those who would rise to the top of society from those who would fall to the bottom. No way in hell was he going to wallow in the pits of society again. He'd clawed his way to the top of the heap for the past thirty years, and he damn well planned to stay there.

He nodded at his hired guns. "Get me that journal in the next twenty-four hours and I'll double your money."

Avarice suddenly gleamed in the mercenaries' saber-sharp gazes.

"Consider it done," the team leader said aggressively.

Tessa had never been so afraid in all her life, not even when those jerks looked as if they might succeed in raping her. The cliff at her left was nearly vertical rock, and open air fell away on her right. The path they trod was literally no more than a foot wide. And then her mare slipped. The horse's right front foot rolled off a loose stone and shot out from under the beast, sending Tessa pitching forward over the animal's right shoulder. A black abyss yawned before her.

But then the mare flung up her head, caught herself on her right knee and staggered back to her feet with Tessa hanging halfway off her neck. Cygna stopped, obviously waiting for Tessa to right herself before continuing.

"Are you all right?" Rustam asked quickly. "What happened?"

No, she was *not* all right! She'd nearly pitched over a cliff, she felt like throwing up, she now officially hated heights, and there wasn't even room to turn around and go back down! Tessa squeezed her eyes tightly shut. She was absolutely sure that nowhere in the job description for time traveler did it mention dying a horrible death by being dashed to pieces on rocks at the bottom of a freaking mountain. She released a shuddering breath and managed to force a reply past her clenched teeth. "Cygna almost went off the cliff. And I almost fell over her head."

"Stay there. I'm coming," Rustam announced.

"There's no room for you to get off your horse on this stupid path," she snapped.

He said nothing, merely slid backward over Polaris's rump and to the ground before her mare. He knelt, examining the horse's legs. "She's cut her knee. It's not deep, but it's bleeding freely. The smell will draw predators, not to mention leaving a trail for our pursuers if they happen to come up here. I'll need a moment to stop the bleeding."

He fiddled with the mare's leg, but Tessa couldn't see what he did to it. She felt a brief flare of…something…across her skin. An electric tingle. The mare threw her head up but did not otherwise move a muscle.

"You're a good girl, Cygna," Rustam murmured a moment later, massaging the mare's forehead gently. And then he looked up at Tessa. His black gaze was hypnotic. She could lose herself in those eyes. "Be brave a little longer." His mouth twitched with humor. "And don't look down."

"No way!" she retorted.

"It's not much farther."

He was lying, but she'd pretend he wasn't. She knew full well they were only about halfway up the cliff. And from here on, a fall would only be larger and deadlier. She sighed. "Let's get on with it. I'm ready to be back on level ground."

He nodded and turned, placing his hands on his horse's rump and vaulting easily back into the saddle. Why the animal didn't bolt at a stunt like that, she had no idea.

The nightmare journey up the cliff resumed. Cygna moved more cautiously, testing her footing with each step before placing weight on it. There were no more near-death experiences before Rustam murmured from ahead of her, "There's the top of the cliff. I'm clear of the path. A few more steps and you will be, too."

She sagged in relief, sensing that Cygna did, too. Tessa reached down and patted the horse's neck gratefully. "You're a fine girl. Well done."

They moved far enough from the cliff edge to be safe, then halted the horses to give them a moment to catch their breath after the hard climb. The view below was spectacular—the entire Persian army was arrayed at their feet, poised on the brink of history.

"Shall we be on our way?" he asked quietly.

"Last chance to back out, Rustam."

She still had no idea why he'd chosen to come with her but wasn't about to drive him off if he wanted to. He'd already proved himself more than handy in a fight. And frankly, he made her feel safe. Tonight's events had thoroughly brought home to her just how dangerous a world she'd jumped into. But in good conscience, she had to give him a chance to change his mind.

If she were being really, really honest with herself, she'd admit that she had purely selfish reasons for being glad he'd come with her. They had to do with the flutter inside her whenever he looked at her, and the way her toes curled when he kissed her.

He answered grimly, "No thanks. I'm not going anywhere without you." Then he added more lightly, "Besides. No way am I riding back *down* that cliff!"

She laughed quietly to cover up her shock at his bold statement. Not going anywhere without her, huh? Wow.

"So. Do you have a destination in mind, my lady fair, or was your goal simply to get away from court?"

She sighed. The medallion. In tonight's insanity, she'd all but forgotten about it. "What lies to the south and east of here?"

"Mount Oeta. Beyond that, the Gulf of Euboea, which is a narrow body of water running down the entire eastern coast of the Greek peninsula."

She said carefully, "My understanding is that Xerxes plans to march down the coast to Thermopylae and then south to Athens, while his fleet sails down the coast alongside."

"That would be my understanding, as well," he replied drily.

"Then we probably need to head inland before we make our way south."

He chewed on his lip, the first sign of indecision she could remember seeing from him. "The farther inland we go, the more impassable the terrain becomes. Vegetation for the horses is scarce and water even more so."

"What do you suggest?" she asked.

He sighed. "We could go west and hide for a few days, then circle back to the north behind Xerxes, once his army has passed."

She shook her head decisively. "I definitely have to head south."

"Why?"

And wasn't that the sixty-four thousand dollar question? She thought fast and finally answered, "Because merchant ships are avoiding Xerxes's army but are probably still stopping at various Greek ports. I'm hoping to find one headed toward my homeland."

"How long a journey is it to your home?"

"The distance isn't the problem," she mumbled.

He nodded. "Sometimes the best way home is not the shortest one, just as the shortest path between two points is not always a straight line."

"You've studied geometry?" she asked, surprised. Her impression was that only a few Greek scholars were students of what was a relatively new form of math at this time. Hard to think of geometry as newfangled...but it had been in 480 B.C.

He shrugged. "I suppose we could parallel Xerxes's army,

but slightly inland from it. If we can get to Thermopylae ahead of him, maybe we can squeeze through there before the battle."

She started. He said that as if it were a foregone conclusion there would be a great battle at the narrow pass, bounded by the sheer wall of Mount Oeta on one side and a cliff dropping into the sea on the other. She had history to tell her what had happened, but how did he know? "You're sure there will be a battle there, then?"

"Where else? The Greeks are vastly outnumbered. They dare not meet Xerxes on an open field. But if they can reach a narrow gap first and plug it up, they might stop the Persian army. A tiny cork can stop an entire amphora of wine from pouring forth when it's hammered into the bottleneck."

She nodded. He was right, of course. "You can't seriously be thinking of going through the pass ourselves, though. The battle will commence in just a few days. Won't the Spar— Greeks already be there, setting up their defenses?"

That earned her a strange look. Dammit, she had to stop making comments like that! It was so hard to separate her foreknowledge of history from the moment she stood in now.

He said, "The two of us are well mounted. If we're quiet and move fast, I think we can beat Xerxes to the pass and slip past the Greeks. It'll be a close thing, but we're up to it."

"What about advance scouts from both armies? Surely each side will send out patrols to keep watch for their enemies."

"We must avoid them. I did not say using the pass would be easy or free of danger, merely that it was possible."

She grimaced, gazing out across the jagged landscape to the northwest. "I don't suppose we have much choice if I insist on heading south, do we?"

"No," he answered bluntly.

She sighed. "Thermopylae it is. Full speed ahead, then."

He looked at her sharply. "You have experience aboard ships?"

She swore under her breath at her big mouth. "A little. You?"

If she wasn't mistaken, that was a wistful look that crossed his mobile features. "Oh, yes," he answered softly. "I have a great deal of experience with ships."

A sailor? Yes, she could see him sailing the open seas. Pitting himself against the untamed elements... "You'd make a great explorer."

He all but fell off Polaris. He whipped his head around fast to stare at her. "Why do you say that?" he demanded sharply.

She frowned. "You're smart and strong and independent. You strike me as being brash enough to think that you could take on Mother Nature and win."

He relaxed slowly in his saddle, but it looked as if he forced himself to do so, one rigid muscle at a time. He was silent for a long time after that.

They rode all through the night, Rustam and Polaris leading the way, she and Cygna following behind. It felt good to be moving, at any rate, to be taking positive action in finding the medallion. Even if it was putting her smack-dab between two of the greatest armies of all time on the eve of their titanic clash.

Rustam and Tessa stopped periodically to rest the horses. A little before daybreak, they took a longer break, actually unsaddling their mounts in a small grove and letting the animals graze and drink at the tiny stream meandering through the sheltered spot. Rustam stretched out beneath a stunted olive tree that was little more than a bush.

"Aren't you going to tie up the horses?" she asked in surprise.

"Polaris won't leave me and Cygna won't leave him."

"But if you're wrong, we'll be in a world of hurt."

"A world of hurt? An interesting turn of phrase. Where exactly do you come from, again?"

His eyes were closed, his big body relaxed beside her, his tone of voice casual. But something about his...aura, for lack of a better word, was on full alert, focused with predatory intensity on her answer to his question.

"I told you. Far away to the north of here, in what the Persians and Greeks consider untamed wilds."

"Not so wild to have produced a female as intelligent and educated as you."

"Ahh, but I attained much of my education on my journey to this place." Which was also mostly true. Athena had planted in her mind much of the knowledge she was using to survive here during the time jump.

Rustam cracked one eye open. "Are you exceptional among your people?"

Sharply aware of his ability to sense when she was lying, she answered carefully. "I am not exceptional for my intelligence or education."

"But…" he prompted.

Darn his perceptiveness, anyway.

"But I am not typical of the females of my people, no."

"How so?"

He just wouldn't leave it alone. She remembered what General Ashton always said—the best defense was a good offense. "What about you?" she asked. "You're a sorcerer. Are you common among your people?"

Apparently, her tactic worked. He frowned deeply, looking nearly as uncomfortable as she felt right about now.

He answered slowly. "Among my own people, I am not strange. But among these Persians, I seem to be a rare and fascinating creature."

"They did seem more than a little afraid of you," she commented.

He abandoned his attempt to rest and sat up, plucking a long stem of grass and twirling it idly between his fingers. "I cultivate that fear. They leave me alone that way."

She nodded. That made sense.

"Why are you not afraid of me? Are magicians commonplace in your home?"

She jolted. He'd turned the tables on her and gone on the offensive himself. She shrugged. "People like you are not common but neither are they unknown."

"Do your people fear them?"

"*I* don't."

"Yes, but you are a sorcerer, too, are you not?"

She gaped at him. A sorcerer? She supposed that wasn't a bad label for her psychic abilities, to someone of this time period. She shrugged. "I guess so. My talents don't run in exactly the same vein as yours seem to, though."

"What vein *do* your talents run in?" He pinned her with an intense look, making no effort now to hide his interest in her answer.

She sighed. "I have a talent for finding lost things. Or at least I used to. Coming here seems to have dulled my ability somewhat."

He snorted, as if he knew exactly what she was talking about.

Was he implying that this place had dulled his psychic talents, as well? She asked eagerly, "Have you found your skills to be less here?"

He grunted. "You have no idea."

Her jaw sagged. So it wasn't just her! She'd been so upset that she'd let down the entire Anasazi Project. But it was this place that was the problem! She leaned forward intently. "Have you discovered any trick to magnify your skills here?"

He glanced up at her, startled. "I can still do things when I'm in close proximity to people, particularly when I touch them."

She nodded. "Like that shape-shifting thing you did. Could you have projected the image to anyone outside that room?"

He shook his head.

Interesting. Maybe all she had to do was get closer to the medallion to be able to sense its exact location. Athena had sent her to Xerxes's court because it was practically on top of the

Karanovo piece, and indeed, that first night when she'd arrived, it had definitely been nearby. But since then, it had just as definitely moved away from her...and out of her sensory range, apparently.

Mightily relieved, she was suddenly eager to get going again, despite her aching legs and lower back.

Rustam laughed quietly. "Relax, Tessa. The horses need a good hour of rest and grazing before we continue. We have a long ride ahead of us. Be grateful for and take advantage of this stop, for you will not get much rest later."

It was hard, but she followed his sensible suggestion. She closed her eyes, her thoughts spinning, and was surprised to find when she opened them later that some time had passed. She'd actually fallen asleep. The sun was up in the eastern sky and the air was already warming around them.

Rustam was not beside her.

She sat upright in alarm but relaxed when she spotted him across the clearing, saddling her mare. Polaris already was tacked up and ready to go.

"Good morning, fair goddess of my heart," Rustam called teasingly.

Okay, he'd said that as a joke. There was no reason at all for her pulse to trip over itself and then take off racing like that. But there was no denying the fact that just looking at him made her heart beat faster. Almost as if he could sense her reaction to him, he grinned at her over Cygna's back. She restrained herself from sticking her tongue out at him.

"Shall we be off?" he asked, after giving the girth a last tug. "If we ride hard through the day, we should have enough of a head start to stop for some rest tonight."

"Why not ride at night when it's cooler, and rest during the heat of the day?"

"Terrain's too rough ahead. The horses need to see where they're going. Besides, Polaris and Cygna were bred for and raised in this heat. They'll be fine." He added, "But thank you for your concern for them. Many humans care nothing for beasts of burden."

Her joints creaking painfully, Tessa climbed to her feet. *Note to self:* sleeping on rocks did nothing for her overall health and well-being. But Rustam had suggested that the bare slab of rock would be less likely traversed by scorpions or spiders than the inviting patch of grass beside the stream. Besides, now that patch of grass was cropped short, and both horses bore green stains around their lips.

She moved over to take Cygna from Rustam.

"Need a leg up?" he murmured.

"One wouldn't hurt. I'm depressingly stiff at the moment."

Instead of reaching for her bent leg, though, he placed his hands around her waist. She glanced over her shoulder at him, startled.

Mistake.

Their gazes met.

She could no more have stopped herself from turning in his grasp to face him than she could've stopped herself from breathing. As a new day broke around them in this isolated little pocket of nowhere, it suddenly felt as if they were the only two people in the entire world. A sense of peace enfolded them. A songbird of some kind twittered nearby, and one of the horses snuffed quietly.

She gazed up at Rustam, and he gazed down at her, a slow, easy smile lighting his eyes. His hands continued to rest on her waist, warmth radiating from his palms. She laid her hands on his chest, and felt his heartbeat thudding, slow and steady against her fingers. Oddly enough, her own pulse exactly matched the rhythm. She felt connected to him at the most fundamental level. As if one blood supply flowed between them, one circulatory system. One heart.

The sparkling display of fireworks she usually spied out of

the corner of her eye whenever they touched each other was quieter this morning, a blue-and-violet swirl that flowed around them like water, caressing them both and drawing them gently closer to one another. Instead of the usual prickle across her skin, this morning it was a light tickle, like gossamer butterfly wings fluttering around her.

Rustam murmured, "Have I told you today how beautiful you are?"

Her lips curved. "No. And seeing as the day is a whole half hour old, I'd have to say you've been seriously negligent."

The smile in his eyes spread to his mouth. His right hand drifted up, his fingers slipping under her hair to cradle her neck, his thumb caressing the line of her jaw. "You are moonlight and marble, a goddess of beauty and love, as cool and pure as fresh fallen snow. And yet there is fire within you. The strength and heat of new-forged steel."

Tessa inhaled in surprise, and he leaned down, capturing the sound with his mouth. His lips brushed across hers, undemanding yet beguiling. As tall as she was, she still had to rise onto her tiptoes to turn the touch into a full-blown kiss.

This morning a new tenderness blossomed between them. Maybe it was just her gratitude that he'd rescued her from the attack and had come with her on this uncertain journey. But it felt like more than that. Much more.

His hands skimmed up her bare arms, chasing away the goose bumps caused by the chilly air, replacing them with goose bumps of delight. His languid sensuality enveloped her, expanding to fill the entire golden morning. She swayed against him, and he absorbed her weight easily.

"You make me think of romancing a woman," he murmured. "Of courting you and winning you over."

"Mmm. That sounds nice."

His chest rumbled with a chuckle. "Yes, but I don't *do* that. Women fawn all over me and I grant them my attention."

She frowned up at him. "I'm not much good at fawning. And arrogant men turn me off."

"For you—" he dropped a light kiss upon her mouth "—I will do my best—" another kiss "—not to be arrogant. Or make you fawn."

Laughing against his lips, she echoed, "Make me fawn? You think you could *make* me do so?"

"Without question."

"No way."

His grin curved against her mouth. "I am really trying not to be arrogant. But it is a simple fact that I could do it."

"Nuh-uh," she mumbled, unable to tear her mouth away from his long enough to form words.

He lifted his head to look down at her. Abruptly, his gaze had gone black and inscrutable. "Tonight," he murmured.

She blinked up at him. "Tonight what?"

"Tonight, I will make you fawn all over me, as you put it. You'll beg. I vow it."

Her right eyebrow shot up. "Or else what?"

He considered for several seconds. "I suppose you shall claim the right to say you are the only woman who has ever made *me* fawn over *her.*"

"You never fawned over Artemesia?"

He snorted in disgust. "She's too power hungry for my taste. Too selfish."

"She would say that for a woman to get ahead in this world, she has to be that way."

He shrugged. "Perhaps. But she lives to accumulate influence. After tonight, you will live to please me."

Tessa burst out laughing. "I'll never live purely to please any man. There's a whole lot more to life than that."

Rustam's already dark gaze went even blacker. This time he smiled with his mouth, but the expression did not reach his eyes. "We shall see, shan't we?"

Chapter 9

The day's trek was every bit as hot and dusty and hard as Tessa had expected it to be. What she hadn't expected was to spend the entire day speculating on what Rustam had in store for her tonight. By lunchtime, she was in an agony of curiosity. By midafternoon, her imagination had run completely wild. She spent *hours* envisioning the best sex she could conjure in her mind's eye.

She had to admit it sure helped the time pass.

The mountains around them continued to be jagged and mostly barren. Somehow, Rustam found game trails and nearly invisible paths, and they picked their way across the rugged terrain far more easily than she'd anticipated. She was forced to admit to herself that she never would've been able to make this journey alone. As traveling companions went, he was a fine one, never complaining, and alternating between periods of pleasant conversation and silence.

He didn't seem at all fixated on tonight's promise. But she

couldn't get it out of her head. Every time she glanced at him, her thoughts galloped away with her, stripping him naked. Him stripping her naked, them stripping each other naked, them already naked…

At one point, he asked in concern, "Are you all right?"

She jolted back to the present moment. "Why do you ask?"

"You made a sound of…I don't know—pain, maybe."

She squeezed her eyes shut, praying that the sunburn overtaking her fair skin would hide the hot blush she felt exploding across her face. That was not a groan of pain he'd heard. It was a sound of pure, sexual frustration. And there was not a chance in *hell* she was going to admit that to him.

She replied as casually as she could, "I'm fine. How about you? You didn't get any more rest last night than I did, and I'm afraid I haven't been much help today in finding our way."

He shrugged. "No problem. I'm good at navigating."

His voice sounded oddly strangled as he said that. He must miss his life as a sailor. No surprise, then, that he changed subjects abruptly. "Tell me more about your people."

Not a topic she was fond of. "There's not much to tell. We're pretty typical of folks everywhere. We raise our families, do our best to have enough food and money to take care of our needs, try to find a little happiness along the way. What of you? Tell me about your travels."

He muffled what sounded like a choking sound. Wow. The business of his shipwreck and subsequent slavery must really be upsetting to him. To distract him, she asked, "How did you come to be in the…employ…of Queen Artemesia?"

"My ship wrecked in her domain, stranding me upon her shores. Her soldiers arrested me, declared me a Greek spy and nearly beheaded me before I was able to talk them out of the idea. After that, it seemed prudent to attach myself directly to the queen to avoid a repeat performance of my near death, and she made me her slave. Artemesia is deeply suspicious of men of noble rank. She fears that one will attempt to steal her kingdom—or worse, force her to marry him so he can steal her kingdom *and* enslave her."

Tessa grinned at that. "I knew from the moment I met her that she was a smart woman."

Rustam glanced at her with interest. "Women are as independent as she is where you come from, then?"

"More so."

He made a face. "In my home, a woman wouldn't dare to imagine ruling a clan, let alone a nation. No woman has ever attempted it. No man would follow her."

"These Persian men are pretty chauvinistic, but Artemesia seems to do all right being a queen among them."

"She has to be a lot smarter, a lot tougher and a lot more manipulative than a man to hold her crown. Why, she even uses sex to further her ends."

Tessa laughed. "You sound offended by that. If men are willing to let her use sex as a weapon against them, why shouldn't she?"

Rustam frowned, thinking about that. "Sex has its proper place. It's up to the men to keep it there."

The question popped out before she could stop it: "And exactly where is the proper place for sex?"

He shot her an amused glance that was so full of promise for later, she all but fell off of Cygna. "The proper place for sex is anywhere. Absolutely anywhere. At any time."

A vivid image of him dragging her over into his lap aboard Polaris, peeling off her leggings and pulling her down on top of his engorged shaft burst into her mind. The horse would surge beneath them, and he'd surged up into her....

"Stop that," she snapped, realizing belatedly that he'd been projecting the image into her mind. "That's not fighting fair."

The image faded from her thoughts, but not the lingering sexual irritation vibrating throughout her. Rustam commented mildly, "Who ever said I fight fair? I fight to win, my dear."

And darned if she wasn't half hoping he did win tonight. Was there actually such a thing as sex so fantastic she would beg for more?

Rustam chuckled beside her, as if he'd picked the thought out of her head. "What?" she asked him a tad crankily.

"I've already won, Tessa. Stop fretting about it and enjoy your defeat."

"Arrogant man."

He smiled unrepentantly. "And yet you want me, anyway."

She resorted to rolling her eyes because to disagree with him would be a bold-faced lie, and he'd hear it in her voice. There was no sense feeding his ego until his head exploded from it.

By the time the last streaks of sunset faded in the west and the sky began to turn dark blue overhead, she felt as if she were going to explode. Rustam declared that they'd made good time today, and that the horses really did need a solid night's rest. He stopped in a narrow sandstone gully that held them close in its embrace.

She unsaddled and groomed Cygna, carefully checking the horse's feet for stones and bruises before turning her loose to graze beside Polaris. As tall as the mare was, she was dwarfed by the mighty stallion. When she approached, Polaris struck lightning fast, teeth bared, and bit the mare on the neck, then used his weight to shove her closer to the spring trickling down the stone wall behind him. Tessa lurched forward to defend her mount, but Rustam's calm voice stopped her.

"He won't hurt her. He's just reminding her who's in charge."

Would Rustam do that with her? Dominate her without hurting her, to remind her that he was in charge? The man maddeningly gave no hint of his plans but went about the business of laying a small fire, with deadwood he pulled from the stand of olive trees clustered around the spring. Meanwhile, Tessa spread out their bedrolls on opposite sides of the fire. She caught the glint of humor in his eyes at the arrangement, but he said nothing.

She dug in her packs for hard bread and dried meat and fruit.

"Save that," Rustam told her. "I've got a barley stew mix we can cook. And since we can have a fire tonight, we should use it. We'll need those dry provisions later when we cannot build fires."

She did as he suggested, commenting, "You can cook, too? You're a man of many talents."

His glance suggested that she had yet to plumb the depths of his talents, and her pulse took off, racing erratically.

While the stew cooked, he inspected the horses, running his hands slowly over them. Both animals seemed more animated and at ease when he'd finished. It crossed Tessa's mind to wonder if he was healing them somehow.

It was odd the way she just accepted his gifts. She'd met some powerful psychics at Project Anasazi, but Rustam's talent was off the charts. She'd love to take him back to Arizona when it was time to go home, to let Athena study him. She'd bet the professor would be thrilled to meet someone of his ability.

He came back to the fire as the pot was beginning to bubble. He stirred some salt from a small leather pouch into the stew, and they sat in silence while it finished cooking. Twilight washed away the vivid streaks of color from the rocks around them, fading them to muted gray.

When the tantalizing smell of the meal had her stomach growling, Rustam finally ladled up a steaming bowl for her. She gazed down at bits of vegetables and meat in a surprisingly thick broth. It tasted great, but then hunger was, indeed, the best seasoning. The first bowl made her feel human again. The second made her feel like a new person.

Out of the blue, Rustam said, "How about a warm bath?"

She exclaimed, "Are you serious?"

"The spring trickles into a stone basin over there, then over-flows to form the stream. The basin is big enough to hold a person, but shallow enough to warm up considerably during the day. The horses have had their share, and I've already filled our canteens for tomorrow. Go take a bath in the basin. It should have cooled off to a comfortable temperature by now."

He didn't need to invite her twice.

She headed for the sound of running water and spotted the knee-deep natural basin easily. Steam was beginning to rise from it as the evening air began to cool. A faint sulfur smell arose, but who was going to be picky about that? It was a bath! Deep enough that if she sat down in it, she'd be up to her waist in water, which was more than adequate for a lovely soak.

She stepped into the shadows beneath the nearest tree and turned her back to Rustam before she stripped. Then she stuck a toe into the water, sighing in delight. It wasn't scalding, but it was plenty warm enough to soothe away the day's aches and pains.

She waded in, sighing as the steaming water embraced her foot, then her calf. She sat down, groaning in nearly orgasmic pleasure as the water went to work on her aches and pains.

Rustam's voice came out of the very shadows where she'd just shed her clothes, and she started violently, throwing her arms across her breasts. "I love it when you make that sound."

Good Lord. She hadn't heard him move, let alone seen his bulky approach. Man, he was good! She peered into the darkness, barely able to make out his broad shoulders.

But then he stepped forward into a shaft of faint starlight, dangling a small cloth bag from his finger. "Soap?"

"You are a prince among men."

He laughed quietly. "You have no idea."

As he retreated back into the shadows, she tipped out the soap, which was scented with rosemary and something sweet and floral, maybe orange blossoms. It was heavenly. She leaned back, wetting her hair. She rubbed the soap vigorously between her hands and then worked the lather into her locks. She smoothed it over her skin, savoring its slippery glide.

"Rinse?"

She jumped again. Jeez. He was right behind her. "Uh, sure." This time she stopped herself from covering her breasts. It was a brazen invitation, but they were both adults.

He held a large cloth in his hand. She watched over her shoulder as he cleverly fashioned it into a rough bucket. He scooped up water and murmured, "Lean your head back and close your eyes."

She obeyed, and he poured a torrent of warm water over her. "Again, please," she murmured.

There was something incredibly sensual about bathing in front of him like this. The water danced over her skin like a thousand shimmering diamonds, its warmth and glide erotic. She threw her head back, and cool air wafted across her breasts. And somehow, all was as it should be. Rustam was her man, and she was his woman.

Except they hadn't established either of those assumptions as fact, and she shouldn't get involved with him at all. She was only going to be here as long as it took her to recover the Karanovo medallion fragment, and then she was going home. To a home so far away he couldn't possibly go with her. And she was *not* crazy about the idea of staying in this time and place for the rest of her life.

But then a wave of soothing emotion washed over her. Apparently, he'd sensed her disquiet and had taken steps to calm her. "I won't hurt you," he murmured.

Perhaps he mistook her apprehension for fear of him. She corrected quickly, "It never crossed my mind to worry that you would."

He continued to pour water over her until her hair squeaked cleanly between her fingers. Then she stood up and he slowly rinsed her entire body with a warm cascade that did nothing to cool the ardor brimming within her. She turned around to face him so he could rinse her front. And she risked opening her eyes to peek at him.

She'd expected lust in his gaze. But she was staggered to see something else entirely.

Reverence. Awe, even.

She was a decent-looking woman, but Venus de Milo she was not. Certainly, after the legions of gorgeous women she'd seen for herself at the Persian court, he was immune to feminine beauty. She murmured, "Hey, I'm not that attractive."

Almost absently, he replied, "You do not see what I see. Your spirit. It's a light that dances across your skin like all the stars in the heavens. You…dazzle me. I have never seen another woman like you in all my travels. Not among my people, not among yours—" He broke off abruptly.

She glanced down at herself and saw only pale skin starting to form goose bumps as the air cooled her wet body. She frowned. "I wish I could see what you see."

"Maybe you can," he murmured, sounding almost surprised at his own words. He took a step closer. "Later. After…"

Her breath caught.

He raised his hands, unfolding a length of white cloth. She stood quietly as he dried her off with the linen. The not-quite-smooth feel of it sliding across her skin wasn't sexual in any way, nor was how he lightly toweled her hair dry. But the very fact that he was tending to her bath was so unbearably erotic she could hardly walk when he murmured that she should return to the fire to warm up.

She was stunned when he didn't go with her. But a moment later she heard the faint splash of water and glimpsed his big body, shrouded in shadows, sliding into the pool.

"Do you need me to scrub your back?" she called out quietly.

"No. You warm yourself. Relax."

Relax? He was kidding, right? She was strung so tight she could hardly sit still.

His bath was quick. Either he didn't need to soak his muscles, or he was more impatient to bed her than he'd let on. He towel-dried his shoulder-length hair into a silky, damp mane. Then he wrapped the towel around his hips and strolled over to the fire. He didn't seem the least bit affected by the chill descending with the night.

The firelight turned his skin to liquid bronze, flowing over muscles a sculptor could not have fashioned more perfectly. Not an ounce of fat marred the rippling contours of his abs or the sculpted definition of his thigh muscles. That towel, hanging low on his hips, was positively tantalizing.

"I knew you were a hunk," she breathed as he drew near, "but wow. No wonder Artemesia hoarded you all to herself."

"She never controlled me. I have always chosen when and with whom I lie."

Tessa forced her greedy gaze upward to meet his eyes. "And do you choose to lie with me?"

"No, I do not." Her jaw went slack with shock, but he continued quickly. "I do not choose *merely* to lie with you, Tessa of Marconi. I choose to make you my lover."

"The two are different?" she managed to mumble.

"Entirely. In the first place, I have not taken a lover since I became stranded here. I have bedded women but that is all. Even back in my home, I've never chosen a consort."

A consort? He was some sort of noble among his own people, then? No surprise. He had natural-born leader stamped all over him.

"I'm honored," she murmured formally. "Should I be worried about any assumed commitments or responsibilities that come with this status as your lover-consort?"

He laughed quietly. "Being my consort is not as miserable as all that. And there is the considerable side benefit of us being permitted to have sex with one another whenever and wherever we want. Did I mention I want you so badly right now that I can hardly stand?"

She blinked rapidly, startled, then rallied enough to quip, "Frankly, you strike me as the kind of man who just throws a woman over his shoulder and has his way with her, not the sort who stands around just talking about it."

His finely shaped black eyebrows arched in amusement. "Are you impugning my manhood, madam?"

"Well, I don't know. I don't have much to judge it by, yet."

"Have my kisses left you cold, then? I seem to recall them differently."

She said lightly, "My recollection of our last one is rather vague and distant. Perhaps you should refresh my memory."

He grinned broadly. "Forward female. Most men in my land would beat that out of you. But I prefer to tame my women by other means."

She rolled her eyes. "I'm beginning to think you're all talk and no action."

He laughed then, his rich baritone rolling up into the mountains around them, as much a part of the night as the stars overhead. No wonder the locals thought this man was a sorcerer or even a rumored god in their midst. He was larger than life. A force of nature.

All of a sudden, he was standing directly in front of her, though she hadn't seen him move. "I believe, madam, that you have failed to return the towel you borrowed from me."

Slowly, she reached for the end, where it was tucked in over her left breast. He folded his arms and watched her uncover herself, his eyes snapping now with unmistakable lust. She tugged the cloth free and unwrapped it slowly from around her.

And then it fell away. The firelight leaped, shining upon her bare skin, lending its faint golden hue to her flesh. How long she stood there, naked before him as he drank in the sight of her, she didn't know. Long enough for her initial shyness to give way to intense awareness of the eroticism of the moment.

If she'd expected Rustam to step forward, sweep her into his arms and kiss her into a sexual frenzy, she was surprised when he did none of those things. Instead, he reached out with both palms, holding them several inches away from her skin. He passed them all over her body, never touching her, just moving his hands alongside her flesh. If she'd been a native of this time period, she'd have sworn he was weaving some sort of magic spell upon her. As it was, she gradually became aware of a shift in the natural energy field around her.

And then she noticed something else. Her entire body felt intensely alive, each and every cell registering and reporting sensations to her brain. How was it that every square inch of her was completely energized and awake like this? It was an extraordinary feeling.

Just when she feared her skin might not be able to contain all of the tingling life energy flowing through her for another second, Rustam murmured, "There. Now you are ready to make love with me."

"What did you just do?"

"I aligned our energy fields. Now we're operating on the same frequency." He added lightly, "And while I was at it, I raised your sensitivity level somewhat. I like my women responsive."

"You make me sound like a horse."

He grinned. "And what's wrong with that? I happen to like horses a great deal."

"Particularly riding them?" she asked wryly.

His voice dropped until it was barely louder than a whisper. "I will not ride you. I will fly with you."

And then he was on his knees before her, startling her with the quick fluidity of the move. He touched her, his big hands sliding around her waist to pull her belly to his mouth. The kiss burned like fire and she cried out with the intensity of the sensation of his lips against her skin. *Oh, my.* This enhanced sensitivity thing was going to be very interesting, indeed.

But then she had no more time to think, for he drew her down to his bedroll, on her knees before him.

He murmured darkly, "And now for the part where you beg."

Chapter 10

Tessa's gaze snapped up to his. She was startled as much by the tone in his voice as by the words he uttered. Gone was all humor. Left only was overwhelming and entirely masculine intensity as he matched her kneeling pose.

"Spread your knees apart. Wider. And lean back." He was all alpha male now, giving orders and expecting her to obey.

A thrill of danger raced through her. Whatever she'd teased and flirted awake within him was fully in charge now. She got the distinct feeling that they'd already passed the point of no return. It was a strange sensation for a woman like her, used to giving orders and being in charge at all times—and over men, no less, in her capacity as a military officer. But this man, he took orders from no one. He expected her to surrender to him. And it thrilled her to imagine doing so.

Still kneeling, she did as he ordered, arching her back and reaching backward to grab her ankles for support. The position was awkward, stretching her shoulders uncomfortably and putting pressure on her lower back. But it thrust her breasts up in blatant invitation, and opened the sensitive places between her legs for his exploration. Her breath hitched with the realization of how vulnerable she was to him in this position.

He reached out with both thumbs and flicked her nipples, which were already swollen hard and so sensitive that she cried out. She lurched and would have snapped upright, but his hands stopped her, capturing her shoulders and pushing just hard enough to force her back into her original position.

"I did not tell you to move. I am not done with you like this yet."

She might have made some retort, but he leaned down and captured her right breast with his mouth, sucking on her flesh until she gladly arched her back, moaning in pleasure, wordlessly offering up her other breast for his voracious attention. Her arms ached with the effort of supporting her weight, but oh, my, was holding the position ever worth it!

When she was literally gasping in delight, he sat back on his heels, studying her intently, not touching her at all. Once again, he didn't react as she expected. She'd thought to see rampaging lust in his gaze. But he still had the towel wrapped around his hips, and his expression was one of intense concentration. What was he up to?

Finally, when she was all but chewing her lower lip to keep from groaning in anticipation, he reached between her legs. A single finger touched her feminine flesh, a long, light stroke of her insanely engorged flesh, drawing the dampness already gathering there forward to moisten the pearl of her desire into a slippery nubbin of pleasure. A jolt of electricity, so intense she nearly screamed, zinged through her.

Another long, light stroke of his finger.

Then a quick flick of his fingernail against that throbbing flesh. She did scream then, as a towering orgasm roared through her. She started to push up off her ankles, to throw herself at him, to kiss him and reach for his male parts, when a rough hand on her shoulder shoved her back.

"Do I need to tie your wrists to your ankles, or will you stay there like I told you to?"

"But—"

"But nothing. You are not ready for me yet."

Not ready? She'd just had her first-ever screaming-caliber orgasm. How much more ready could she get?

Then he proceeded to show her just how little she knew of the limits of pleasure her body could experience. Six, maybe seven orgasms later—she'd lost count—her arms trembled with fatigue. And yet she pressed her hips forward eagerly, offering her most private places to him with utter abandon. She danced beneath his magical fingers like a puppet, pleasured at first, embarrassed at some point by the excess of her lust, and then simply craving more. Without pride, without question, without restraint.

Every muscle in her body had long ago turned to quivering jelly. Every nerve sobbed for more, and yet more, of what he did to her. Her core muscles clenched and unclenched spasmodically within her belly, desperately seeking the fullness of him within her, seeking ultimate completion in this journey of unbelievably erotic sensation.

It didn't even occur to her to swallow the words, to hold out against what he did to her. "Please," she begged. "Please take me, Rustam. Finish this thing. Fly with me."

A small smile broke through his aggressive concentration, but he had the good grace not to gloat. He pressed a fingertip just within her opening. Her muscles clenched frantically around it, then responded in blatant invitation, showering his finger with the moist, slick rush of her desire.

"Ahh. *Now* you are ready for me."

His arms went around her then, and he raised her gently, laying her back upon his bedroll. He knelt over her, bracing his hands on either side of her head and slowly lowering himself until he could kiss her. She sucked at his lips, his tongue, mad to drive him wild with as much lust as he'd aroused in her. He groaned, and she vaguely registered that the towel fell away from his hips.

She made to reach for him, to pleasure him, but before she could, he leaned back on his heels, lifting her knees and positioning himself between them. Something hot and shockingly hard touched her where she most desired to be touched. She cried out, shuddering with yet another orgasm at the sensation. He waited patiently for the tremors to pass.

He seemed to be taking inordinate care to make sure his aim and angle were exactly correct, and she nearly laughed aloud. Did he think she was a virgin?

She murmured, "In my home, most girls become sexually active in their teens. You don't need to worry about hurting me. I've done this before."

He replied in a low growl, "You haven't done this with me. Trust me. I know what I'm about."

Who was she to argue, when that delicious shaft of molten fire was finally pressing exactly where she wanted it?

He muttered, "Relax, or this will hurt."

She noted with satisfaction that his voice and his control sounded seriously strained. Maybe he wasn't as immune to all of this as he'd acted so far. And then he began pushing ever so slowly into her, and all thought fled her stunned mind.

A stretching fullness became almost but not quite painful as he filled her up. Then filled her more. And more. She was impaled on a staff, the hardness and size of which were unlike anything she'd ever experienced. His big hands reached beneath her. Grabbed her buttocks. Lifted her hips with shocking ease, drawing her up to him. And somehow, she took in even more of him. Finally, he was seated to the hilt within her. If she moved a single millimeter, she was going to split in half. But as it was, the sensation was absolutely incredible. Ripples of pleasure spread outward from her internal muscles to the farthest corners of her body.

As if he knew her predicament, he held himself still, only the faintest pulsation of movement in his shaft letting her know it was living flesh within her and not hot steel. Her own body began to pulsate in response. Her hips didn't move—they couldn't, for he held her buttocks firmly in his hands. But her internal muscles began to clench and release, clasping him, drawing him into her, milking his flesh, coaxing him deeper into this unbearable pleasure with her.

He groaned, and his fingers dug into her flesh, but still he did not move.

And then, finally, she understood. He was waiting for her to move against *him.* For her to set the limits of what was pleasurable and what was painful for her. She withdrew slightly, then eased forward.

He groaned again, the sound wrung from deep in his chest. Emboldened by it, she moved again, cautiously finding a rhythm, and then increasing its tempo. As her body gradually accommodated his size, she grew bolder and more athletic. His eyes closed and he tipped his head back, his neck and arm muscles straining, veins standing out in stark relief beneath his skin as she drove him into oblivion.

At some point, she levered herself upright as he knelt, looping her arms around his neck, sliding up and down on him like a wild thing. Without warning, he lunged forward and bit her neck. Hard. He didn't draw blood, but pain shot through her, mingling with and somehow intensifying the latest orgasm ripping through her. He bit her again, marking her as his, and she quite simply exploded.

His arms wrapped fiercely around her, and the two of them zoomed up and out of themselves into the night, so fast her eyes could hardly register planets and stars and entire solar systems flashing past. A planet with a red sky came into view, a brief glimpse of a half human, half horse people, and then she and Rustam were flying again, ever onward. How many alien planets and peoples she saw, how many nebulae, how many swirling spirals of gas and shooting rays of light, she could not say. The brilliance of it was breathtaking.

And then, as soul-deep shudders started to build inside them both, the entire vastness collapsed back in on them, a billion rushing points of light imploding around them as a pleasure she'd had no concept of even imagining broke over them both. Rustam shouted against her neck, surging up beneath her. A keening cry tore from her throat to mingle with his as his seed spilled, hot and thick, so deep within her it filled her womb. For a moment, the entire galaxy whirled around them, fathomless and infinite.

And then Rustam fell backward, pulling her down on top of him, their bodies still joined. And they were back on Earth once more. Lying on solid ground. He drew great, panting breaths beneath her, his chest heaving, while sweat poured from her trembling body to bathe them both. If someone had told her in that instant that the world was coming to an end and she had to move if she was going to live, she'd not have been able to lift a single finger.

How long they lay like that, she couldn't say. It took her a while to recover—that being a relative thing after the performance he'd just put her body through. It took easily ten to fifteen minutes for the shuddering aftermath of her orgasms to finally stop racking her. She eventually regained the ability to move. A little.

He finally slipped carefully out of her and she managed to roll to his side, where he tucked her head against his shoulder and drew her close to his warmth.

Some pillow talk was probably appropriate. She should acknowledge his victory over her, should admit that she'd shame-

lessly begged him for sex and would happily do so again. But
the only words that formed in her mind were things like *Wow.
Unbelievable. Earth-shattering. Epic.*

He surprised her by murmuring, "Thank you. And I agree."

"With what?"

"With what you were just thinking. That was, indeed, epic."

"For you, too?"

He lifted his head enough to look down at her, one eyebrow
arched. "You need to ask?"

"I'd hate to think that the most mind-boggling sex I've ever experienced—by a lot—was just another day at the office for you."

He collapsed back against the ground, laughing quietly.
"No. That was not…the usual."

Thank goodness. As her brain finally began to function
again, albeit sluggishly, she frowned. "What were those images
you sent me?"

He tensed beside her. "What images?"

"The places. The people. You said you were going to fly with
me, but I swear, you just took me on a guided tour of the
galaxy."

He went board-stiff beneath her, so tense it felt as if he
might splinter into a million painfully sharp slivers.

She sat up, startled. What had she said? She'd made the
comment lightly, in jest. But he was reacting as if she'd just
accused him of killing someone…and he was guilty as hell
of the crime.

"What?" she asked.

He stared up at her in nothing less than total shock. "You
remember all that?"

"Well, yes. Why wouldn't I?"

"Because I didn't send you a damn thing. You *took* those
images from my mind. You stole them!"

"I did no such thing," she blurted in alarm. "I would never
steal anything, least of all your—"

Without warning, he surged up over her with that blinding speed of his, flipping her onto her back, his hand encircling her neck. He growled down at her, "Who are you? And how did you do that?"

"Do *what?*" she cried in frustration. "What in the world are you talking about? You're the one who put those images into my head. I have no idea how to do what you're accusing me of. And even if I could do it, I wouldn't. It's not ethical!"

His fingers began to tighten. "Tell me this instant who you are or I swear, I will kill you here and now."

Chapter 11

Rustam glared down at the woman on the ground beneath him. She was no ignorant barbarian, tragically shipwrecked upon the shores of Greece. No woman, of his own kind or foreign, had ever done anything remotely like that to him during sex—or not during sex, for that matter. Tessa had mind-raped him! Those images were *private*.

She looked genuinely confused beneath him. A hint of fear glinted in her silvery eyes. He probed her mind with his, aggressively and without finesse. His truth sense was completely quiet. No doubt about it—she wasn't telling him a lie.

Why, of all the women he could've met, did he have to fall for the one monstrously powerful psychic who had no idea whatsoever how to control her skill?

How could the magnificence they'd just shared have turned, so quickly, into his hand around her neck and enough rage to kill her? Even if she'd blatantly and intentionally stolen his thoughts, he'd already declared her his consort. He couldn't kill her if he wanted to; tradition strictly forbade it. Disgusted, he released her neck and sat up, turning away from her.

He'd known that if he could drive her far enough into the throes of passion, she might turn her power completely loose, accidentally or otherwise. And she had. Ye gods, had she ever. It had all but ripped his mind from his body permanently. He'd had to struggle to draw them back to Earth, to their bodies, at the end. His orgasm had been so overpowering, he'd almost lost them both in it.

It would have been a hell of a great way to die, but he hadn't fought this hard to say alive here for this long to throw it all away in a single moment of admittedly incredible pleasure.

He swore under his breath. He'd had some amazing sex in his day, but what they'd just done had been in another class altogether. He'd never heard of anyone experiencing something like that for real.

His people were frankly sexual, and males in particular took their pleasure freely and often. But in his not inconsiderable experience with partaking of sex, both here and at home, Rustam had never heard of anything like what had just happened to them. What he and Tessa had made between them—that had been the stuff of legends. Mystics among his people talked about bonded soul mates in epic terms of love that transcended the physical body. Of expansion of mental powers into realms most of his kind couldn't fathom. Of awareness that encompassed vast reaches of the heavens and beyond.

But…he and Tessa couldn't possibly be soul mates! They were from totally different places. Their backgrounds and cultures were entirely dissimilar. She barely even knew she was psychic, let alone had begun to harness her abilities. They had nothing in common. Nothing at all!

Nothing except that swirling indigo vortex that built around them anytime they got close to one another. And that impossible flight to the far side of the stars and back… They'd both let down all their mental barriers in that moment of orgasm. They'd both turned their power loose. Completely. Could it be? Was she more like him than he'd realized? In *that* way?

Impossible.

No female possessed his powers. Only the men of his kind did. And yet the incontrovertible evidence of her ability was staring him right in the face. Could she be a—

"I've got it!" she cried out from beside him, startling him badly.

He scowled down at her. "Got what?"

"I find lost things. I told you that, right?"

He nodded.

"Well, I've been looking for something lost. And I just got another read on it. It's that way." She pointed eagerly to the southeast. "Ten or fifteen miles, maybe. What lies in that direction?"

"How far is a mile?"

"A little over five thousand lengths of your foot."

Rustam frowned and did some quick mental math. "That's along the coast, or maybe even a little out into the sea."

She frowned. "Did Xerxes recently send any ships that way?"

Rustam lurched. Only his status as a royal insider gave him the answer to that question. "Yes, in fact. He has ordered part of his personal fleet south to join his main fleet in chasing the Athenian navy."

Tessa frowned. "How much farther until we reach Thermopylae?"

"In your miles, maybe seven or eight as a bird flies. But our route will be far from straight in this terrain. We should reach it tomorrow afternoon."

"Any guess as to how long it'll take Xerxes's army to get there?"

"Maybe two more days. They'll camp overnight to rest, and then attack the pass at dawn the following morn. Many Persians are sun worshippers, and it's good luck to do things with the rising of the sun."

She nodded briskly. "We should have plenty of food and water to reach the pass, then."

Thank the gods. She'd turned her attention to bread and water skins and away from the strange images in his mind.

But then she muttered, "How is it that I can see that stupid medallion when I'm with you, but not when I'm by myself?"

He stared down at her as an awful suspicion planted itself in his head. Was she borrowing more than his thoughts? *Was she stealing his actual power?* There was only one way to tell.

"Rest now. I have to go check on the horses." He pushed himself to his feet and moved away from her, walking to the far side of the clearing, near the trees. Polaris whuffed quietly at him.

He scratched the horse's ears affectionately and murmured, "Go back to sleep, boy." Cygna poked her nose at him sleepily, and he gave it a brief rub, too.

He waded quietly across the shallow stream and found a flat spot on the far side. He sat down cross-legged and assumed a comfortable meditation pose. He sank deeply into the nearly unconscious portion of his mind.

It had been a long time since he had done this. Too long.

First, he rendered his naked flesh impervious to the chill around him. Then he released the residual tension of his love-making with Tessa from his body. The remains of her pleasure clung to him, bits of violet energy that tingled tantalizingly, seducing him anew, begging him to come back and fly with her again. That woman could very easily become an addiction in his blood. To do that with her whenever the urge struck, to show her all the variations he'd learned in his extensive travels…

Focus.

Meticulously, he cleared the violet shards of energy from his aura. And strangely enough, lost something in the process.

With each bit of her he pulled free and discarded, his mind felt less sharp, his perception muddier.

When his aura was finally clear of her, restored to its usual cobalt-blue for the first time since he'd laid eyes on her, he reached deep inside himself to access that inner wellspring from whence came his power.

It was dry.

Empty.

Dark.

He'd done something wrong.

He started over, even going so far as to stand up and walk around a bit before sitting back down and repeating the entire ritual, clearing his mind, releasing all tension and sinking deep into his unconscious.

And it was exactly the same. Except a little more of the color had faded out of his aura.

Not only had Tessa stolen some of his power, she'd stolen *all* of it!

For the first time in his adult life, Rustam panicked. Not even when he'd woken from the wreck and realized he was stranded in this remote corner of the world had he completely lost his cool. He'd still had his power. It gave him a weapon of survival among these strangers, gave him hope that one day he would find his way home. As long as he had his power, he would be all right.

But now...

Now he was well and truly lost.

Tessa woke up groggily a little after sunrise the next morning. She felt as if she'd been asleep for days. Her swim toward consciousness was slow and reluctant. She felt weighed down, as if something heavy lay over not only her body, but her entire psyche.

Dang. Her first love hangover.

Lest she entertain the thought that it had all been an incredible dream, her body protested fiercely as she tried to move. She was sore from head to foot this morning. It had been well worth it, however. She doubted she would ever again in her lifetime experience anything that came close to last night.

Where was Rustam, anyway? The horses were grazing side by side not far away. Last night's fire was dead, and the camp was undisturbed. She bolted to a sitting position in quick alarm. He hadn't left, had he? While her body punished her for the abrupt movement, she looked around frantically.

There. Beyond the trees. He was sitting on the far side of the sluggish trickle of water that ran through the clearing. She sagged in relief. It looked as if he was meditating. She frowned and glanced down at the bedroll beside her. It was unrumpled. Had he spent all night there?

She levered herself cautiously to her feet, wincing every inch of the way. It felt as if she'd gone a few rounds with a heavyweight boxer. She made her way to the bathing basin and poked a toe in. The water was ice-cold this morning. She settled for dipping a corner of one of Rustam's towels into it and giving herself a fast, uncomfortable sponge bath. At least that woke her up.

She spent several minutes doing careful stretching exercises, gradually loosening her muscles to a semblance of functionality. And still Rustam sat on his rock, his eyes closed, his muscular body utterly still. Although there was no expression on his face, strong emotion rolled off of him, visible even over here. If she glanced at him out of the corner of her eye, pale blue light seemed to emanate from him. Strange. The last time she'd seen energy coming off of him, it had been a vibrant violet-blue. Maybe he was just tired. After their rather athletic evening and an all-night vigil, it made sense.

She got dressed, lit the fire and hung the pot of last night's stew over the flames to warm. While it reheated, she packed up their camp. Since Rustam was naked over there—how he wasn't frozen solid, she had no idea—she laid out his leggings and a light tunic.

When there was nothing left to do but eat, tighten the saddles and go, she headed to the stream. "Rustam?" she called quietly.

He didn't give any indication of having heard her. Wow. Must be in a deep state of trance or hypnosis or whatever it was he did. They really did need to get going. The Persian army was not that far behind them.

Sighing, she kicked off her boots, hiked up her pant legs and waded across the stream. She tried again. "Rustam?"

Still nothing.

She reached out and touched his shoulder.

Several things happened all at once. First, a violent explosion of energy passed between them, so strong and bright that even she could see it. Violet beams of light raced all around them. His aura abruptly went from pale blue to brilliant cobalt and back to that indigo mix of violet and blue that she was used to.

Second, a blast of mental awareness burst inside her skull. All of a sudden, she was vividly aware of the smallest sound around her, of the color and energy of the air and rocks and blades of grass. The bronze wedge's signature burned bright and clear, still southeast of their position, a bright beacon of energy calling her to it.

Third, and much more alarming than the previous two events, Rustam surged up off the rock, grabbing her wrist and twisting it with enough force to drop her to her knees before him.

"Why do you give it back to me now, witch?" he snarled.

She snapped, "Would you *please* stop talking in riddles and throwing tantrums when I have no bloody idea what you're talking about?"

He flung her hand away from him. Still on her knees, she glared up at him. "I asked you a question, and I'd appreciate an answer. What the hell are you talking about?"

He glared down at her, magnificent in his unclothed fury. "You took all of my power last night, but you just gave it back to me. Why? What did you do with it all night?"

She climbed to her feet, fists clenched at her sides, and glared back up at him. Their height difference probably diminished the effectiveness of her aggressive stance, but he was a bright boy. He'd get the point. She'd had it with his displays of childish temper.

"Rustam. I slept all night. Like the dead. I didn't take your power. I didn't do anything with it. And if you think I just gave it back to you, bully for you. But frankly, I don't give a damn one way or the other. I've got places to go and things to do, and the day's a'wasting. If you want to sit here on your rock and pout some more, be my guest. But I'm leaving. Now."

She pivoted smartly on her heel and marched across the stream with as much military precision as she could muster. She put her boots back on and stalked over to Cygna. The mare was skittish, and Tessa had to stop and take a deep, calming breath.

"I'm sorry, girl. I didn't mean to scare you. It's just that the man drives me completely crazy." She tugged on the girth strap and started to knot it.

Big hands came out of nowhere from behind her and pushed hers away gently. "Go eat some soup. You need your strength. I'll take care of the horses."

His voice was neutral, betraying nothing—not anger, not calm, not even a note of apology. She nodded stiffly and ducked out from under his arm. She split the soup between their two bowls, ate hers quickly, and then took the cooking pot to the stream to scrub with a handful of sand and rinse clean.

When she turned around, Rustam was holding a set of reins in each hand, his expression stony. She walked over and took Cygna from him in silence. They mounted up, and he turned Polaris's nose to the south. She fell in behind him.

They rode hard through the day, taking only two rest stops. Each time, Rustam worked on the horses, passing his hands over them and noticeably refreshing the beasts. She half wished he'd offer to do the same for her. But after what had happened to her when he'd passed his hands over her like that last night, maybe that wasn't such a good idea. She didn't need to be any more sensitive and tender than she already was.

Sometime in the early afternoon, she became aware of a faint salt smell in the air. The day grew muggy and uncomfortable as the sun rose higher overhead, beating down upon them mercilessly. They must be getting close to the coast. Which meant they were also getting close to Thermopylae. The name sent a thrill shivering through her—it was arguably one of the most famous battlefields in all of recorded history. And she was about to walk upon its hallowed sands. *Before* it was sanctified with the blood of heroes.

Rustam murmured over his shoulder—the first time he'd spoken to her all day. "Bring Cygna up here beside me."

They picked their way along the floor of a winding valley. With the exception of plentiful scree, the going was fairly easy. She urged her mare forward, and Cygna obediently moved up next to Polaris.

Tessa arched an eyebrow at Rustam but said nothing. If he wanted to get over his sulk and be civil with her, he could make the first move.

He surprised her by holding out a hand to her, palm up. Without looking at her, he said, "Give me your hand."

He seemed to be concentrating fiercely on something—something that worried him more than a little. There was a time and a place for picking fights, and one for just following orders. She sensed that this was the latter. Rather than distract him, she reached out for him without arguing.

The moment their hands touched, that wild swirl of energy leaped and jumped around them both. The horses threw their heads up sharply, but settled quickly. Steady beasts, both of them.

Rustam continued to study the mountains intently. Finally, he muttered, "Greek patrol off to the west. They haven't spotted us. If we can get out of this valley in the next few minutes, we'll be clear of them."

His hand dropped away from hers and the indigo energy between them dissipated. He urged Polaris into a careful trot. Cygna followed suit, and Tessa focused all her attention on helping the mare navigate the uneven ground. They slowed only when Rustam spotted an overhang high up the side of the valley and headed for it.

They had to dismount and lead the horses up the last part of the climb out of the valley. But they made it to the deep shade of a broad rock before anyone came along to spot them. Tessa was breathing as hard as her horse and grateful for the rest as they waited in their makeshift hiding spot.

Rustam held out his hand again. Wordlessly, she laid her palm in his. This time, standing shoulder to shoulder with him in the confined space, she felt his mind ranging outward, probing the terrain around them. Her own awareness expanded to encompass the local area. She felt the living creatures nearby, tiny pinpricks of energy crawling, crouching and slithering.

There. Off to the west. Three—no, four—large energy sources clumped together, moving toward the north. That must be the patrol he'd sensed earlier. The scouts were much closer than she'd realized. Rustam didn't need to tell her to be still while they passed by. The two of them and the horses huddled together quietly, waiting. This time Rustam did not release her hand.

A wave of protectiveness passed through his fingers and flowed over her. As angry as he might be with her, he couldn't help being who he was and taking care of her. She supposed it came with the territory of being an alpha male. Still, it must be hard to feel responsible for other people.

The Greek patrol passed perilously close to them, but then began to grow distant once more, moving off to the north, no doubt in search of the Persian army.

"No, it isn't hard most of the time."

She started. Stared up questioningly at Rustam.

He repeated, "It has its rewards, being an alpha male. Better that than some herd gelding who trudges along through life, docilely doing whatever he's told."

Okay, then. So now he could pick her thoughts out of her head.

He snorted. "Like you can't do the same thing to me?"

She jerked her hand away from his. Yeah, but he didn't have a massive secret like she did. If he picked up on the fact that she was a time traveler, she didn't even want to think about how he'd react. An even more alarming realization slammed into her. Sometimes he was able to pick up her thoughts when they weren't touching. She had to find a way not to think about… *that*…at all!

Caution dictated that she get far, far away from this dangerous man, as quickly as possible. Small problem, however, she needed him. No way could she navigate this rugged terrain and work her way past not one, but two, armies without him.

No doubt about it. As soon as they made it through the pass, she had to get rid of him.

He flashed her a sharp look all of a sudden.

Great. Had he heard what she'd just thought?

Chapter 12

Rustam muttered to her, "We've got a problem."

She didn't wait for the command this time but went ahead and stuck out her hand. *What now?*

Over there.

Okay, she'd definitely heard his answering thought. They officially had some sort of telepathic link whenever they held hands now. She reached out hesitantly with her mind to seek life signs nearby like he did, unsure of the skill and how to use it. But it didn't take any great expert to sense the Greek patrol that had passed earlier, running frantically back this way, scrambling over the rocks heedlessly, panicked.

She cast her awareness out beyond the men.

Oh, no.

A great, teeming mass of energy surged southward, not more than a mile away. Xerxes's army.

They aren't supposed to get here until tomorrow!

Rustam looked disgusted as he thought back, *This is*

*probably an advance guard. He no doubt sent them ahead at
high speed to seize the pass. He can only bring a few hundred
men into the narrow gap at a time, so there's no need to have
a hundred thousand troops at Thermopylae before he engages
the Greeks.*

Doing her best to keep panic under control, she transmit-
ted, *Any thoughts on what we do now?*

*Let those Greeks pass back to the south of us and then
follow them.*

To Thermopylae?

*We'll have to find another way around the pass. We can't
go through it now.*

Her stomach plunged. There was always the fabled goat path
that a Greek traitor had supposedly shown to the Persians and
which had spelled the demise of the three hundred Spartans
holding the pass. How could she suggest they search for it
when nobody was supposed to know about it yet?

Rustam muttered aloud, "Those Greeks aren't heading for
the pass proper. Perhaps they came around it another way.
Let's follow them."

The patrol was ahead of them now, racing south to warn
their generals of the arrival of the Persians. Problem was, they
were on foot, and Rustam and Tessa had two big, impossible-
to-hide horses with them.

They couldn't abandon the beasts—they needed Polaris and
Cygna for the rest of their journey. The horses could make
twice the speed and three times the distance of a man in a day,
and they could do so day after day.

The Greeks stayed inland, fleeing through the mountains,
following a chain of gullies and narrow washes that led generally southward. Behind Tessa and Rustam, a small party broke
off from the main Persian force, following the same route. It
became increasingly hard to move stealthily between the two
forces and conceal the presence of the horses.

Finally Rustam stopped. "This isn't working," he murmured. "Take off Cygna's bridle and stow it in your saddlebag."

"Take off—" she started to ask. What did he have in mind?

He flashed her one of those military-commander looks that she used on her own troops when there was no time to explain, but she knew what she was doing. She shut her mouth and reached up to unbuckle the mare's bridle.

Rustam muttered, "Take your water skins but leave everything else on the animal. Tie it down securely."

She did as he instructed. He made a quick visual inspection of her work, nodded his approval and gave her girth a tug to tighten it. Then he did the oddest thing. He laid his forehead against Polaris's. The mighty stallion closed his eyes, and for all the world it looked as if the two were communicating with one another. Rustam did the same with Cygna, who jittered nervously at first, then closed her eyes and tolerated his forehead against hers.

Rustam straightened, then breathed, "Go."

Tessa opened her mouth to protest as the two horses turned around, to head back down the slope they'd just climbed. He was letting the horses go? Was he insane?

Lightning-fast, Rustam reached out to clap a hard hand over her mouth, and an image of a half-dozen new human signatures close behind them flooded her mind. She looked up fearfully at Rustam and nodded to indicate she'd seen the new threat.

The Persians. He sent the message silently.

We're trapped! she sent back.

Not yet. Follow me. He moved off, easing up the slope before them, making his way mostly below the broken profiles of the plentiful boulders littering the slope. The barren, rocky terrain and incredible heat reminded her of summer in Afghanistan. She'd pulled a tour there a while back and had done her share of patrols in the hills around their base camp. It was hard enough scrambling up and down mountainsides like this but to do it quietly and without being seen was ten times as hard.

Rustam was indomitable. He never wavered, never became fatigued. When she flagged, he'd offer her a hand and half drag her up the next slope. But he never stopped.

In a perfect world, they'd have moved off perpendicular to the path of the Greek patrol ahead and the Persian patrol behind. But the terrain was horrendous as they traversed the face of Mount Oeta. They were lucky to have even one direction of possible travel. For better or worse, they were all making their way inexorably east. Tessa might get to see Thermopylae after all, as all three parties were stuck following the exact same course.

The shadows lengthened around them. The two patrols were evenly matched and moving at approximately the same speed. Whether each knew of the other's existence was anyone's guess, but both groups were advancing at a brisk pace. It was grueling work trying to maintain a reasonably equal distance between the two. But the alternative—being caught by either patrol—was unacceptable.

With sunset, she hoped the teams would stop or at least slow down. But neither did. Exhausted, Tessa dragged herself up yet another near vertical cliff, blindly placing her hands and feet in the holds Rustam sent her mentally. As long as they stayed within a foot or two of one another, they could send each other their thoughts telepathically. But as the trek dragged on and her fatigue deepened, she had to be practically brushing against him to hear him.

The moon rose. And then the unthinkable happened. The Greeks in front of them stopped…and the Persians behind them kept on coming. Rustam and she were about to be trapped between the warring parties.

The two of them looked around frantically for somewhere to hide. They stood on a relatively flat stretch of the narrow trail. The Greeks were less than a hundred yards ahead now, just over the crest of the plateau.

"The West Gate," Rustam breathed.

Her breath hitched. In her study of this period prior to time-jumping, she'd learned that the pass at Thermopylae was a narrow path with three choke points along its length. The Spartans had made their famous stand at the middle one. The West Gate was the first of the three, when approached from the northwest. If Rustam was right, that meant there'd be a vertical rock face climbing to one side of them—yes, there it was, just yonder. And on the other side…

She gulped. There should be a sheer drop-off to rocks hundreds of feet below.

As if sensing something amiss, the Persians behind them slowed, easing cautiously up the slope toward this open area.

Rustam grabbed her hand and sprinted for the only cover along the path, a few knee-high boulders with a little scrub beside them. They dived behind the bushes, plastering themselves against the ground just as the first Persian poked his head up over the north lip of the plateau.

She watched for the rest of the patrol to join him, but surprisingly, they didn't materialize. And then Rustam stiffened beside her. She reached out to touch him. Her fingertips encountered his forearm, but it was enough. The contact and shared auras were all it took. An image flooded her brain that made her blood run cold.

At least fifty more Persians were closing in behind their advance patrol. Fast.

Panicked, she cast her mind to the south. Of course. More Greeks were streaming in this direction. Great. This might not be a rock and a hard place but it was just as bad. They were caught between a cliff and a death plunge with two war parties closing in on them. It appeared that she was going to witness the first skirmish in the battle of Thermopylae.

Tessa felt Rustam's frantic thoughts sifting through and discarding various options. He, too, understood the seriousness of their predicament.

The night took on a tense, waiting quality as the two forces massed on either side of that plateau. No creatures disturbed the silence—no chirping insects or nocturnal birds, not even a breeze ruffled the stillness. She and Rustam dared not move. Each faction had lookouts posted just below the ridge lines, and any movement whatsoever would be spotted in a second.

The fifty soldiers from each side massed, weapons bristling. Tension grew until the air crackled with it.

If she and Rustam were lucky, this skirmish would happen at the far side of the plateau, and no one would stumble across their hiding place. Ideally, the Greeks and Persians would kill a few of each other's men, and then retreat to lick their wounds and let their superiors know where the enemy was.

If they weren't lucky, Tessa's mission might end tonight. Careful not to touch Rustam as she did it, she fingered her belt pouch and the all-important cuff inside. Worst case, she'd use the armband and bug out before she got killed. But what about Rustam? If he was touching her when she used the cuff, would he come back to the future, too? Problem was, she didn't know for sure. Would his powers mess up the time jump for both of them? She'd give anything to save them both, but she knew what his take on her dilemma would be—he'd insist that she save herself and not risk killing them both to make a try at saving him. But the idea was a bitter one.

She hated to abandon Rustam to die alone, and she hated to admit defeat. But she wasn't stupid enough to die for no reason. If nothing else, she had important information about the current location of the Karanovo stamp fragment that she could relay to the next time traveler who came back here to try to find it.

Rustam spoke, a bare breath of sound, "Here they come."

Her blood ran cold. The two of them were out of time and out of options.

A mighty roar erupted on their right as the Persians charged. Two ranks of men raced forward, shouting at the top of their lungs. The soldiers held round shields and short, thick swords.

The Greek reaction was immediate. They came charging over their side of the ridge, yelling their heads off. The din was impressive. The lines crashed into one another, and the clash of steel on steel, the grunts and groans and screams of the wounded, rose to join the battle cries of both sides. At first the combat stayed mostly over by the cliff—well away from the drop-off. But gradually, the Persians wheeled to the right and the outnumbered Greeks were forced left to face them. Tessa and Rustam were now behind the Greek line.

The Persians gradually began to press forward, forcing the Greeks step by bloody step toward the precipice. The Persians were intending to drive their enemies over the cliff—with Tessa and Rustam among them!

Rustam's hand gripped hers. *Get ready to retreat. Stay flat on your belly and crawl backward like a centipede. And keep your head down.*

They'll push us over the edge, too!

He responded, *If we're lucky, there's some sort of a ledge or toeholds on the cliff face.*

They hadn't been particularly lucky so far, however. Several more Greek soldiers went down. Tessa's military training told her that a critical shift had happened in the balance of the battle. The Persians now held a distinct advantage over the Greeks, and pressed their attack with renewed frenzy. Tessa winced at the viciousness of the fighting. This was no Hollywood-choreographed play of swords and shields, politely clanging against one another. Men shoved and kicked and bit and hacked brutally. Soldiers were disemboweled, while others slipped and slid through their bloody entrails. The thick, metallic smell of blood filled the air.

Rustam inched backward beside her. When he tugged on her tunic, she started to crawl backward, too. It was awkward and painful as her forearms and palms scraped across the rocky ground. Thankfully, no Greeks were looking back over their shoulders to spot the two strangers sprawled behind them. The Persians, although clearly winning, still seemed fully occupied with their opponents, as well.

Tessa's feet abruptly popped out into open air. She stopped crawling at once. She'd almost pushed herself backward off the cliff!

Turn around and help me search for a way down, Rustam told her mentally.

A few seconds later, she lay on her belly, staring out into space. Her head spun. The ground was so far below she couldn't see it in the dim starlight. *Oh, God.* Worse, the cliff below slanted inward a good six to eight feet. They were lying on an outcropping of rock, suspended in space. Tessa suddenly felt as if she were trapped in a bad cartoon. This wedge of rock could give way at any second and she'd plunge to her not-so-cartoonish death on the rocks below.

Anything? Rustam asked silently.

No.

Slide to your left. Look there.

But no matter where along the cliff they searched, they could find no way down. They were trapped. Worse, the Greek line was starting to buckle. Any minute now, the Persians were going to overrun the their enemies. It appeared that the invaders did intend to toss the Greeks over the cliff.

It was not looking good for the home team.

And then the unthinkable happened. The Greek commander shouted an order to his men that made Tessa's jaw open in shock.

He'd just told his men to fling themselves off the cliff rather than be taken by the Persians.

Appalled, she and Rustam turned to look over their shoulders. Here they came, some twenty soldiers, running grimly straight at them. If the Greeks hadn't spotted them yet, they soon would. And they would no doubt sweep her and Rustam over the edge with them.

This was it. They were about to die.

"It's been a pleasure knowing you," she murmured. "Had we met in another place and time, I'd have fallen desperately in love with you. As it is, I've relished every moment with you. You're one hell of a man."

His eyes widened in surprise. "It's not ove—"

The Persians, as if sensing the intent of their enemies, roared with glee just then and charged, lest the Greeks change their minds at the last minute and balk.

Rustam looked down at her.

Tessa expected despair. Instead, she saw grim determination. He had an idea of some kind. But she couldn't fathom what he planned to do. Whatever it was, it would have to be soon. The Greeks were close enough to spot the two strangers who had been behind them all this time. As clear as day, she saw the soldiers' indifference to the fact that she and Rustam were going to be pulled over the cliff with them.

"Hug me," Rustam shouted over the cries of the Greeks, who were now calling out greetings and prayers to their favorite gods. "Hang on tight to me!"

She turned into his chest, reaching blindly for her belt pouch. The Greeks were almost upon them. The precipice loomed no more than a foot away on her left.

"Give me all your power!" Rustam shouted. "It's our only chance!"

Dammit, she really wished he'd stop saying that. Her fingers groped for the crystal.

And then, his arms crushing her against him, Rustam stepped off into space.

A scream tore from her throat as they plunged into the abyss.

Chapter 13

Athena Carswell looked up sharply from the desk in her makeshift office as a loud alarm bell rang out in the main lab. The emergency recall.

She bolted from her desk, scooping up the headband and putting it on her head as she raced for her chair. She sank into it and quickly went through the mental routine to prepare herself for a time jump, while a technician worked frantically at the new computer console.

"It's Captain Marconi," the tech reported tersely. "All systems ready. Go!"

Athena nodded, already deep in trance. She reached out, seeking urgently with her mind, following the signal of Tessa's armband. *Hang on, girl. Almost there.*

And then a violent burst of energy exploded in front of Athena, both visually and mentally blinding. An indigo flash threw her backward, slamming her back in her armchair and mentally ripping her out of the time stream.

"What the hell was that?" the tech exclaimed as the console lit up like a Christmas tree in front of him.

Horrified, Athena reached out again. *No. Not another one.* She'd lost twelve travelers, but that was before they worked out the bugs in the system. Time travel was safe now, dammit!

Nothing.

Tessa's signal was gone. Whatever that massive energy flux had been—and the professor was dead certain it hadn't been a random glitch in the time stream—it had snatched her right out from under Athena's nose, ripping her signal away and tossing it God only knew where or when. For all the world, it looked as if the link between them had been *attacked.*

Athena sagged in her chair, drenched in sweat. In the reflection of the newly cleaned and polished time-travel booth, her face looked gray.

Finally, she roused herself enough to order, "Call Beverly Ashton. We've got a problem."

The sickening sensation of free fall nearly paralyzed Tessa. But then awareness that she had only a few seconds to activate her cuff spurred her past the horror of what was happening.

As she and Rustam fell through space, she plunged her hand into the bag. Cool metal met her fingers. She felt for, and found, the smooth, round crystal of quartz. Her fingertip touched it. Pressed.

Screams erupted above her. The first Greek soldiers had leaped.

A shout erupted from Rustam's own throat.

Without warning, Tessa was ripped from her body and thrown into a blackness so intense and so cold, she couldn't breathe. It crushed her, immobilizing her in frozen terror. What was Athena doing to her? This wasn't what her first jump, coming to Persia, had been like at all! Pure panic claimed Tessa then and she could form no more thoughts. She struggled desperately to move. To breathe. To catch herself and stop the horrible falling sensation that went on and on and on.

And then there was nothing. No sound. No light. No taste or smell. No sensation of body or not-body. No passage of time. How long she hung out in this featureless void, she had no idea. She was aware of existing, but had no capacity to form conscious thought beyond *I am*.

And then all of a sudden, a painful impact slammed her back into her body. She was assaulted by sensations—hard ground tumbling sharply beneath her. An unpleasant taste of soil in her mouth. Dirt. Sky. Dirt. Sky. She was rolling over and over. She caught momentary flashes a of rock-strewn, sloping terrain in the dark. She began to register the alternating cushion of a big body beneath her, and then its smashing weight as she and another person tumbled together down the hill.

Conscious thought began to return. *Rustam*. He was still clutching her against his chest. Were they alive, then? Shock coursed through her. How had they managed that? They'd just fallen off a five-hundred-foot cliff into a boulder-filled gully below.

Their rolling progress slowed, and she glanced around at the mild slope they lay upon. Where in the heck were they? This wasn't the terrain at the bottom of that cliff. There were no dead Greek soldiers around her. Had she passed out? Had they survived the fall by some miracle, and had Rustam carried her here?

As she continued to return to her senses, her awareness of time came back next. She knew without a shadow of a doubt that they'd stepped off that cliff only an instant before. So how had they ended up here? And where were they? Or maybe the pertinent question was *when* were they?

Had Athena rescued them from that plunge toward death and sent them to this place instead? Tessa had never heard the professor mention being able to do such a thing. In fact, she seemed to recall Athena commenting longingly that someday she hoped to learn how to do more with the headband than just send people back in time, and then retrieve them again.

Deeply alarmed, Tessa sat up. Or at least tried to. Powerful arms held her in a viselike grip, preventing her from going anywhere. Sprawled on top of Rustam, she stared down at him now.

"Are you all right?" he rasped.

"Yeah. You?"

He was breathing shallowly. Like someone in severe pain or bad respiratory distress. Or both. Even in the scant starlight, he looked deathly pale, his cheeks hollow, his eyes sunken in their sockets. He looked *terrible*.

"Let me go. I'm crushing you and you're obviously hurt," she ordered sharply.

His arms fell away without protest, which was a glaring admission from him that he was in serious trouble. He never obeyed her like that.

She scrambled off of him and quickly ran her hands over his body, searching for mortal wounds. His limbs were intact. His rib cage was not collapsed. He seemed to be breathing normally, if she discounted the fact that he sounded as if he'd just sprinted a marathon with a bunch of broken ribs.

She found no bumps on his head, no gashes, nothing to indicate a serious injury there. He had the same minor cuts and scratches that she did from their pell-mell roll down this hill, but that seemed to be the extent of his visible wounds. Why then, did he look like hell? He must have some sort of internal trauma.

"Tell me where it hurts," she urged him. She began pressing gently on various parts of his abdomen. He didn't answer, but neither did he flinch at any of her pokes and prods. A brain injury, maybe?

Squinting in the dark to see his eyes, she made out his pupils.

They were large and black—but then it was really dark out here. They *should* be fully dilated. She pulled out her fire-starting stones.

"Look at these." She struck them together, throwing off a shower of bright sparks. Momentarily, his pupils contracted—quickly and symmetrically. Not a concussion, then. She leaned back on her heels and stared down at him. Then it hit her. She was looking at the wrong thing.

She gazed at the ground beside him, so that her peripheral vision encompassed him. Dear Lord. His aura was practically nonexistent. It was a pale, shell-gray color, and paper-thin, barely clinging to him. Even as she watched, more of it faded, until she could barely make out any energy at all around him.

She lurched, laying her hands on him urgently. "Take my energy, Rustam. I don't know how you do that, but it's yours. Take all you need."

She stared down at her own hands in shock. She saw nothing when she looked directly at them, and had to remind herself to turn her gaze away from where her palms lay on his chest. Only a thin layer of lavender clung to her hands. It wasn't as depleted as Rustam's aura, but her energy field wasn't in a whole lot better shape than this.

He shook his head weakly.

"Don't argue with me," she snapped. "We'll share whatever I've got. I don't know a lot about all this energy stuff, but even I can tell you're dying. Take some of me, dammit!"

She slid her hands up, pressing her palms to either side of his head. Mimicking what he'd done with the horses earlier, she laid her forehead against his.

If that draining feeling, the sudden weakness, the abrupt fatigue weighing down her limbs was any indication, she'd successfully transferred some of her energy field to him. Too exhausted all of a sudden to stay upright another moment, she collapsed on top of him.

And slept.

Sometime later, something shifted beneath her, rousing her enough to crack one eye open. She was looking up at the stars. They had rotated almost a full night's turn overhead. She tensed her muscles to sit up, when something warm and heavy landed across her shoulders.

"Stay," Rustam murmured. "You need more rest, my brave little fool. Especially now that you're carrying—"

He broke off. She murmured, "Now that I'm carrying what?"

"Nothing."

"Are we safe?" she mumbled.

"For now."

She closed her eyes and went back to sleep.

The next time she woke, it was because something warm and velvety nudged her cheek. Insistently. She reached up to push it away, and cracked one eye open.

"What do you want, Cygna?" she mumbled.

The mare nudged her again, this time on the shoulder. The sun was bright overhead. It had to be at least midmorning, if not later.

Cygna? Tessa sat up, startled. How had the horses found them? Rustam was still out cold on the ground beside her. Both Polaris and Cygna stood over them, providing welcome shade.

Tessa looked around. They were in a gentle valley, completely unlike the rugged landscape they'd spent the past two days traversing. Whereas the terrain at Thermopylae had been of gray-black rock, volcanic in origin, this valley was beige sandstone, and the silhouettes of the nearby peaks, and even the scree beneath, were worn smooth with time. Tufts of wiry grass grew here and there, and a few wildflowers poked up their cheerful heads. This was *not* the same place they'd looked down on last night from the top of that cliff.

Rustam woke up beside her. One moment his presence was quiet and subdued, and the next his vibrant mind was active and awake, as dynamic and forceful as always.

She glanced at him. "Feeling better?"

He squinted up at her. "I'm alive. Still feel like I've been through a gauntlet of barbarians with clubs, though."

She nodded in commiseration. "So. Are you ready for a shock, or do you want to rest a little longer?"

He sat up quickly, groaning under his breath. "What's wro—" He broke off, gazing around him. He swore under his breath.

Oh, he sounded roundly annoyed, all right, but he was definitely not freaked out. He should be coming out of his skin right about now. They weren't anywhere near where they'd been last night.

Why wasn't he panicking?

He glanced at her quickly. *Guiltily.*

"Is there something you'd like to tell me?" she asked ominously.

He shot her a thunderous scowl. "Funny, I was thinking the exact same thing."

It went without saying that they hadn't borrowed each other's thought on this one.

"You first," she snapped. "Last thing I remember, we stepped off that cliff. And then I woke up here. How did we *get* here, Rustam?"

He winced. The guilty look intensified. "I cannot answer that question."

"Yes, you can," she exclaimed. "And you will."

"You wouldn't believe me if I told you."

An awful suspicion tickled the back of her mind. Surely not… But how else…? If not Athena Carswell, then who…

"Try me," she growled, suddenly furious. Too agitated to sit still, she leaped to her feet and glowered down at him.

He sprang to his feet, as well. The horses danced away from them, perhaps sensing the humans' growing agitation. Rustam took off pacing, marching in a circle around her, gazing at the terrain in all directions.

"I shouldn't have been able to do that," he muttered. "It's shattered. Unusable. I already tried everything before—"

"With all due respect, what in the hell are you talking about?" she demanded.

He shook his head. "It can't be."

"What can't be?"

"We shouldn't be here. We should be dead. Lying at the bottom of that cliff with those Greek soldiers."

"I'm well aware of that," she replied with scant patience. "So how did we end up here? What did you do?"

He continued to mutter to himself. "Our imminent death must have cut our full powers loose, the same way making love did. Perhaps even more strongly. It's the only explanation. But if I could do this, can I do more? Is it possible—"

She stepped in front of him, physically blocking his path.

He pulled up short, glaring at her irritably. "Don't interrupt me. I'm thinking."

"Too bad. I want some answers. And I want them now. How did we get here? *What did you do?*"

His gaze narrowed as he studied her intently. Finally he announced, "You're some kind of warrior princess, aren't you? You give orders as only a military commander can. You have an astonishing grasp of tactics, and you know when to stay silent and when to obey. You know your way around weapons and horses and camp gear as no normal female should. And you fight like a man." He nodded to himself. "You're soldier trained! Where do you come from?"

She rocked back on her heels, startled by the accusation. She shrugged. "What of it?"

His voice rose in indignation and he threw up his hands

in irritation. "Yet again you avoid the question. Name your homeland, woman. Draw me a map and tell me exactly where it is."

"Nice try, buddy. I refuse to be distracted from the issue at hand. You tell me how we got here. You know, don't you? I can see it in your eyes." When he didn't answer, she continued forcefully. "You're absolutely right. I'm a military commander back home, and a damn good one. And part of my training includes being able to spot a lie at a hundred paces. You're evading the question. Cut the crap and start talking."

As she'd expected, her strident tone aggravated the living snot out of him. He was not accustomed to anyone speaking to him that way, particularly a female. And he didn't appreciate it. His nostrils flared, and he seemed to swell up, growing even taller and wider than he usually was. Excellent. Time for one more nudge to push him over the edge.

"You're not *scared* to tell me the truth, are you? Are you actually afraid of me?"

His eyes snapped with fury. He snarled, "I fear no female, and certainly not you, human."

Human? Her jaw sagged. What in the bloody hell did he mean by that? If she was "you human," then what did that make him?

Oh. My. God.

Chapter 14

Tessa took a horrified step back from him. Another. "Who are you? *What* are you?"

Glaring, he growled, "I'm a traveler. I got stranded in this place by accident, just like you."

No. Not just like her. She was a time traveler. He couldn't possibly be...or could he? She was familiar with all the Project Anasazi time travelers—even the lost twelve. And they were the first ever to master time travel. Could he be from a future earth sometime beyond the twenty-first century? Possible but unlikely. He should have seen her face in files of previous time travelers, or at a minimum, known her by her coloring and modern name. Which meant...

She swore under her breath.

"You're not from here, are you?" she demanded.

"I already told you—"

She interrupted him. Time to cut to the chase. "You're not from this *planet*, are you?"

He stared. "How do you know what a planet is? Only a few astronomers understand the concept."

Rage began to build, roiling upward in her gut. "But you understand it, don't you, Rustam? You understand a great deal about the galaxy. Now that I think about it, you didn't even bat an eyelash when I used that term last night, did you?"

He opened his mouth to speak, then snapped it shut.

She took off pacing, circling him this time. "Oh, it all makes sense now. Your crazy psychic abilities. Your uncanny knowledge of what happened—what's going to happen—at Thermopylae. I suppose it even explains your ability to talk to horses!"

While she ranted and raved, he stalked over to the nearest boulder and sat down on it, his arms crossed over his chest. His alert gaze followed her every movement.

"So. Are you some alien observer who's been sent here to watch us stupid humans evolve? Or maybe you're one of those extraterrestrials who came to Earth to mess us up?"

He lurched, and she pounced in response. "You *are* an alien, aren't you?"

He said nothing, but his jaw muscles rippled visibly.

She was too agitated to press him for an answer just yet. "Or maybe you're just some exceedingly unlucky galactic schmuck who happened to crash-land here. But either way, let me be the first to officially welcome you to Earth, you alien bastard."

"Are you done?" he bit out.

It was her turn to cross her arms defensively.

"Sit down, Tessa. We need to talk."

"No, *you* need to talk."

"Sit."

The whiplash command in his voice was hard to resist. But resist she did.

He sighed. And said more politely, "This is going to take a while. I think you'll be more comfortable if you sit down. Please."

Dammit, she hated logical requests when she was this mad.

Reluctantly, she did as he suggested. "Start talking," she said truculently.

"You are right. I come from the stars. The reasons for my arriving here are not important. But my craft malfunctioned and I crash-landed as I said I did, on the shores of Halicarnassus. My ship was not repairable, so I dragged it out to sea and sank it. Eventually, my people will figure out that I've gone missing and come looking for me, I hope. The emergency signal I got out before I went down will take a few more years to reach them. But until then, I'm stuck here."

To hear him confirm what she'd already surmised was still a severe shock to her system. She stared at him in disbelief. She was sitting in front of a no-kidding, one-each alien. All the science fiction stories were true. Mankind was not alone in the universe.

Someday, if she didn't screw this mission up any more and found that blasted Karanovo medallion piece, humans might, indeed, take their place among the peoples who traveled the stars.

Her entire existence shifted on its axis as the truth sank in. Too agitated to sit, she jumped up and paced yet again, her mind racing. To his credit, Rustam said nothing, giving her time to absorb the immensity of it.

Finally, she stopped, staring intently at him. He'd almost managed to distract her completely from the question of what he'd done to get them off that cliff alive. "What did you do last night? We should have been dashed to death on the rocks when we hit the ground."

Confusion clouded his vision. "We… I believe your word for it is *teleported*."

"Tele—no way! It's physically impossible for people to just blink out of one place and suddenly be in another. Not without some serious alien technology…. Oh, wait. You've got that. You did it, didn't you? You brought us here."

His frown deepened. "My *technology* is broken. Otherwise

I wouldn't be stuck on this godforsaken chunk of iron and water you call home. My people can perform time and space displacement, but we need certain equipment to do so. We do not have the capacity to do it spontaneously. In fact, no race anywhere in the galaxy has such ability. Mind power must be greatly amplified through mechanical means to affect physical objects strongly enough to disrupt their conductive field patt—"

He broke off, as if realizing he was about to digress into a technical discussion that was not germane to the conversation at hand.

And in that moment it all fell into place in her head. Her cuff. She'd reached for it at the exact moment he'd made a last-ditch effort to teleport them away from that cliff. Because of the whacky psychic link they seemed able to share, he must have tapped into the power of her cuff by accident.

Curious, she asked, "As we went over that cliff, did you try to teleport us without your...technology? When we were falling, did you do whatever it is you usually do to travel?"

He nodded tersely.

That explained it.

It was his turn to lean forward aggressively. "How did you power the jump? *You* had to have amplified my thought waves."

She shrugged. She wasn't about to tell this alien traveler that she had a piece of his technology in her pocket. He would snatch it and boogie out of here. And then *she'd* be the one stuck in this place, waiting on an improbable rescue from the gang back in Arizona.

"You still haven't told me where you come from," he prompted.

She stared at him long and hard. A certain rueful humor glinted in his dark brown eyes, and gradually, the bizarre humor of the situation they found themselves in overtook her. The only two aliens on the entire planet, and they'd managed to run into each other and promptly get themselves into a horrible pickle. Of all the people alive in this place and time, the two of them should've been able to use their superior educations and foreknowledge of history to their advantage. And yet here they were, stuck in the middle of nowhere, running for their lives.

Oddly enough, they had even more in common currently than they'd had before. If anything, she felt closer to him, now that she knew how alike they really were. She studied him idly. She had to admit that, for an alien, he was one serious hunk.

"Is that what you really look like?" she asked. "Or is this some sort of mental projection to hide your six octopus arms and your innards worn on the outside?"

He grinned. "When beings travel to other places, their energy fields, and hence physical appearances, align to the local field patterns. Nobody really knows why it happens. But you arrive with an ability to understand local language, too."

She nodded. "We're familiar with the concept. We call it Intent."

He continued, "This is mostly how I look at home, with a minor adjustment or two to make me look fully humanoid here on your planet. Normally I have a bony ridge down the back of my neck and spine that's slightly more pronounced, and hair grows down that ridge, too. But the rest of me is as you see it."

For some reason, she was abjectly relieved. Not because she was worried about the looks of the creature she'd slept with but purely for selfish reasons. He was *such* a good-looking guy... Ohmigosh. She'd *slept* with him. Could they have made a baby together? She remembered belatedly—and gratefully—that she'd gone on the pill as one of the many health precautions she'd been required to take before this mission.

He was in front of her in a flash. "What's wrong?" he asked urgently.

She stuttered, "I, uh, was, uh, wondering about our...genetic compatibility."

"Ahh." Laughter glinted in his gaze.

"It's not funny!"

His arms went around her, gathering her lightly to him. "Our races are entirely compatible genetically. Most of the life forms in this part of the galaxy are loosely related through various planetary seeding and settlement projects."

Whoa. Seeding and settlement?

"Humans are native to Earth, of course, but other DNA was introduced to help advance the species more rapidly."

Had he just accounted for the jump from cave-dwelling near-ape to fire-lighting, tool-making, talking modern man?

He murmured into her hair, "When are you from?"

She sighed. She supposed it would do no harm to tell him at this point. He had come clean with her. Fair play dictated that she do the same with him. "I'm from a couple thousand years in the future. My home is on the other side of the planet, in lands that these ancient people don't have the faintest idea even exist."

He nodded, kissing his way across her temple and distracting her thoroughly. Liquid heat warmed her lower body and melting need made her knees suspiciously weak all of a sudden. He was mesmerizing. Even when she was so mad at him she could spit, she still couldn't get enough of him.

"Why did you come here?" he asked, his tongue swirling around the shell of her ear, causing her body to arch into his of its own volition.

"Research," she managed to mumble.

"What did you lose?"

That startled her partially out of her sexual haze. "I beg your pardon?" She hedged, thinking fast. How was she going to answer or avoid that without lying to him?

"You're looking for something you said you lost."

Inspiration struck. She said smoothly, "It's a modern map. I accidentally lost it, and it has to be recovered. I can't interfere with the natural development of mankind, and leaving that kind of information behind could affect human progress."

Rustam nodded in understanding. "Tricky stuff, time travel. We try to do as little of it as possible for the very reason you're talking about. Time paradoxes are difficult to untangle and put right."

"They can be fixed, then?" she asked with interest. "We haven't gotten that far yet."

He smiled wryly. "Then I guess I'd better quit talking about that, and not set your own history awry by giving you information your civilization isn't ready for yet."

She couldn't help but laugh. The irony was too rich. She looked around the valley curiously. "Do you know where we are?"

He followed her gaze. "I told the horses yesterday to head south as far as they could and still avoid any humans. When we went over that cliff last night, I willed us to appear wherever the horses were. I imagine we gave them a hell of a shock when we showed up beside them."

She nodded, thinking aloud, "So if the horses did as you said, we're somewhere to the south of Thermopylae. Hopefully, well clear of the battle, which should start in earnest today or tomorrow."

"Tomorrow if my race's histories of Earth are accurate."

His people kept histories of Earth? That was interesting. She'd have to remember to ask him about that later. Tessa continued her line of thought. "A horse without a rider would travel fifteen, maybe eighteen miles in a day. So we're still thirty or forty miles from Athens, somewhat farther inland than we were last night."

"Based on this terrain, I'd say your estimate is correct."

"Too bad you didn't imagine us landing at the Parthenon."

He grunted. "Xerxes is going to sack the place. I have no desire to be in Athens when he does."

His arms fell away from her with a last caress of his fingertips along her wrists. Shivers rippled through her that had nothing to do with cold. He murmured, "We ought to get going.

I don't know how far we are from the battlefield, and more Greeks may be moving through this area. As I recall, several local tribes joined the Spartans for their stand at the pass."

She nodded. "The Thespians and Thebans."

"Exactly."

She nodded again and headed wearily for her mare. Apparently, teleporting really took the starch out of a person. It would explain why both of their auras had been so badly drained last night. Rustam looked tired, too, as he headed for Polaris.

They went through the simple motions of checking the horses and repacking gear that had been jostled about during their time away. Then the two mounted up, and Rustam turned the stallion to the south. In this open terrain, Tessa was able to ride beside him easily.

"Need to check anything?" she murmured, holding out her hand to him.

He smiled ruefully. "I still haven't figured out why, ever since you showed up, my powers have been so messed up. Care to share what you've done to me?"

She blinked in surprise. "You're the one who's been messing up *my* powers."

"Okay, so we've messed each other up. Any hypotheses as to why?"

"Maybe our mental energies operate on conflicting wave-lengths," she tossed out.

"Could be. Although, meaning no offense, humans aren't advanced enough to generate wave lengths in the same spectrum as my people."

"And yet I'm here," she said lightly.

With a faint frown creasing his brow, he reached out and took her proffered hand. As usual, awareness of the local area promptly flooded her. She didn't sense any large life signs in the vicinity. Rustam let go of her hand. Darned if she didn't miss the contact with him.

"So what's up with you needing to touch me to do your thing?" she asked as the horses settled into a ground-eating walk.

"I'm not sure. I just know that when our energies mingle, I recover a portion of my old abilities. The rest of the time, I seem to have lost my skills."

Alarmed, she said, "Do you need me to stop touching you, then?"

He sighed. "Ahh, my dear. I don't think I could go more than a few hours without touching you even if I tried."

Warmth shot through her. Was it possible that he craved her the way she craved him? But then her thoughts derailed. He was an *alien*. She had yet to figure out if he was one of the good-guy Pleiadeans or the bad-guy Centaurians. Not to mention that anything between them would give new meaning to the phrase long-distance relationship. This was a short-term fling they were having, and that's all it could ever be.

She clamped down on her rampaging feelings for him. She could never pursue them. She could have epic sex with him, even like him. But *nothing more*. He'd go his way and she'd go hers, once she recovered the medallion. She was an army officer, for heaven's sake. She had a vitally important job to do. Not the least of which was to return home and report the presence of this shipwrecked alien in ancient Greece.

She reached out with her mind to see if she could sense his thoughts, but got nothing at all from him. Did that mean he was sensing none of her thoughts, either? Hopefully, that was how it worked.

They made good time through the afternoon. It wasn't as hot as the day before, and as the gentle hills continued, the terrain was immeasurably easier to traverse.

When the sun sank in the west, a bloodred ball of fire, Rustam spotted a damp spot near the base of a large rock formation. "A seep," he pointed out. "We'll have to stop and spend the night collecting water, but it smells like the only moisture nearby."

Gotta love that alien sense of smell of his.

They dismounted, and he started to set up camp and build a fire while she went to rig a collection system. The seep turned out to be a small spring, bubbling sluggishly from a crack low in the rock wall. She only needed to move a few large stones to get better access to the sheet of moisture trickling down the wall.

She'd lifted a big slab of rock, dumping it aside, when a flash of movement out of the corner of her eye made her freeze. A gigantic black snake, as thick around as her wrist, had lurched back violently, coiling itself defensively before her. A good three feet of the serpent lifted up off the ground as she watched, its head fanning out into the distinctive flat hood of a cobra.

Rustam!

She didn't dare take her eyes off the agitated snake and didn't dare move a muscle. She was no more than six feet from the creature, surely well within its striking range. She could only pray this wasn't a spitting variety of cobra. The snake wove back and forth slightly, its forked tongue darting out every second or two. Tessa's terrified gaze followed the beast.

Don't move. Rustam's voice flowed through her mind reassuringly.

And then a strange whooshing noise came from behind her and something whisked past her cheek, so close it stirred her hair. The snake flew backward, pinned against the wall. It writhed wildly for a few seconds and then subsided, hanging by what looked like three steel spikes lodged in its throat. Each spike was maybe four inches long and slightly thicker than a toothpick.

Rustam lunged to her side, gathering her in his arms. She turned to the comforting bulwark of his chest, shuddering in terror. She was a military officer, for crying out loud. She shouldn't lose her cool like this! But man, that had been a huge snake, and it had been so close she could see the vertical slits of its pupils expand and contract as it had watched her.

"I've got you," Rustam murmured. "You're safe."

She turned her head to look at the snake again. "What are those?"

"The flechettes? I shot my needle gun at him. It uses compressed air to fire metal spikes at hypersonic speed. I kept it when I sank my ship."

"I'd ask to see it, but humans are just starting to experiment with that technology. I'd better not." She paused. "Thanks for saving my life, especially given how much simpler yours would be if that snake had killed me."

He went rigid against her. A fist under her chin forced her gaze up to meet his. "You are my consort. I will protect you with my *life.*"

Wow. She had to give the macho, alpha alien male credit. He sure knew how to make a girl feel special. "Uh, maybe we better have a little talk about this consort business. What exactly does that mean in your world?"

"You belong to me."

Belong— "Come again?"

"You are mine. I own you. No other male may mount you."

"Whoa. Stop. Rewind, big guy. You *own* me? Nobody *owns* me."

Chapter 15

Rustam stared down at Tessa in shock. What did she mean, he didn't own her? Of course he did. She'd given herself to him. She'd specifically accepted his offer to make her his consort. True, she'd done it deep in the throes of passion, and that maybe wasn't the most fair time to ask a female to take the title. But there was no rule saying a male had to play fair. And accept his offer she unquestionably had.

He was just infatuated enough with her to hold her to her word, even if it was unchivalrous of him.

She stepped back, violet sparks flying from her hair and fingertips. God, she was glorious when she was riled up like this. "Humans don't tolerate slavery."

He snorted. "Have you looked around? Xerxes rules the greatest empire on Earth on the backs of slaves. The Greeks take slaves, the Egyptians, they all have them. And as for owning women, every great prince on this planet has a harem of women whose lives he utterly controls. He can have them all killed on a whim if he likes."

Tessa visibly checked her outrage. Still throwing plentiful sparks of anger, she said carefully, "You forget. I am not of this time. In my own era, two-thousand-plus years hence, slavery has been abolished for the most part on Earth. I will not be your slave."

"That's an entirely different thing from a consort. You are not my slave. You are my woman."

"What's the difference?"

He frowned. He'd never had to explain the concept before. Everyone understood the layers of social order in his home world. "There are drudges who do manual labor. They are not slaves in the Earth sense. They are paid modestly and can change employers at will, but I admit their lives are hard and mostly unpleasant."

Tessa frowned but refrained from commenting.

"Then there are the working classes. They comprise most of society. Those males take a single female to wife and maybe receive licenses to have one or two offspring if they show a special talent."

If her eyebrows went much higher, they'd disappear over the top of her head. He ignored her disapproving look and plowed on.

"Then there is the breeding class. The nobility. Within it, males compete fiercely for wealth, prestige and power. The more of each they amass, the more females they may take into their…*harem* is probably the closest equivalent word on Earth."

"And you're one of these males?"

Despite him trying not to let it, his mouth twitched into a smile. He answered drily, "I am."

"So you have a *harem* of women waiting for you back home?"

He nodded. "Of course. But I have no consort. Or at least I didn't until I found you. A male may only have one of those. She is first among his females. It is a position of great prestige. And power, I might add."

"Do males of your class marry, or just collect females and toss them into their harems?"

He drew back, insulted. "We do not marry...nor do we collect females. The genetics are thoroughly analyzed, and matings chosen to maximize the potential of the offspring. In my case, because I am a star navigator, all females I take must exhibit genetic potential in that area."

"Then how do you explain me?" she challenged. "I'm no star navigator. I'm just some human who can find lost things."

"I—" He broke off, frustrated. There *was* no explanation for her. He was drawn to her as to no other woman he'd ever met. She exasperated him much of the time and infuriated him the rest. She was too smart for her own good. Too independent. Too stubborn. Completely unlike the docile, obedient females of his own kind, who understood their place as the mothers and nurturers in society.

Even now, with Tessa tapping her foot in agitation, glaring openly at him, he wanted nothing more than to throw her down and mount her wildly, to lose himself in all that crackling energy and untamed power.

"Never mind," she said sharply. "Don't answer that." She turned away and jerkily went about setting up a funnel beneath the seep for water collection.

He was unaccustomed to restraining himself around a female like this. Did she not know how hard it was for him to keep his hands off her? In his society, breeding males were expected to take their pleasure whenever and wherever the urge struck them. In certain venues, such as a business meeting, the pair in question might withdraw to a discreet side room, but it was entirely acceptable for the alpha male in a meeting to call for a short recess that he might indulge his whim.

Particularly star navigators. They were the lifeblood of his people. Without them, the Centaurian stranglehold on interstellar travel could very well be lost, and with it all the wealth and power of Centaurian society.

As Tessa bent and straightened before him, lust pounded through him, grating across his skin like sandpaper. Frustrated beyond all imagining, he stalked forward, recovered his flechettes from the throat of the dead serpent, and dragged the snake back to the fire. At least they'd have fresh meat for dinner.

Tessa came over to the fire sometime later and held out a full water skin to him. "Drink as much as you like," she murmured. "I'll refill it overnight."

He tipped up the soft container, sending a stream of water into his mouth. Over its curving top, he caught sight of Tessa watching his throat as he swallowed. She swallowed convulsively herself. Of a sudden, he felt much better. At least he wasn't alone in his sexual frustration.

A bowl of steaming-hot stew made from the snake seemed to soothe Tessa's bad temper somewhat. He ventured a conversation with her. "Tell me of your people. How is human society in your time arranged?"

"I'm afraid it's not so easily categorized as yours. I suppose you'd find it entirely chaotic. We are arranged into geographic and political divisions called nations. But people travel freely from one nation to another and work, live and marry as they wish. Traces of old ways—more like your layered society— linger here and there in the world, but for the most part, such views are fading."

"What use are these nations, then?"

"The government of each is supposed to look out for the best interests of its people. But some governments are corrupt or paranoid or selfish, and fail to do so. Increasingly, Earth's economy and political dealings are becoming more global in nature, and the importance of individual nations is beginning to diminish somewhat. I expect that when we join the intergalactic community, we will simply become 'mankind' and stop worrying about the various flavors of humans."

He managed to keep the expression on his face bland, but

just barely. Humans join the intergalactic community? The very idea made his blood run cold. It was that exact thing he'd been sent to Earth to help prevent. Of all the indigenous races ever discovered, only humans had shown a widespread, if nascent, talent for star navigation. Worse, the talent seemed to reside in human *females*. They must not be allowed to develop it, or Centaurian primacy would be destroyed!

"And for the record," Tessa continued, thankfully not seeming to notice his panicked reaction, "men and women are widely perceived as equals in my time. Earlier, women were thought to be second-class citizens, but that belief is disappearing fast."

A shudder of horror rippled across his skin. Women were weak. Governed by their emotions. Totally incapable of acting as the equals of men! Except…

Images of Tessa over the past several days flashed through his head. She'd kept her cool this afternoon when confronted by that snake. She hadn't run screaming or fainted or reacted in any other way a Centaurian female would have. Back at the palace, when those randy boys had jumped her at the feast, she'd fought like a tiger. She'd even absorbed the revelation that Rustam was an alien with relative calm, and quickly started asking intelligent and insightful questions of him. Even now, she'd rapidly gotten over her snit at the way Centaurian society was organized and seemed to have accepted their differences with a certain grace.

She spoke reflectively. "I actually am a military officer. I command dozens or even hundreds of men at a time and am expected to be able to lead them in war as well as manage them in times of peace."

He stared openly at her. "Truly?"

She nodded, grinning. "Truly."

He shook his head, muttering to himself, "We not only failed, we failed colossally."

"I beg your pardon?" she asked.

"Nothing," he replied quickly. "Do you want more stew before I smother the fire?"

"No." He caught her wistful look at the flames. It was already cold and the sun had set an hour ago. "We can't leave it going, a beacon announcing our presence to anyone who passes within a mile or two of us."

She sighed. "I know. But after that snake, I was rather enjoying the critter-repelling qualities of a nice fire."

He chuckled quietly. "If you'll sleep close to me, I'll keep an eye out for any approaching critters through the night. The horses will let us know if any large predators get too close."

Quick alarm flitted across her features. "I'm not sure that's so good an idea, for me to sleep next to you."

He quirked an eyebrow. "Why not?" he asked blandly, masking his amusement. His keen Centaurian sense of smell detected the quick surge of desire in her at the mere thought of lying beside him.

She surprised him by looking him square in the eye. "I want to make love with you again. A lot. But no way can we do it, especially knowing what we know now."

He leaned back against his saddle, lounging casually. "What has changed that we could make love last night and we can't tonight?"

"Well, we know who we are now."

He laughed. "I knew who I was last night, and I suspect you knew who you were, too."

"You know what I mean. We're not even the same race...."

She trailed off, as if unsure how to finish that argument.

He commented casually, "My kind have mated with humans before. We breed with most of the races we discover, to test the genetic interaction. My kind and humans can produce offspring, and they're not monsters, if that's what you're worried about. They appear like humans, with a slightly pronounced spine. Or, if you will, like my people, but with a smaller spinal ridge than usual."

"I wasn't even thinking about children!" she exclaimed.

"Then what's wrong with us sharing sex? If we both enjoy it and it makes us feel good, why not indulge?"

She paused, as if debating inwardly. She seemed convinced it was wrong but wasn't having any luck coming up with a good reason why. He didn't feel at all inclined to help her out. In fact, wickedly, he nudged her in the other direction. "Are you sore from last night? There are many other forms of pleasure in which we can partake. I'd be happy to show you a few of them."

Her eyes went dark as her pupils widened sharply. Violet sparks flew off of her, and the musk of her desire filled his nostrils.

He shrugged, feigning a casualness he did not feel. "We're all alone. It's going to be a cold night, and at a minimum, we ought to share blankets and body heat."

She scowled at him. "I'm not so gullible that I'll crawl into the sack with you, all innocence, and let you seduce me."

That surprised him. Centaurian females either were that gullible, or they joyfully crawled into his bed, pretending to innocence, but knowing full well he planned to mount them. It was a common ploy among females to worm their way into a prestigious harem, in fact.

He frowned at Tessa. "What do you want to do, then? Freeze?"

She sighed, and with that shocking honesty of hers, replied, "You are right. It is going to be cold tonight. But I don't trust myself with you. If you kiss me and start doing some of those things you did to me last time—"

Her breath hitched at the memory, and he smiled knowingly. "You and I both know what would happen."

It was incredibly difficult to sit here and do nothing, when every fiber of his being was shouting at him to go to her. To kiss her and stroke her to climax and lose himself in her. He clenched his fists, concentrating ferociously on the pain of his fingernails digging into his palms.

"Will you promise to behave yourself?" she asked abruptly.

He blinked, startled.

"We really ought to sleep together," she explained. "I'm already shivering and it's going to get a lot colder than this. But there can't be any hanky-panky between us."

He'd never heard the term *hanky-panky,* but what it meant was self-evident. "Are you trying to kill me?" he muttered.

She laughed ruefully. "No. I'm trying to do the right thing."

"Right in your world," he grumbled. "Emphatically not right in mine."

She studied him quizzically.

"What?" he retorted a bit irritably. He couldn't help it. She was resisting his charms far too well, and it made him cranky. There wasn't a Centaurian woman alive who wouldn't be crawling all over him already, what with these sexual vibes flying thick and fast between them.

"It is a little presumptuous of me to assume that we have to do things my way, isn't it?"

Yet again she'd managed to surprise him. He mumbled, "It is not the way of my culture to rape women. If you are not willing to lie with me, I will not force you. Since your culture seems to be the one with a prudish attitude toward sex, I suppose yours will have to prevail."

He watched in silence as she kicked dirt over the fire and then, in the darkness, drew her bedroll over beside his.

"Thank you for being such a gentleman about this," she murmured, as she stretched out cautiously beside him.

He didn't feel much like a gentleman. He felt like a damn fool. This woman was a fire in his blood...and he couldn't have her. He was worse than a fool. He was insane to have agreed to this arrangement.

"It's strange that you should accuse me of being prudish about sex," she commented from the shadows.

He about jumped out of his skin. She could stop talking about sex now. He was already so aroused he was in physical pain.

She continued, blithely unaware of her effect on him. "Back home, I've been known to argue passionately against some of the more conservative opinions held in my country about sexuality. Other parts of the world are much more laid-back about it all and seem to have healthier societies because of it."

"Laid-back?" The visual image he formed all but made him growl in frustration.

"It means relaxed. Free of stress or tension."

Exactly like they'd be if they made love tonight— *Stop that*, he ordered himself. He'd given her his word.

They lay there side by side in silence for a long time. They were both as stiff as boards. If she was one-tenth as uncomfortable as him, she was utterly miserable. And the longer they remained, the thicker and more overpowering her scent became in his nostrils.

Finally, she broke the silence, whispering, "Are you awake?"

He grunted. "You're kidding, right? I won't sleep all night. Not when I'm this randy."

She sighed. "I'm sorry. This really is ridiculous, isn't it?"

"How so?" he said cautiously.

"We're both adults. I'm assuming we're all alone out here—"

He accessed her aura quickly and cast his mind out. "There's no one within at least three of your miles."

She propped herself up on his chest, a pale, unearthly figure in the light of the new moon just rising behind them. She flung one sleek leg across his thighs, and every part of him jolted to full attention.

"What the heck?" she murmured.

"I beg your pardon?" he asked cautiously.

She laughed. "How about this phrase? In for a penny, in for a pound."

That one he got the gist of. Hope leaped in his chest, but he held himself perfectly still beneath her.

"You may have promised not to make love to me, Rustam, but I never promised not to make love to you."

He gaped up at her, stunned. Relief flooded him that she was going to end his torture. But more than that, the idea of her making love to him galvanized his mind. He'd never conceived of such a thing before. Such a thing would *never* happen on Centauri Prime. It had to be forbidden here, too…taboo somehow…but apparently not. The idea of her pleasuring him—ye gods…

And then all thought fled as her soft, warm hands closed around his rigid flesh, and her mouth…oh, stars, her mouth…

He reached for her, but she pushed his hands back down to the ground. "Oh, no, big guy. Tonight it's my turn. You keep your hands right there. Just lie there and don't move anything. Promise?"

Too stunned by what she was doing to think straight, he muttered, "All right. Fine. I promise."

She slid down his body deliciously, and he all but spilled his seed right there. Her lips and tongue and teeth wove magic around him unlike anything he'd ever felt before. The sensations were beyond intense, verging on painful at times, so achingly wet and soft and seductive at others that, despite his promise, his entire body arched up off the ground, desperately seeking more and yet more of what she was doing to him.

Just when he thought he couldn't take another second of it, she would drift away from his male parts, stroking her fingernails across his belly, kneading and massaging his body from head to foot. She even sucked on his toes, which all but sent him over the edge.

And then she'd move back to his throbbing, rock-hard shaft and start her ministrations all over again, until he was stretched so taut upon a torture rack of pleasure that he thought he might explode into a million pieces.

"End this," he finally ground out from between clenched teeth. "For the love of man and horse, release me from this torture."

The vixen laughed. "Not yet," she purred. And then, using both hands and mouth, she drove him nearly to the point of unconsciousness.

"No more," he gasped. "You're killing me. I shall die if you do not let me spill myself now."

She rose up over him, smiling triumphantly. "I do believe the man begged. And for his troubles, he's earned his reward."

He watched in abject relief as she threw her leg over his hips and positioned herself above him. "Say please," she murmured.

A groan tore from his throat. "Please, woman. Release me from my promise."

"I release you."

He reached up, grabbed her hips and yanked her down on top of him. Thankfully, she was mostly ready for him, wet and relaxed. She gasped, and, gritting his teeth, he forced himself to give her a moment to adapt to his size. Then she did the unexpected.

She started to ride him. Fast, then slow. Hard then gentle. Rocking easily, and driving mercilessly. He thought she'd plundered the depths of his being and wrung the last drop of pleasure out of him, but apparently, there was more.

Showers of light began to spin around them, faster and faster, higher and higher, forming a towering vortex with them at its center. And then it exploded, casting them up and out of their bodies, into the darkest night of space, far beyond any place he'd ever been before, past the margins of the entire galaxy, far out into the vast expanses of the universe.

A moment of utter stillness came over them.

Just the two of them were in this place, two halves of a perfect whole, together, complete. There was no past, no future, just this moment and them. They could go anywhere; do anything. Her mind, as much a part of his as his was hers, mirrored his thoughts.

What shall we do? Where shall we go?

Anywhere. Everywhere.

A shared flash of humor faded away, leaving only a peaceful intimacy between them. And then, eventually, a sigh.

Back to our bodies now? Another shared sigh at the necessity of existing as separate entities in separate bodies part of the time....

Rustam slammed back into himself with a jolt that knocked the wind out of him. He lay on hard ground, with tiny stones digging into his back. Tessa sprawled on top of him, only semi-conscious, whether from an excess of pleasure or from the shock of returning to her body after that massive jump, or both, he didn't know. He gasped, sucking air into his lungs convulsively as he began to breathe again.

What...in the hell...had that been?

Never had returning to his body after star travel been a *choice.* It was the natural end of a jump. Out of body into energy form, then almost instantly back into physical form. The first time they'd made love, he'd recognized the out-of-body instant as it happened, had reflexively limited the length of the jump to something safe, and had just as quickly dragged himself and Tessa back again. After all, every star navigator knew how dangerous it was to spend more than an instant in-between.

But tonight, with her in control of the vortex, they'd broken free of the limits of time and space entirely. She hadn't contained the jump, nor had she taken them back to body right away. According to every bit of training he'd ever had, the two of them should have just died.

How had she done that? What did this extraordinary human woman know about star-jumping that he and his kind did not?

Chapter 16

Tessa sprawled on top of Rustam, his heart pounding like a jackhammer in her ear. *Wow.* That had possibly been more incredible than last time. That suspended chunk of time, where nothing existed but the two of them, had felt so right. She'd never wanted to come back from that place. Already, she wanted to go back as soon as they could possibly get there.

It was humbling to have a man like him give himself completely over to her. He didn't strike her as the type to allow himself to be vulnerable often. And yet he'd opened up his very soul to her, given her an intensely private and personal piece of himself tonight. He'd said please to her, for goodness sake. That had to come hard for him.

In return, she'd let go of all her inhibitions and fears, diving headfirst into that whirling indigo maelstrom they created between them. And it had been…transcendent. She wasn't sure there actually were words for what they'd shared. It was almost as if they'd become part of one another.

He murmured something in a tongue she didn't recognize, but she didn't have to. From his tone of voice, the meaning was obvious. She smiled lazily, too sated herself to do much more than that. The poor boy had just gotten a thorough initiation into Earth-style lovemaking, and it appeared to have blown his mind. He seemed completely poleaxed by the idea of the woman taking the lead and giving pleasure to the man.

"Great spiraling Milky Way," he finally breathed.

She murmured against his perspiration-slick skin, "I take it you liked that?"

"I am your slave, woman. I shall serve you to the end of time if you but do that to me again."

She laughed outright. "I'm glad to have done my part to broaden your romantic horizons." Although she hoped she hadn't ruined his enjoyment of his harem forever. Tessa was quickly coming to the conclusion that no Earth man was ever going to match up to him in her lifetime. Maybe he'd take the concept of letting the woman have her way in bed back to his females and share it with them. Who knew? Maybe she'd started a revolution that would sweep his society and revolutionize the role of alien females.

A pang of jealousy shot through her. This was a man she would want all to herself if she were to have a long-term relationship with him. She wouldn't do well in a harem. She couldn't see herself sharing him nicely with the other women.

She frowned. How could his people, with their rigid, layered view of society, be the same enlightened race that had planted the pieces of the Karanovo stamp on Earth, and who'd nudged mankind—human females in particular—for millennia toward developing into a race capable of star travel? Was he Centaurian, after all? But how could he be? They hated humans, by all accounts, and particularly hated human females. The man who'd just surrendered himself entirely to her was no hater of human women.

He dragged her blanket over both of them and locked an arm at the small of her back to hold her in place when she would have rolled off of him.

"Am I too heavy? Should I move?" she murmured.

"Stay right where you are. I wouldn't have you anywhere else."

"Mmm. I like the sound of that."

"What am I going to do with you?" he muttered.

"I think we've established at least one thing you like to do with me."

He laughed. "We've established several things I like to do with you."

Rapidly becoming drowsy, she murmured, "Don't worry about it tonight. Sleep now. There'll be time enough tomorrow to ponder the question."

Except tomorrow turned into a long, hot day of dodging Greek soldiers streaming north. Once the Persians fought their bloody way past Thermopylae, the Greeks would fight a guerilla-style delaying action, pestering Xerxes's army all the way to Athens. Oh, the city would eventually be sacked and burned to the ground, but the constant harassment would buy the citizens of Athens enough time to evacuate, taking with them their culture and their great stores of knowledge.

Unfortunately, the Karanovo fragment, which had been steadily moving south along the coast, had stopped overnight, somewhere in the vicinity of Chalcis. Chalcis sat at the narrowing of the gulf about halfway down the Greek peninsula. Tessa had discovered by accident, once when Rustam was holding her hand and searching for soldiers nearby, that if she reached out with her mind to search for the medallion piece at the same time, she got a strong, clear reading on it. Frustratingly, though, she continued not to be able to pick it up on her own.

They stopped early that night. Rustam parked her and the

horses in a shallow cave—which he'd thoroughly checked and declared free of snakes before they entered—and then left to scout the area. She'd argued that she ought to go with him so they could combine their powers, but he would hear none of it. Sometimes there was just no reasoning with him; he set his jaw in that stubborn manner, and there was no budging him. She'd eventually thrown up her hands and retreated to the cave to chew on stale biscuits and stringy jerky of God-knew-what form of animal protein.

After her initial irritation wore off, the worry set in. Not only was she afraid that something bad might happen to him, but it felt horribly wrong to be apart from him like this. As if a vital part of her was missing. Tessa missed the vibrant energy of his presence, the tingle of excitement that skittered across her skin whenever she looked at him, the mental challenge of verbally sparring with him. Her world was a drab and colorless place without him in it.

Desperate not to be quite so desperate, she resorted to giving both of the horses a good, long grooming. Brushing Polaris soothed her a little. Remnants of Rustam's aura clung to his horse, and she gathered the bits of energy greedily, hoarding them and savoring the feeling. Eventually, the horses glistened, even in the near darkness. And still there was no sign of Rustam.

"Polaris, what am I going to do? I'm sorely afraid that I've fallen for your master. And that's going to throw a giant monkey wrench into everything."

The big horse rested his chin heavily on her shoulder until she reached up and scratched the base of his ear, where he liked it. "You're just as sure of yourself as he is, aren't you?" she murmured.

The stallion nipped at her fingers, and she jerked her hand back, laughing quietly. "Behave yourself. You and your master both need a good woman to keep you in line." Polaris tossed his head at that. If she thought there was a chance he understood her, she'd accuse the animal of being indignant at her suggestion.

Restless, she wandered around the cave until she finally flopped down on her bedroll in frustration. She buried her face in the wool folds, greedily inhaling the faint scent of Rustam's body. He smelled of sweet grass and sunshine and leather and honest sweat. Good grief. She was smelling him now? She really was desperate.

What she really was was in trouble. She'd fallen head over heels for an *alien*. And it wasn't like they had any future together. By his own admission, he was a prince among his kind. They wouldn't tolerate some backward human female from a planet that was just barely beginning to experiment with time travel. Heck, had it not been for the lucky accident of the Roswell UFO crash, humans wouldn't be even remotely close to having time travel, either.

She sighed. If they were the only two people in the universe, she had no doubt they could be deliriously happy together for the rest of their lives. They balanced each other perfectly. She was strong enough not to let him bully her, but likewise, he was intelligent and complex enough to challenge her emotionally and mentally. She found him endlessly interesting, and he seemed to feel the same about her.

But unfortunately, they both had lives in their own worlds. He had a harem to get back to breeding baby star navigators with, and she had a job to do. As if that weren't enough, who knew what intergalactic forces would come to bear upon the two of them if they went public with their relationship? Athena Carswell would have Tessa's head on a platter if she got tangled up with some alien observer she happened to run into while time traveling into the ancient past. And General Ashton—Tessa winced to think of the butt-chewing the former marine would give her.

Why couldn't everyone just leave them alone? They'd found something rare and special and perfect…and they were going to have to give it up. Sooner rather than later, if she didn't miss her guess.

Sometime during the night, Rustam returned from his scouting and slid under the blanket beside her. He gathered her close, and she vaguely registered his warmth and comforting strength before slipping back into a lovely dream where the two of them soared among the stars together and no one could touch them.

"Good morning, my lady." Rustam's warm, familiar mouth moved across her skin, effortlessly stirring the ever-glowing embers of desire within her into flames.

She cracked one eye open to see the gray of predawn encroaching upon their shelter. "It's not morning yet, and it's not good yet, either. But we can fix the latter." She stretched languidly against him and trailed a hand down his chest, across his magnificent abs, and lower still. No surprise, he was as ready for her as she was for him.

"I don't want to make you sore today. We have a hard ride ahead of us," he murmured.

"Then don't make me sore. But don't make me frustrated and grumpy all day, either, if you know what's good for you."

He laughed under his breath. "Yes, I'm familiar with that phenomenon in human females. In my kind, the harem females who aren't getting enough attention have mechanical devices to ease their discomfort."

Tessa grinned up at him. "We have those in my time, too. But I don't happen to have one in my saddlebag. It's either you or frustrated me. Take your pick."

Today, her body accommodated him more easily and comfortably, although he had to put his hand over her mouth when the screaming part of her orgasms came upon her. Likewise, he bit down hard on her shoulder rather than shout out in turn. Their out-of-body flight this time was short, and Rustam tightly controlled it, but the pleasure was so piercingly intense that she could hardly draw breath when they returned.

"Will that hold you for a few hours?" he murmured when he had recovered enough breath to speak.

She laughed quietly. "A few. You may yet talk me into this notion of jumping each other's bones whenever and wherever the mood strikes." As his eyes lit with a fierce, possessive light, she continued, "But I have to confess, I have a really hard time with the idea of sharing you."

He pressed his forehead to hers, wordlessly. Something warm, gentle almost, passed between them. It flowed peacefully over her like a warm bath, cocooning her in…what felt a whole lot like love. She didn't know exactly what he'd just done. She got the distinct impression it was something native to his culture, and that it was potentially significant.

"If it makes you feel better, I haven't thought about another female since I laid eyes on you, and I most certainly haven't desired one."

"What about Artemesia? That last feast—"

He cut her off quickly. "Did I look like I was enjoying myself? At all?"

"Well, no."

"And did you not notice that I was not…otherwise engaged that night when you summoned me to help you?"

"Summoned? Is that what I did?"

"Indeed. And thank the heavens you did. I do not want to think what would have happened had I not come." He crushed her against him until she had to squirm to get a little room to breathe.

"Honestly, I didn't notice how quickly you came. I had my hands full dealing with those boys."

He grunted in displeasure. "Randy swine."

"Oh, come on. It's not like you weren't enjoying the bountiful and readily available sexual pleasures of Xerxes's court."

He shrugged. "I never forced any female into my bed. It was better than nothing, but mostly I found it boring and vaguely depraved. At least at home, I know my sexual endeavors result in strong children who will be a credit to my lineage."

"How many children do you have?" she asked, curious.

He shrugged again. "I do not know. When I left, I had four hundred thirty-eight."

Four hundred? He really was a breeding machine!

He continued, blithely unaware of her shock. "Shortly before I left on this mission, I mounted a dozen of my females to impregnate them. By now I should be up to four hundred fifty or so."

She winced at his choice of words and the bald imagery it created. Rather than leaping to judgment about his culture, as she had before, she instead said lightly, "Four hundred? Good grief. You must live in a state of constant exhaustion if you have to have that much sex with that many females."

He frowned. "It only takes once. Whenever I choose to impregnate a female, I merely prepare her womb properly and fill it with my seed, and it happens."

Tessa's jaw dropped. "You have control over that?"

He frowned. "Of course. There is sex for pleasure and then sex for impregnation. The first night you and I made love, and I claimed you as my consort, that was for impregnation. But last night and this mor—"

She lurched upright, tearing free of his grasp to stare down at him, appalled. "Whoa, whoa, whoa. Back up there, big guy. Are you saying you tried to get me *pregnant?*"

"I did more than try. I succeeded."

Chapter 17

"What?" Tessa squawked, outraged.

He retorted with rising indignation, "I am a potent male. I have never failed to impregnate a female when I wished to."

She spluttered, alarmed, "But human biology doesn't work that way. We—I—am only fertile for a very small window of time each month. Even if I were to have sex with a man during that time, I still might not get pregnant. It can take months or even years for human females to achieve pregnancy. I'm not even sure you and I could create a viable offspring." Her voice continued to rise as her agitation increased. "We're different races, for goodness sake—"

He pressed a finger over her mouth, stilling her incipient tirade. "Keep your voice down. These hills are far from deserted and sound carries forever out here."

"I can't possibly be pregnant," she hissed. Frantically, she was casting back in her memory for the first day of her last period. It had been nearly four weeks ago. In fact, her period was due to start in another three or four days. Even if her birth control pills didn't work on aliens, the timing was all wrong. *Whew*. Some of her panic abated.

"Nonetheless, you are with child," he said certainly.

"You don't understand my biology. I have these things called ovaries. They store my female genetic material. They release an egg only once a month and the egg survives for just a day or two. That window of opportunity has passed for me this month."

He sighed. "Do you recall that first night when I stroked you with my hand…until you felt a series of deep spasms inside you? If you're built like a female of my kind, it would have been low in your belly, between your hip bones. I'm not talking about pleasure feelings. It would have been deeper within you, where your reproductive organs lie."

Her cheeks began to heat up. More than a little taken aback at this turn of conversation, she nodded cautiously. She did, indeed, recall the sensations he described. She'd been kneeling before him with her knees spread wide, while he'd played her body like a fine violin.

"Those spasms you felt were me drawing forth an egg from within your…what did you call them? Ovaries?"

Her jaw dropped. "But eggs have to mature. They need exposure to the right hormones. It's a terribly complicated sequence of events…."

"And you think a race capable of star travel can't learn to control a simple biological sequence?" he asked easily, his voice laced with humor.

"You didn't."

He nodded at her solemnly. "I did. I drew forth one of your eggs and prepared it for my—I'm sorry, I don't know your word for them—seeds?"

She interjected quickly, "I get the idea."

He continued patiently. "Of course, I prepared your body to

accept a child, as well. Given that your race is directly descended from mine to more than a small degree, that, too, is a process I can and did control."

Her jaw dropped. "But…implantation depends on certain proteins being present. My body has to be producing them at the right time…." Although she made the argument, she had a sinking feeling that he was trying to tell her that her body's chemistry didn't matter a heck of a lot. It sounded a great deal like he was trying to tell her he was capable of completely overriding her body and hijacking the entire process of impregnation.

"If I so choose, you have no choice chemically or biologically but to accept my seed. Trust me, my dear. You are pregnant even now."

Somehow she didn't doubt for a moment that he was telling her the truth. "You…you son of a bitch!" she exclaimed.

He leaped to his feet, clearly offended. "What's wrong with you? Do you have any idea what an honor it is to carry one of my offspring? To bestow that upon you, an alien woman… I risked everything—my political standing, my rank and status as commander of the Fifth Centauri Star Regiment—"

"Ohmigod. And you're *Centaurian* to boot?" The news just kept on getting better. She was *pregnant*. The father was an *alien*. And to top it all off, he was a *hostile* alien!

"You…you…" She stepped forward and punched him as hard as she could in the gut. Of course, her fist barely dented his rock-hard abs, but it made her feel a whole lot better.

"What's gotten into you?" he demanded furiously. As she flailed her fists at him again, he captured them and forcibly held them at her sides.

"You didn't ask me if I wanted to have your precious offspring, you arrogant bastard! I have a career, dammit! I don't have time for a child. And we're not even married. And as I understand it, you don't *get* married. You just collect whatever females happen to catch your fancy and force them into your…your herd of broodmares."

He reared back, mortal insult etched on his face. "I do not…mount…common broodmares." He snarled each word individually. "I only breed with women from the very best lineages, from the greatest of the noble families. Their daughters fight for my attention. They throw themselves at me in hopes that I'll gift them with my child! I even stand a fair chance of becoming the Primus if my career continues on track. Kentar himself has hinted that I might replace him when he steps down."

Her fury was unappeased. "I don't care if you're the king of the universe. You had no right to foist a child on me without my consent."

He yanked her against his chest, hard enough to rattle her teeth. "You did consent. You agreed to be my consort."

"I hadn't the slightest idea what it meant. You can't possibly hold me to that."

He glared down at her, blue lightning flying off him in all directions. His eyes were black, and violence snapped in them, barely contained. His entire body vibrated with fury, every muscle clenched—whether in anger or rigid control, she couldn't tell. She had to admit, Rustam in a towering rage was an impressive sight. Intimidating, even. But then she clamped her teeth and glared back at him.

Their battle of wills howled and blew around them like the mightiest of tempests. It was a silent thing, but no less turbulent for the lack of raised voices. They didn't even bother to fling words at each other. They threw raw emotion instead until they'd both spent the worst of their fury. Eventually, the energy vortex around them calmed slightly, settling down to, oh, tornado proportions.

Gradually, their separate blue and violet energy streams merged once more into the usual indigo haze whirling around them.

At long last, Rustam glanced away. He looked back at her.

Took a deep breath. "I apologize. I did not know your customs. I would have asked, had I known."

She released a long breath of her own. What was she supposed to say to that? *What's done is done?* In this case, it really was. If she was, indeed, pregnant...

Her mind balked at finishing the thought, but reluctantly she made herself do it.

If she was indeed pregnant, what in the world was she going to do? This changed everything.

Athena Carswell opened her kitchen door and stepped inside. A wave of blessedly cool air hit her. It was blistering hot outside today, and the contrast between the 108-degree heat and her house made goose bumps rise on her skin.

She set her satchel down on the kitchen table, her mind on a tall glass of iced tea. She turned toward the refrigerator, and froze.

Something was wrong. The goose bumps on her arms weren't going away. In fact, they prickled, screaming an alarm at her brain. She listened carefully. Only the hum of the air conditioner and the quieter sound of the refrigerator broke the silence. She opened her cell phone and dialed a *nine* and a *one*. With her finger poised on the *one* button for one more punch that would summon help, she eased over to the kitchen door and peered around the corner. The dining room and living room were empty. She glided through them toward the short hallway leading to both bedrooms and the bathroom. Mental alarm bells clanged wildly inside her head as she did so.

No sound. No movement.

She spun fast through the doorways to all three rooms and even checked the closets. Nothing.

What in the world? Her psychic warning system never went off like this for no reason. Athena closed her eyes and reached out with her mind for the cause of her alarm. *Her bedroom.* She stood in the doorway, gazing around the room. Something was…not right. It was subtle. But things didn't seem to be in exactly the same place she'd left them. She didn't remember her hairbrush being that close to the edge of her dresser. And she usually didn't make her bed quite that neatly.

She frowned. Her bed.

Oh, no.

She shoved at the bed frame with her shoulder, sliding it back to reveal the safe mounted in the floor beneath it. Quickly, she spun the combination, pressed her thumb to the recognition pad and pulled up the heavy door. She breathed a sigh of relief.

All the papers appeared to be there.

She reached in to inventory them, and prickles skittered across her skin again.

She closed her eyes.

A clear impression of a lean, hard stranger handling the files flooded her mind. His energy signature was still fresh on the papers. And then a second image came to her. Another man photographing them. All of them.

Fury and a dose of terror at having her privacy so violated rushed over her.

And a smirk of satisfaction. Yes, they'd gotten some of her proprietary research data, and it might give someone a decent idea of what she was up to. But the bastards hadn't gotten their dirty hands on the *Ad Astra* journal.

She cleared her cell phone and dialed Beverly.

"I've had an intruder at my house. Some guys broke into my safe and copied my papers. But they didn't get what they came for."

The general's voice was alarmed. "Are you all right? Did you call the police?"

"No. They didn't take anything. They just photographed my research papers."

"And the—"

"I'm not dumb enough to leave it lying around someplace so obvious, Bev."

"Didn't think so. I was just checking."

Athena grinned at the relief in the woman's voice. Then she grew sober. "But we do have a major problem. Someone's onto our work, and they want to know what we're doing. They're clearly not friendly."

"Do you think the Centaurian Federation is behind it?"

Athena frowned. "The energy signatures in my house are human." She added grimly, "But I wouldn't put it past the Centaurians to be meddling again. Wouldn't surprise me in the least to find out they're pulling some human's strings on this one."

Bev replied, "First the fire at the lab, and now this. I'm beefing up security for both the project and you immediately."

"Fine. Just don't ask me to suspend the work. We're too close now to stop."

"Not if you die," the former marine retorted sharply. "Come back to the lab so we can go over new security measures and I can get a guard detail assigned to you."

Athena sighed. She'd known it would come to this. Just not this soon.

Rustam packed up their camp while Tessa perched on a large rock at the cave opening, staring out pensively at nothing. He glanced over at her occasionally but left her to her thoughts. Who'd have guessed that human women would ultimately become so independent? The steady stream of observers sent from Centauri Prime was supposed to prevent this exact kind of development in human females.

What a hash he'd made of it. He'd genuinely thought she would be thrilled and honored to realize he'd given her a child. He hadn't been kidding when he'd told her Centaurian women fought for the privilege.

And what was this about her having a career? Females had

one purpose, and one purpose only. Even on Earth, a woman like Artemesia, who was queen and general and able ruler of a kingdom all by herself, was an extreme rarity. If modern women had abruptly become this strong and self-sufficient, no wonder the Centaurian council was so worried they might go after the Karanovo Stamp.

Recovering a piece of the stamp was why he'd been sent here in the first place. If the humans failed to recover all twelve pieces of the medallion, they would not be able to signal the Intergalactic Council. Just one piece of the stamp. That was all his kind had to find and remove from Earth.

He'd wondered why the sudden urgency when he'd been given this mission to time-travel back to ancient Earth, to find and recover a piece of the medallion. He was too skilled and high-ranking a star navigator to rate such a trivial assignment under normal circumstances. But it made perfect sense, now. Unfortunately, staring at the back of Tessa's head while she gazed at a distant hill wasn't getting either of them closer to their respective goals. He interrupted her reverie quietly. "It's time to go."

He didn't know why she was so hell-bent on recovering a simple map. Sailors in this time already had reasonably complete charts of this part of the world. Even if her map of unknown seas and continents on the far side of the planet were found, the locals would likely put it down to inaccurate drawing or some sort of imaginary document of the gods' underworld. A context existed for explaining away her map to these ancient people. If discovered, it shouldn't derail the development of mankind. But if the map was that important to her, so be it. After all, she was his consort, and the mother of his child. He owed her a certain amount of consideration.

The females of his kind didn't usually become irrational and demanding until late in their pregnancies. Maybe these humans started earlier. But, in her defense, Tessa had good cause to be angry with him. It hadn't even remotely occurred to him that first night that human females might want some say in their reproductive processes. Now that he knew her better and understood how intelligent and *liberated*—that word had a sour taste in his mouth—a woman she was, he could see her point. Not to mention that every star navigator learned in his first days of training never, ever, to involve himself with an indigenous species this personally. But damned if the woman didn't completely bewitch him. It wasn't an excuse for his behavior, of course. But it did help him unravel how he could've ended up in a mess like this.

It was midmorning before they finally cleared a long line of Greek soldiers off to their east. Rustam glanced over at Tessa, who was riding beside him stoically, steadfastly ignoring his existence. He sighed. "Tell me of this human custom of marriage."

She glanced at him, naked surprise flashing in her gaze. To her credit, she swallowed her anger for the moment and answered civilly. "Most humans take a single mate for the long term or life. Marriage is a ceremony wherein they promise to spend their lives together and forsake all others."

He stared, shocked. "You would ask me to give up all my other females for you?"

She lurched in her saddle, startling Cygna badly enough that Rustam had to send out a quick calming to the mare lest she dump her rider off her back.

Tessa glared at him. "I haven't asked you to marry me nor have you asked me."

"But on your planet, the mother and father of a child are expected to marry, are they not?"

She blinked in apparent surprise. "'Tis customary, but not required. Many people choose to be single parents in my time. You don't have to marry me."

"But you will be angry with me until I do?"

"Good Lord, no!" she exclaimed.

He frowned, deeply confused. Contrary woman. She railed at him for impregnating her without marrying her; and then when he offered to do so, she turned him down! "Do you want me to marry you or not?" he demanded, roundly frustrated.

"I—no—well, maybe— No!"

A glimmer of amusement shone through his frustration. He said drily, "Forgive me, but perhaps you could be slightly clearer in your answer? This ignorant alien hasn't the faintest idea how to interpret that reply."

She huffed. "It's not that simple. People who get married love each other. They want to spend their lives together. They have things in common. They like sharing time together. They want to raise a family together."

"Ahh." He turned all that over in his mind. It was the way the commoners among his kind lived. Supposedly, they were happy with that. He'd even heard they scorned the lifestyle of the nobles and called it empty and debauched.

Not that debauchery was all bad. He rather enjoyed that aspect of his status as a star navigator. But what she was asking of him— to give up all of that—to live like a commoner... His political status depended heavily on the number of star navigators he sired. To date, he'd produced an impressive twelve. Only Kentar had produced more, and the man was nearly twice Rustam's age.

Love, huh?

His kind never spent enough time with a single female to develop feelings remotely akin to love. He wasn't *allowed* to spend that kind of time with a woman. As soon as one was pregnant, he was expected to move on to the next female who was ready to breed. Viewed from Tessa's perspective, he could begin to understand how nobles could be seen as shallow and incapable of real feelings. Perhaps the critics among the commoners were right.

Rustam didn't even know if he was capable of giving Tessa

this love she demanded of him, if they were to marry. What in the hell was he supposed to do now? He was completely at sea in a foreign culture, playing a game whose rules he didn't have the faintest idea of. And his future with the most extraordinary woman he'd ever met lay in the balance.

The thing was, he couldn't leave one of his children behind on this planet, especially now that mankind had mastered time-jumping. Star travel would not be far behind if a person with the right kind of talent came along. Such as the child of one of the greatest Centaurian star navigators of his time and a wildly talented human female who might very well carry the star-travel gene herself.

The thought broke across his consciousness with the force of a tidal wave.

Tessa had the star navigator gene. What else could explain the incredible, inexplicable star flights they took every time they made love? It had been right there before his eyes the entire time, but he'd been too besotted to see it or perhaps had intentionally ignored the evidence right under his nose.

She was a nascent star navigator.

And his orders from the Centaurian Federation were crystal clear.

Eliminate every human female who displays a talent for star navigation.

He had to kill the woman carrying his dreams and his child.

Chapter 18

The next week fell into an exhausting pattern for Tessa of nearly round-the-clock travel with Rustam only calling for short rests every few hours. She ate in the saddle, drank in the saddle and even dozed in the saddle. The horses were tired, but Rustam poured energy into them every time they stopped.

She didn't complain about the brutal pace, however. If she stood any chance at all of catching up with the medallion fragment, she had to get to that pinprick of energy to the south before the main body of the Persian army reached it. The good news was that the winds blew steadily in their faces, which would significantly slow the progress of the Persian fleet down the coast and make it easier to catch.

Every time she sensed the bronze wedge now, she got a clear impression of water. There was no doubt about it, the bronze piece was traveling by ship. How they were going to get from shore out to the vessel, she had no idea. She'd figure that out when the time came. For now, it was enough to get close to the darn thing.

Hour by hour, the grueling journey stripped her anger at Rustam from her, leaving behind only exhaustion. It was impossible to stay furious with someone who was so unfailingly courteous and considerate. In spite of the horrendous heat and his obvious fatigue, he steadily engaged in pleasant conversation with her, telling her of his home world and people, and asking endless questions about modern human culture. They compared politics and philosophy and the arts…not to mention a hundred other subjects from children's education to sports to foods.

Despite her best efforts to hate him, she learned to see him and his race as not so very different from mankind at all. They had the very same hopes and dreams for their children and their future. It just so happened that humans and Centaurians were going to end up competing for the same slice of intergalactic power someday.

And in the meantime, as much as she hated to admit it, Rustam really was a noble, kind, courageous man whose humor and intelligence made him completely irresistible to her.

After yet another of their all-too-short power naps, this one taken during the worst of the afternoon heat to spare the horses, Rustam muttered, "Are you really sure a lost map is worth all this? The horses are about done in."

She winced. There wasn't a chance in hell she was telling a Centaurian that she was chasing down a piece of the Karanovo Stamp his race desperately didn't want mankind— or womankind, to be precise—to get its hands on. She certainly wasn't into cruelty to animals, but time was against her in a big way. "How much farther until we catch up with the Persian fleet?"

He looked at the hills around them. Scattered huts had begun to dot the region, and here and there rows of olive and fig trees striped the hillsides. "We're getting close to the southern tip of the Greek peninsula. Once the Persian fleet rounds the end, it will sail against Athens. According to our records, the Persian ships get bottled up in channel islands near the city."

Tessa nodded. "That's what human histories relate, as well." And *there* was a line she'd never thought to hear herself utter in her lifetime!

"The Persian fleet will hug the coast as it rounds the southern cape since the Aegean winds and currents offshore are treacherous. We might be able to flag it down there. I'd guess that by tonight we'll reach it. The horses have made good time, but I have no way of knowing if we've beaten the ships there or not."

"Is that our best bet to catch up with the fleet?" she asked.

He shrugged. "It's probably our only bet if you want to join the ships before they engage the Athenian navy."

"Let's ride, then."

Rustam looked over at her in quick concern. "You aren't overexerting yourself, are you? After all, you have my child to look after."

She rolled her eyes. They'd had this argument a dozen times already. She kept insisting that she wasn't necessarily pregnant, and he remained adamant that she was. Exasperated, she said, "We won't know for a few more days if I might be pregnant. And even then it's not a sure thing. With the amount of physical strain I've been under, I could easily skip a period and have it mean nothing."

"I have never met a woman as stubborn as you."

She flashed him a grin. "And you love the challenge, don't you?"

He grinned ruefully. "I am learning to. I must say, you human women are never dull."

A strange thing happened then. His smile faded and a regretful, almost haunted look passed through his expressive eyes. She'd caught him gazing at her that way a couple of times during the past few days.

She asked quietly, "What's on your mind?"

He started guiltily. "Uh, nothing."

Riigghhtt. What could possibly put that much worry in a Centaurian star navigator's gaze? She wasn't at all sure she wanted to know.

Dusk was turning to night around them when they rode around a large outcropping of rock. Tessa stopped in surprise. Moonlight illuminated a broad expanse of water before them. The Aegean Sea. Only a steep shale slope separated them from the shore.

Rustam murmured, "The fleet's not here yet. It'll stretch for miles when it comes."

She nodded in relief. They'd done it. Now all they had to do was intercept whatever vessel carried the Karanovo fragment before the great naval battle of Salamis happened. With her luck, the ship bearing the medallion would sink, and she'd have to introduce scuba diving to ancient Greece to recover it. She mumbled, "May I borrow your hand?"

Raising his eyebrows in surprise, he offered his big, callused palm to her. She took it, reveling in his warmth and strength in the instant before the power flowed through her, overwhelming all other sensations. She closed her eyes and reached out with her mind, seeking the distinctive sharp emanations of the metal object she sought. *There. Off to her left.*

She started. "It's close."

"How far?"

"A few miles at most."

Rustam swore quietly under his breath. "If you're right and your map is on a ship, we'd better make our way down to the shore right away."

The ride down the hill was wild, with the horses sitting practically on their haunches and sliding down the slope as much as walking down it. When they finally got to the water's edge, she was surprised to see that the beach, such as it was, was mostly boulders scattered upon the shore as if a giant hand had tossed them there. This land certainly was conducive to legends of gods and mythic heroes.

She cast a sidelong glance at Rustam and smiled. She, for one, knew where the stories of guys like Zeus and Apollo came from.

"What?" he asked in response to her silent look.

"I was just wondering if you or others of your kind are the source of certain mythic characters from the human literary tradition. In particular a man called Hercules."

"The legendary hero who did the various labors?"

"That's the one."

Rustam shook his head. "Silly children's tales."

"Those tales will survive until my time and beyond. Maybe not so silly, after all."

"In my travels, I have found that most myths and legends have at least some basis in fact. I'm convinced that primitive cultures use fictional stories to explain away actual occurrences they are not yet ready to understand or accept as real."

She raised an eyebrow. "Are you trying to tell me that magic and fairies and the abominable snowman really exist?"

"In some form or another, yes."

She snorted. "I wish magic existed. I'd wave my wand and find that stupid map."

"And then what?" he asked.

The question brought her up short. "And then I'll go home, of course."

He nodded slowly. "Of course. And how are you planning to get there?"

He asked the question lightly, but it didn't take a rocket scientist to know he'd be intensely interested in her answer. She gave him the response she'd carefully crafted over the past few days. "I have a small device. It's like a pager and sends a one-way signal. Are you familiar with what that is?"

He nodded tersely. "So you activate this signal, and then what?"

"Then the scientists back home in their lab do their thing and pull me home."

"You don't power the jump yourself?"

"Heavens, no!" she exclaimed. "I'm just a simple psychic who can find stuff. I'll be along for the ride when it's time to go."

He frowned thoughtfully. She wished she knew more about time travel and could ask him a few intelligent questions about what thoughts were racing through his head so fast his ears were all but smoking.

But he changed subjects abruptly, surprising her. "What do you plan to do when the Persian fleet sails by?"

She frowned. "Hopefully, I'll be able to isolate which ship has the map on it. Then I have to find some way to get out to that vessel."

He grunted. "You think you can just flag it down and it'll pull over to pick you up?"

"When you put it that way, no, I don't suppose that would work." The corner of his mouth curled sardonically, and she added, "Gimme a break. I'm winging it here. Next order of business is to get on the right ship and find the damn thing. Then I'll worry about getting it back."

Rustam murmured, "Time to rest the horses."

He'd stopped on a tiny patch of sand that barely qualified as a beach. But a small dune rose behind it and sparse grass dotted the sandy slope. She and Rustam unsaddled the horses and stripped off their bridles to let the animals forage for what food they could find. Frowning, Tessa watched Rustam gather driftwood until he had a substantial pile of the stuff. Three substantial piles, in fact. Spaced evenly along the spit of sand.

Finally, her curiosity got the better of her. "What are you planning to do with that?"

"Light signal fires."

"To signal whom?"

"The Persians when they get here."

"You think they'll come investigate a lone fire on the beach?"

"They will when it's three separate fires."

"What's to keep them from killing us when they get here?"

That earned her an arch smile. "I'm the Sorcerer of Halicarnassus. My fame is widespread within the empire, and certainly anyone in the Persian fleet has heard of me."

"Yeah, and last they heard, you were a runaway slave."

"I do not think Artemesia will have admitted to anyone that I've run away. She'll have concocted a tale of sending me off on an errand after I paid too much attention to the pale foreigner. No one will question her story. It's unthinkable that a high-profile slave like me would slip from her grasp."

"Maybe," Tessa said doubtfully. "You're screwed if you're wrong, though."

"Ahh. Screwing. I know this one." His grin flashed as quick and dangerous as lightning. "I had thought you too fatigued for such athletics, but if you insist, I stand ready to serve."

"Yeah, I bet."

He closed the distance between them and swept her up against his powerful, and indeed ready-to-serve, body. She gasped at the sensation of his impossible length pushing impudently against her belly through their clothes. "Don't taunt me, woman. I have my limits."

"But Rustam," she said sweetly, "if I'm carrying your child, you dare not hurt me. We human females are fragile and miscarry easily."

He muttered something to the effect of "Fragile, my ass," under his breath as he turned her loose. He stalked over to the first of his woodpiles and began to lay a fire with sharp, violent movements.

Silently, she moved to the second pile and did the same.

For the first time in days, he made an actual camp, spreading out their bedrolls side by side over a patch of soft sand. After they gnawed the last of their jerky and washed down handfuls of dried fruit by drinking from their water skins, there wasn't much to do but go to sleep.

Rustam took off his boots and sighed in appreciation as he lay back on the sand. He held out his arm to her. "Come, Tessa. You need rest. The horses will watch for the fleet for us."

She'd long since quit marveling at the distinctly non-horselike things he got the beasts to do for him. And she did need sleep. But she wasn't sure cuddled up with him was the way to get it.

"I promise to leave you to your dreams," he murmured, grinning boyishly. "Unless, of course, you have other ideas."

She couldn't help but grin back at his ridiculously hopeful expression. "You're incorrigible."

"No, I'm Centaurian."

And so he was. For better or worse. And for better or worse, she was addicted to every arrogant, masculine, alien inch of him. There was no use trying to fight it. As soon as she fell asleep, she would promptly curl into his warmth and strength as surely as she was standing here.

"What am I going to do with you?" She shook her head as she sank down beside him and laid her head on his shoulder.

"Laugh and fight and love with me, but never leave me," he murmured sounding already more than half-asleep.

Never leave him? What in the heck was that supposed to mean? She was a twenty-first century human and he was… well, he was not. There was no way the two of them had a future together. Was there? Her head spun with the prospect. How would that work, anyway? Would he stay on modern-day Earth with her? Did he expect her to go back to Centauri Prime with him? Her, traveling across the galaxy to some alien planet? The first human in history to do so?

On second thought, maybe not the first. There'd been plenty

of stories of alien abductions over the years. She was beginning to think some of them might just be true. Stranger things no doubt had happened, like a time-traveling human bumping into a stranded Centaurian and having epic sex that might have resulted in a baby.

If Athena Carswell or Beverly Ashton found out about that, they were going to *kill* her.

She lay there, wide awake, long after Rustam's breathing had settled into the long, slow rhythm of deep sleep.

Never leave him, indeed. Impossible.

But a tiny voice in the back of her head wished that somehow the impossible was possible. After all, she'd time-traveled to ancient Greece, and that hadn't been remotely conceivable even a few years ago.

She fell asleep praying for a miracle.

Chapter 19

Rustam woke up abruptly, not sure what had disturbed him. A wordless mental pressure intruded insistently upon his rest. Not human. *Polaris.* He'd set the horse the task of guarding them and watching the sea.

Rustam reached for his short sword, which he slept with ready at hand, while he flung his awareness outward. With Tessa plastered against him, it was an easy matter to channel their combined power and determine that no intruder approached by land.

But the sea was a different matter entirely. A massive, unending flow of humanity covered the Aegean like an enormous algae bloom, choking out all other signs of sea life. It approached from the east and was nearly upon them.

"Tessa, wake up! The fleet is coming."

She jolted up beside him and he scrambled for the first signal pyre, using his fire-starting stones to light the tinder. He blew on it carefully, fanning the blaze. It caught the dry wood quickly and flared up. Soon Tessa had the second fire lit and was fanning it gently. He moved to the third and repeated the process.

When all three fires were burning strongly, sending columns of flames and sparks up into the endless halls of night, he commenced packing. "It won't take them long to come investigate. The entire sea is covered with ships. We should practically be able to walk deck to deck until we find your map."

"What about the horses?"

Regret stabbed him. "They have served us faithfully and true. They have earned their freedom."

He was no stripling lad to mourn the loss of a horse. But Polaris had been one of the few familiar entities in a foreign world, a loyal friend in a place and time where precious few souls could be called that. Although Rustam had been accustomed to the swirling intrigues of a palace—Persia and Centauri Prime were not so different in that regard—he'd grown lonely from time to time. And Polaris had always given him affection without reservation.

Would that Tessa would do the same. He felt her holding back on him all the time. Whenever the topic of the map came up, she mentally pulled away from him. And whenever he tried to talk about the two of them, she shut down completely. But maybe she had cause. Maybe she'd caught an inkling of the Centaurian directive in his turbulent thoughts and knew that nothing good could come of their relationship.

His mind rebelled, roaring in silent frustration. No way could he kill her. He'd planted his child in her, for star's sake. There had to be another ending to this story. If only he could find it! Time was running out on them. As soon as she found that blasted map of hers, he had no doubt she would activate her retrieval signal and leave him. There *had* to be a way to bind her to him. A way to neutralize her star navigator talent without killing her. A way to be with her forever…

Her voice, quiet and tense, interrupted his chaotic thoughts. "I think a small boat has broken away from the fleet."

He held out his hand at the same time she did. Their palms connected, and he reeled, startled. Apparently, both of them had been accessing their respective powers simultaneously, he to search for an approaching boat and she to scan for the map. The result was a burst of energy that ripped through him, burning like lightning across his skin.

"Oww!" she yelped.

"Sorry," he rasped. "You first."

She frowned for a moment, and then her brow cleared. "Got it. The map's still off to our left by a half mile or so. Your turn."

He reached out with his mind. Six men. Coming this way quickly in a shallow-bottomed pole barge. Armed. Cautious. Prepared to kill.

"Let me do the talking," he muttered under his breath as they stood waiting for the landing party in the flickering shadows of the fires. The heat warmed his back but not enough to make up for the night's chill on his front. He channeled a thin stream of energy into rendering his body impervious to the weather.

Tessa fingered her belt pouch nervously, but otherwise was still. She was a brave woman. As the waiting stretched out, a realization broke over him. He admired this Earth female. *Respected* her. Which was probably a good thing. After all, she was the mother of his child. His consort. His woman. He would do whatever it took to protect her, even if it meant taking on the entire Persian fleet.

"Who goes there?" a voice called out in Persian.

He replied in the same tongue. "Rustam of Halicarnassus."

"The sorcerer?" another voice squawked in surprise.

"Aye," Rustam answered evenly. "Queen Artemesia's man. I have important information to relay to her right away. Can you give us passage to her vessel now?"

"I dunno," the first man answered. The shallow boat scraped

the sand, and the soldier jumped out, steadying the prow without pulling it ashore. "Who's that with you?"

"The pale foreign woman. Her highness sent the two of us out on a scouting mission for her."

"Why would the queen send a stranger—and a female, no less—to do such important work?" the man demanded.

Rustam grinned. "Don't say that in front of Artemesia if you value your life. She'll flay the hide off your back for suggesting that a woman isn't the equal of a man in all things."

Snorts of agreement floated from the back of the boat.

Rustam took a casual, nonthreatening step forward. "Time's a'wasting, and our news won't wait. Let's get going." He pitched his voice in a tone of persuasive command. He backed it with a mental wave of willingness to do his bidding.

The soldier nodded obediently.

Rustam took Tessa's hand and helped her into the boat. He seated her in the prow. "Hand me an oar. I'm willing to pull my weight if it'll speed us back to my queen."

He felt Tessa's body clench more than saw it. Jealous of Artemesia, was she? Surprise and fierce pleasure burst over him. Maybe there was a bit of Centaurian in her, after all.

It took only a few minutes to reach the first Persian ship. Indeed, the entire channel between the Greek shore and the nearest island was quickly filling with vessels. A jumble of masts striped the sky, silhouetted starkly against the night like a burned out forest. Or maybe it was just death clinging to the fleet that his mind's eye saw.

General Mardonius was waiting when Rustam planted his hands on the rail and vaulted aboard the vessel. The man blurted, "You? What's Artemesia's sorcerer doing lighting signal fires to the fleet?"

"I have news. Who commands this expedition?"

Mardonius replied wryly, "That would be the emperor, boy."

"Is Xerxes aboard one of these boats?"

"Aye. Back a few ranks. Your lady queen's ship is there-abouts, as well."

"How do we get back there?"

The general grunted. "Ye could walk, most likely. Damn crush. I told 'em to spread the fleet out. Arrange it in separate flotillas. But no, they've got to move the whole mess at once. Gotta make a grand show of force. Gonna get us all drowned out here if the gods send a storm."

Rustam refrained from mentioning the narrowing straits ahead and the logjam of ships that was sure to follow. The Persians would figure it out, to their detriment, soon enough. "Can we take a small barge to the emperor's vessel?"

"I wouldn't try it myself. You'll likely get run over and drown."

Rustam glanced at Tessa, who seemed to be concentrating on something else. Probably seeking her map. "I wouldn't ask you to risk any of your men, General. I will take the lady with me. Unless you'd like her to stay aboard your vessel—"

"No, no!" Mardonius answered hastily.

Rustam grinned to himself. So. A tradition was already established here that women were bad luck aboard a ship in battle? The Centaurian propaganda effort was starting to take root, apparently. For several Earth centuries already, the federation had been sending spies to this planet to spread the view of women as immoral, untrustworthy creatures fit only for serving men and bearing babies. Anything to keep Earth females from rising to enough prominence to be allowed to explore their star navigator talents. Too bad it seemed to have been a wasted effort. But maybe it had bought his kind some time to prepare their defenses against these wildly talented human women.

Then he snorted to himself. And if he was any indication, that effort was doomed to failure, too.

He murmured, "Let us go, my lady." Grasping Tessa by the elbow, he steered her back to the rail where the small barge had yet to be hoisted aboard.

"I'll take those oars, boy," Rustam told the young seaman who was steadying the barge against the side of the ship. To Tessa he murmured, "Can you climb down a rope, or do I need to carry you?"

She muttered back irritably, "I'm a freaking army officer. Of course I can climb down a rope."

He grinned. "After you."

Manning a pair of oars, he fought the current and dodged ship after ship bearing down upon them, beginning to question the wisdom of trying to reach Tessa's map by sea. Lookouts yelled at them continuously and their tiny vessel was in constant danger of capsizing.

"Where's the map?" he called forward to Tessa.

"Off to our left, toward the center of the fleet."

Of course. And it was going to be a gentle morning stroll to cut across the ranks of vessels. Risking life and limb, he turned their tiny craft. An annoyed captain hollered epithets at them, and Rustam and Tessa squeaked in front of the prow of his ship moments before it would have cut their little barge in half.

They repeated the maneuver a half-dozen more times before Tessa murmured excitedly, "It's close. Very close."

"Talk to me, sweetling."

"One more ship over."

He looked up to gauge the speed of the next oncoming ship, and jolted. The prow of the vessel bristled with soldiers pointing long spears down at them. Tessa gasped.

"I think we found the imperial barge," he muttered at her.

"Who goes there?" one of the soldiers growled.

"Rustam of Halicarnassus," he called back. "I come with tidings for my lady queen, Artemesia. Can you point me to her vessel?"

"She sails starboard and aft of his imperial majesty. Make way for this ship and steer clear of it or we will skewer you and your passenger."

"I would not advise doing that," Rustam replied evenly, stacking his voice and energy emanations with cold menace.

The imperial barge was close enough for him to make out the uncertain scowls on the soldiers' faces. But then the undertow of the larger ship sucked at them, and he had his hands full for a few moments, rowing for all he was worth to keep them from being pulled under. This was madness. No map was worth this risk.

"There!" Tessa called excitedly. "That's the ship! That's where it is!"

Rustam looked up as Xerxes's barge finally passed by. "You're kidding, right?"

"No. That's it!"

Tessa was pointing at a low-slung vessel flying the red and gold colors of Halicarnassus. Artemesia's ship. And here he'd been so relieved to have gotten clear of the woman's web of intrigue and control. "Are you certain?" he asked sharply.

Tessa clambered forward, setting their keelless barge to rocking wildly.

"Be careful!"

She dropped to her knees, lowering her body weight fast lest she dump them both out into the sea. "Sorry," she gasped. "Give me your hand."

He dragged one oar aboard quickly and thrust out his left hand to her. She grabbed it, and a look of sexual pleasure passed over her face as their energy fields melded. His body hardened, ready to take her, as her violet aura flowed over him, hot and sweet.

"Oh, yeah," she groaned, sounding nearly orgasmic. "We're practically on top of it. It's there."

Damn. He sighed. "All right. Let me hail her men. And again, let me do the talking. She's likely to slit your throat if we're not extremely careful. Stay close enough to me that I can access your energy. I may need it with her."

And then there was no more time to talk. A sentry from Artemesia's ship spotted them and a shout went up on the vessel, announcing that the queen's sorcerer approached. A flurry of activity erupted and, in short order, he and Tessa were thrown a pair of rope ladders. He was startled that she knew how to climb one properly, going up the outer side of it, straddling one of the long support ropes between her legs. Must be more of that army training of hers. He harrumphed. Completely inappropriate for a woman.

Tessa grinned over at him as she gained the low, wide deck, almost as if she sensed his thoughts. He scowled back at her. And then the charismatic—and highly angry—red aura of Artemesia exploded across his brain. She was awake. That violent flash of crimson must be someone telling her that her missing sorcerer had returned.

Suffice it to say she was not happy.

"Stand behind me," Rustam muttered under his breath to Tessa.

Thankfully, she had another one of those military-officer moments of knowing when to follow an order without question and scooted behind him just as Artemesia stormed up onto the deck.

"Well, well, well. Look what the gods have brought me on the tide. My runaway slave…and his mistress. This is too rich. I shall give thanks to the gods in the morn for the return of that which left me without my permission. Perhaps I shall make an offering of your black heart, sorcerer mine."

Artemesia strolled around him to glare at Tessa, who stood tall and proud behind him. *Not defiant,* he sent her urgently. *Not fearful. Be calm.*

"And the blond bitch, too."

"You may call me Princess, Your Highness. And I would like to thank you for the loan of your slave. He saved me from rape and protected my virtue. In my land, this is a woman's single greatest treasure. And mine is safe because of your man."

Rustam snorted to himself. Taking her virtue had been one of the greatest pleasures of his life.

Behave, Tessa sent him. Aloud, she said, "As we fled my attackers, your sorcerer discovered vital information about the invasion that he knew you would want him to investigate. He said something about gaining you great glory with the emperor if you were the one to bring the news to Xerxes."

The queen's fury abated momentarily. Nice ploy on Tessa's part. The only thing Artemesia enjoyed more than wielding power was gaining more power.

Her sharp gaze swung to him. "What news is this?"

Rustam went blank. Quickly, he sent to Tessa, *Okay, smartie. What's this news I supposedly have?*

Artemesia barked, "Explain yourself this instant or die. Guards, seize them!"

Chapter 20

Tessa thought fast. She shot back mentally to Rustam, *Tell her Athens is being evacuated by sea right now. If the Persian fleet hurries, they can trap the Athenian navy and force it into battle to protect the retreat of the citizens. That's what happens, anyway.*

Rustam retorted, *We risk speeding up how soon the Persians get to Athens. For all we know, it'll cause Xerxes to annihilate the Athenians.*

As a guard grabbed her roughly by the arms and yanked her elbows behind her back, she responded frantically, *The fleet's too unwieldy and the straits are too narrow for it to speed up, as long as it stays together in one flotilla.*

"Off with their heads!" Artemesia snarled.

Rustam laughed lightly. "Temper, temper, my dear queen. Trust me. You want to hear what I have to say."

Artemesia threw up a hand, stopping the soldier beside her in the act of lifting his scimitar for a swing. Tessa exhaled carefully. With her arms held behind her back like this, she had no access to her emergency cuff. Of course, she had no idea if Professor Carswell could get her out of here fast enough to avoid a beheading, anyway. Athena had said she could usually pull out operatives in a few seconds. But what was "usually" and how long was "a few seconds"? At the moment, one or two extra heartbeats could mean life or death. And that was assuming Tessa could wrench her arms free and activate the cuff at all.

"Speak," Artemesia purred to Rustam, her voice silky and dangerous.

He nodded. "Athens is being evacuated. It's an exodus by ship. The city's entire navy is assembled in a mass to protect the retreat of the civilians. If Xerxes strikes now, he can wipe out the Athenian navy and most of its population in a single blow."

Artemesia stared. "Truly?" she half whispered.

"I swear it upon my life and my honor," Rustam replied solemnly. Tessa felt the wave of sincerity he sent the queen to reinforce his vow.

"How do you know this?" the queen demanded.

He stepped forward, and Tessa, sensing his intent, dragged her guard forward a step so she could stay in close proximity to Rustam. He'd need the extra strength she could lend him for this stunt.

"May I touch your exalted highness?" he murmured deferentially.

Artemesia started. Cautiously, she held out her hand. "You may. But take no liberties with my person," she added sharply.

Tessa grinned inwardly. Always had to be in control, that lady. But she supposed she didn't blame the queen. The woman held her own in a time and place that gave new meaning to male domination.

Ignoring the proffered hand, Rustam reached out and gently placed his fingertips on Artemesia's temples. As the queen's eyes drifted closed, Tessa carefully pulled her right arm free of the guard's grasp. She was surprised when he let her go. But apparently, permission to touch the queen put the two of them firmly in the class of non-threats. And then, of course, there was the soldier's fear of and fascination with Rustam's "magic." Regardless of the reason for her release, Tessa reached out quickly and laid her hand on Rustam's back. She allowed her own aura to flow over him, blending with his in a familiar swirl of indigo.

As Rustam shaped the energy and formed a mental image, which he projected into Artemesia's mind, the image also flowed through Tessa. For someone who hadn't actually seen the evacuation of Athens in person, he created an amazingly vivid image of it. The Parthenon stood proudly on the Acropolis, bathed in moonlight, its white marble architecture so perfect it stole Tessa's breath away. Is *that* what it looked like new? It was one of the most beautiful things she'd ever seen.

The view shifted to an Athenian port. Long lines of people crowded the shore, waiting impatiently to board small rowboats that would shuttle them to larger seafaring ships moored close by.

Artemesia's eyes grew wide as the vision flowed through her mind. Tessa's mouth twitched with humor when Rustam blasted the queen with the absolute belief that what she'd just seen was real. Heck, it probably was close enough to real.

The monarch whirled away from Rustam to face the captain, who'd come up on deck by now, rubbing sleep from his eyes, "Take me to the imperial barge," she ordered.

The man looked alarmed. "I cannot maneuver in this crush. If we get broadside of the fleet, we'll get rammed and sink."

"Then put a barge in the water," Artemesia ordered impatiently.

Rustam cleared his throat. "With all due respect, my queen, I would not see you risk life or limb in such a flimsy craft."

She shot him a suspicious look. "A barge was good enough to bring you to me."

"Ahh, but I would gladly risk my life to return to your side, my lady."

Tessa winced at the heavy wave of sexual attraction he sent along with that remark. Artemesia visibly preened for a moment, but then turned her formidable mind to the problem at hand. "Shout word to the next ship that the Queen of Halicarnassus has tidings of great import for the emperor. At his earliest convenience, I request an audience to relay my news."

Obediently, the ship's captain bellowed to the next vessel over. In retreating volume over the next several seconds, Tessa heard the message shouted from boat to boat. Hopefully, the meaning wouldn't get too mangled by the time it reached Xerxes's ears.

"Now what?" the captain asked.

Artemesia shrugged. "Now we wait." She cast a speculative glance at Rustam. "And in the meantime, my slave shall attend me. Come to my bed, slave."

Tessa had to clench her jaw—hard—to stand there and listen to Rustam being called that. He was such a magnificent, intelligent, powerful man, a star navigator, for heaven's sake. It was obscene to hear his name and the word *slave* in the same sentence. And she didn't even want to think about him in Artemesia's bed.

Tessa couldn't help herself. Her aura surged, flying around her in shades of violet and angry purple.

Easy, love, Rustam warned. *Artemesia can sense a strong enough energy field. Do not give her a weapon like your jealousy to wield against you.*

Tessa had to dig her fingernails cruelly into her palms to distract herself, but she managed to wrestle her emotions back under control by sheer dint of will. She counted backward from ten to one, forcing her expression to go blank as Rustam stepped away from her, following the queen toward the hatch that led belowdecks. And it was a good thing she did so for, without warning, Artemesia cast a triumphant look over her shoulder at her.

Go ahead, Your Highness. Pretend you've won and the man is yours. I am the one he named his consort and put his child into.

A cobalt-blue wave of amusement so strong it nearly made her burst out laughing slammed into Tessa.

As Artemesia disappeared down the hatch, Tessa scowled fiercely at Rustam, who was grinning back at her like a cat with a big, fat canary in its mouth.

Petulantly, she flung at him, *I hope she makes you have sex with her.*

No, you don't. Do not be ashamed of your jealousy. It pleases me.

Go to he—

He cut her off. *Search the ship for your map while I've got her distracted, my love.*

The Karanovo fragment. Her mission. She'd completely forgotten why she was here, in her irritation at Artemesia taking *her* man to bed. Tessa froze. Her man? Since when was Rustam *her* man?

Grimly, she turned to face the ship. She glanced over at the captain, who hovered unhappily on deck. He looked as if he'd love to go back to bed but wasn't sure he had permission from his queen to do so.

"My dear sir," Tessa said sweetly, "would you do me the honor of showing me your most excellent vessel?"

The man looked relieved to have something to do. Tessa reached out with her mind to search for the medallion…and realized all of a sudden that she was getting absolutely nothing. No pinprick of energy, no general direction, nothing. Dammit. As soon as Rustam had left, he'd taken every bit of her skill with him. Well, she could always do it the old-fashioned way and hunt with her eyeballs. With a sigh, she turned to follow the captain.

At night, with no moon, and no torches nearby, she didn't stand a chance of spotting the medallion. And it didn't help that her stomach was roiling and queasy in short order. She'd never been prone to seasickness before, but then, she'd never been on a tiny Persian ship in the middle of the Aegean Sea with her lover below her feet, in bed with another woman. She had every right to be seasick, thank you very much.

It was a long night. As Artemesia had made no provision for her to have quarters, the ship's crew wasn't inclined to offer them to her. She eventually dug Rustam's big cloak out of his pack and wrapped herself in it, but it wasn't quite enough to stave off the damp chill as the wee hours of the night came and went.

It was silent belowdecks, but her mind still conjured any number of lurid scenarios involving Rustam and Artemesia. And every successive one made Tessa a little crazier. It shouldn't matter to her that Artemesia had reclaimed her lover. Tessa knew they'd slept together before, and she also knew that Rustam wasn't particularly fond of the woman in bed. He'd expressed respect for the woman's mind and her leadership abilities, but a closed, unpleasant look entered his gaze anytime the subject of Artemesia's sexual proclivities had come up in conversation. Not that it had more than once or twice.

Still, Tessa was miserable. She paced the decks, swathed in Rustam's voluminous cloak, surrounded by his scent and residual bits of blue energy that clung to the coarse wool and suffered the torments of hell.

Eventually, a single thought coalesced and took root in her brain. This had better not be love, because if it was, it sucked.

But as the stars wheeled about overhead and the Aegean Sea slapped the sides of the vessel, she gradually came to accept the truth. Somewhere along the way, she'd fallen in love with the big lout.

And without a shadow of a doubt, that was an enormous mistake. He was Centaurian, the enemy. From what Professor

Carswell had told her, the Centaurians were actively trying to interfere with mankind's progress toward space travel. For all Tessa knew, Rustam was one of those sent to Earth to impede mankind's progress!

A person did have to wonder why his spaceship was even in this corner of the galaxy when it crashed in the first place. Without his overwhelming presence to distract her from rational thought, she actually chewed on that question seriously for the first time.

She didn't like any of the possible answers she came up with.

Had he intentionally played on her intense attraction to him to keep her completely distracted from his purpose—distracted from *her* purpose, too—in being here? Had he managed to pick out of her brain what she was actually searching for and realized he had to prevent her from succeeding? Yes, he'd helped her make this journey through a war zone. But here she was, potentially mere feet away from the fragment, yet with no means of actually locating the wedge, thanks to him stealing her skill.

Funny how he'd accused her time and again of stealing *his* psychic abilities, when all along he'd been taking hers. Clever man. Had she really been that blind to what he was up to?

The gall of betrayal blossomed, hot and bitter.

Oh, yes. She'd been blind, indeed.

She found an out-of-the-way corner on the crowded deck between a pair of massive, fat-bellied amphoras of what smelled like lamp oil and sank down, huddling into the folds of Rustam's cloak.

Now what was she supposed to do?

It was time to get back on track. Do her job. Find the disk, activate her cuff, and get the hell out of here.

It would be a relief to leave behind the temporary insanity that had taken hold of her and return to her own place and time. Rustam was good, all right. He'd completely befuddled her.

She probably owed Artemesia a giant thanks for dragging him away from her and distracting him so he couldn't maintain the control he'd obviously insinuated into her mind.

Tessa swore under her breath. She'd been so gullible. The first sexy, handsome man who'd ever given her the time of day, and she'd fallen head-over-heels for him. Had she been the least bit suspicious when he was freely bedding the greatest beauties of an entire age yet mysteriously turned his affections upon her? Noooo. She'd believed he actually found her that attractive and had blithely jumped into his bedroll, swallowing his whole "I choose you for my consort and to be the mother of my children" line. By his own admission, scores of women mothered his children. She was just another conquest to him. And an easy one at that.

Worse, he'd managed to divert her from her original purpose in coming to Greece. Tessa might physically be close to the fragment, but she may as well be halfway around the world, given how much progress she was making at actually finding it.

Renewed resolve flooded her. If it took searching the entire ship from stem to stern on her hands and knees, so be it. When the sun came up, she'd find that wedge, come hell or high water!

She must have dozed at some point because she jerked awake with sunrise blasting light into her eyes. She felt like hell. She needed another four or five hours of sleep. The grueling pace of the past week and the unfamiliar strain of riding a horse for hours on end had apparently caught up with her. She was hungry for real food. Right now, a big stack of pancakes smothered in maple syrup with bacon and orange juice, and a steaming hot cup of coffee, sounded like manna from heaven. She wanted to drink water that didn't taste of goat skin or dust, and she wanted a hot shower with real shampoo.

And then last night's long vigil and its unpleasant realizations caught up with her. She dragged herself to her feet, her heart heavy. Time to search the ship. She was near the rear of the vessel, so she started there with the intent to methodically work her way forward. She'd do the top deck first. If need be, she'd figure out a way to sneak below and search there, too.

She'd been at it for maybe a half hour and had worked about a third of the way to the front of the ship when the sound of a horn drifted across the water. The single long blast was followed by two short, sharp ones. The ship's crew responded with alacrity, racing to drop the sails and hurrying aft to throw the anchor overboard. Startled, she gazed across the water and saw that all nearby ships were doing the same.

Apparently, the fleet was coming to a halt.

Artemesia burst up on deck wearing a barely there gauze gown that left absolutely nothing to the imagination. Tessa had to admit the woman looked pretty good for having never heard of aerobics or macrobiotic diets. Rustam came up on deck behind the queen, his tousled hair loose about his shoulders. He yawned and stretched like a sleepy lion. Tess scowled. The two of them could have each other, for all she cared.

Someone from the next ship over shouted, and Artemesia jumped as if a bee had just stung her. She turned and raced back belowdecks, dragging Rustam with her. Tessa had caught part of the message, something about an immediate audience. Indeed, a few minutes later, the queen returned, fully dressed in a gorgeous red gown, her hair pulled back from her face with a pair of beautifully jeweled combs. The woman really was lovely. Even in harsh morning light with no cosmetics, she was exotic. Commanding.

A good-size rowboat pulled up beside Artemesia's ship just as Rustam stepped back up on deck, fully arrayed in an elaborate scarlet toga. He wore a gold circlet around his forehead, and his bare, bronzed biceps were clasped by a matching pair of gold cuffs encrusted in thumbnail-size rubies. He looked every inch the prince he claimed to be.

Tessa's traitorous heart flip-flopped before her head reminded it sourly that he'd used her and played her, shamelessly distracting her and preventing her from accomplishing her mission. Still, he was beautiful to look at. She felt his mind reach out to her, but she forcefully cut off her own response. No more freebie mind reading for the alien, thank you very much.

His gaze went bleak. Hard. He spared a single, arrogant glance at her and then turned to murmur in Artemesia's ear. The queen laughed, a throaty, seductive sound that set Tessa's teeth on edge.

She turned away from the lovers and watched the sailors below expertly guide the rowboat close and hold it steady while Rustam and the queen were lowered aboard. The vessel pulled away.

Pain stabbed Tessa like a dagger in the gut, and she forced her mind away from naming it. Who cared if it was envy or loss or a broken heart? *It didn't matter.* She had to find the disk and get out of here...hopefully before those two returned.

She took the opportunity to duck down the stairs and search belowdecks in the queen's absence. The space was dark and damp, the ceilings so low she had to duck every time she came to a support beam. Rustam must have had to crouch over like a hunchback to move around down here at all.

Stop thinking about him!

She explored every inch of Artemesia's quarters, to no avail. A large, locked chest in one corner of the space worried Tessa. It looked like something that might contain jewelry and valuables...and the Karanovo fragment could easily have ended up in something like that.

Tessa got chased out of the crew's sleeping quarters by a grumpy, half-conscious soldier who told her to ply her whore's trade elsewhere. But not before she'd had a quick look around and seen nothing that looked even faintly like a bronze disk emblazoned with an image of a constellation.

She was appalled at the sight of the twin rows of oarsmen amidships, slumped over, asleep at their oars. She surreptitiously checked their ankles for shackles as she looked for the piece of bronze. The men weren't chained at their posts, thank goodness. But still, they were skinny, filthy, bearded and pale. None of them saw the light of day often, apparently.

The ship's cargo hold was a pain in the butt to search, but search it she did, barrel by barrel, crate by crate. The disk was nowhere to be found down there.

Frustrated, she returned to the top deck to continue her search. She'd finished about another third of the ship when the imperial rowboat returned, interrupting her.

Rustam lifted Artemesia aboard, her presence overwhelming everything and everyone aboard the ship, including him. The woman was a force of nature. She could probably give Rustam as good as she got from him.

Tessa sighed. Yes, she'd been an idiot to think he'd actually fallen for her. She'd been convenient. A tool to be used and discarded when it wasn't needed anymore.

Artemesia's crew hauled up the anchor and hoisted the sails with fascinating efficiency. In a few minutes, their ship was under way again. Tessa frowned as she noticed that their vessel was passing all the other nearby ships, which were still at anchor.

Relenting on her vow never to speak to Rustam again, she sidled up beside him and murmured, "What's going on? Why are we moving and the others holding their positions?"

"Because the queen brought such valuable tidings to the emperor, his generals are giving her the honor of leading the fleet."

Tessa frowned. "Isn't that the most dangerous position?"

"Aye."

"So they're rewarding her by putting her in harm's way? That makes no sense."

Rustam glanced down at Tessa wryly. "From her perspective, she has the most chance to gain glory by leading the fleet.

From the generals' perspective, maybe they remove a pesky thorn in all of their sides if she happens to drown gloriously."

"Lovely."

"Any luck finding your map?"

"Not yet. And I've been over most of the ship."

Rustam silently held his hand out to her, hiding the move by angling his body closer and using a fold of his toga to disguise his hand.

She really didn't want to touch him, lest she fall under his spell again. But did she have any choice? She *had* to find the disk. Exhaling hard, she took his hand.

Power flowed over her and through her, more intoxicating than ever. It was infused with his desire for her, the explosive lust between them dancing through her like chain lightning.

"Do you have this effect on all the girls?" she ground out between clenched teeth.

He laughed quietly. "I sincerely hope so."

She scowled up at him. Dammit, he was doing it again— distracting her from the job at hand! The fragment. Where was it? She focused her mind and received a reading on it so piercingly sharp and close it stabbed the insides of her eyelids like ice picks. Jolted by the discomfort, her eyes flew open. *Directly in front of her. At eye level. No more than a few feet away.*

"Anything?" Rustam muttered.

She dropped his hand. "It's close, but we already knew that. I'm not even sure it's on this ship, at this point."

Meanwhile, her gaze flitted back and forth in front of her. The sides of the ship swooped together into a sharp, ironclad prow that curved up into a sharp point like an eagle's talon. Mounted just behind that claw was a not-quite-life-size carving of a woman, leaning forward as if into a strong wind. It appeared to be done in some sort of hardwood, inlaid with metal and semiprecious stones. Her robes flowed back behind her, and her face showed determination. Her left hand pointed forward as if she were gesturing troops into battle. Her right hand held a spear at the ready.

The spear.

Its tip was a wedge of bronze…with a series of bumps across its surface. Tessa squinted to make out the marks more clearly. That was the constellation Virgo.

Elation leaped in her chest.

She'd done it! She'd found the Karanovo fragment!

How she was going to climb out onto that narrow, precarious tongue of wood and get the damn thing, she had no idea. But one step at a time. It was a huge milestone to have even found it.

Another series of horn blasts drifted across the water, and ships all around them began to weigh anchor and hoist sails. The front edge of the fleet appeared. But, with the forward momentum it had, Artemesia's ship passed most of the others before they got under way.

Now that Tessa knew where the bronze piece was, she probably shouldn't stand here staring at it until Rustam took notice of what she was doing. She wandered aft to watch the progress of the fleet. She was relieved when he didn't follow her but rather chose to stay up front and gaze out across the open water before them. The fleet at their back was an impressive sight. As far as she could see, ships blanketed the sea. Hundreds, even thousands, of them. Ancient histories reported that Xerxes had fifteen thousand ships. It was possible his army numbered three hundred thousand or more, as Rustam said it did.

A sailor, perched high in the rigging overhead, shouted all of a sudden. The Athenian fleet had been sighted.

Artemesia's voice rang out from behind Tessa. "Prepare for battle! Wake the oarsmen and arm yourselves! We fight for the glory of Persia!"

Tessa's heart leaped into her throat. How in the world was she going to climb out onto the prow of the ship and get that disk in the middle of the greatest naval battle of ancient times? What if the ship sank? Then what was she supposed to do, assuming she didn't drown or get run over by another ship in the process?

As soon as crewmen on the ships behind them sighted the Athenian fleet, the race was on. Every captain wanted to be the first to engage the enemy, apparently. Bigger ships gradually gained on Artemesia's low-slung vessel.

Tessa had spoken with the captain during the night about how its lower center of gravity made it more stable on the open sea or in a storm than the other Persian ships and more nimble to maneuver. However, what it gave up in momentum and surface area of sails was quickly becoming apparent as the other Persian ships bore down on them.

She gazed ahead anxiously. There it was. The first of several channel islands that angled in toward shore, creating a natural—and deadly—funnel for the Persian fleet.

Tessa turned to speak urgently to the captain and was startled to find herself facing Artemesia.

"Speak," the queen commanded when Tessa drew up short.

"See that island over there?" Tessa pointed to the one she'd been looking at. "It angles toward shore, and this strait gets narrower and narrower ahead. The fleet behind us is going form a massive logjam—" She broke off. "Do you know that term? When logs float down a river and get smashed together—"

Artemesia waved a hand, cutting her off, her assessing gaze already taking in the bigger ships bearing down upon them. She grasped the problem in an instant and quickly ordered, "All sails aloft. Now! Full speed ahead on the oars!"

The faint rhythmic sound drifting up from below picked up speed and urgency, and Tessa abruptly realized what it was. A drum, being used to coordinate the strokes of the rowers.

Artemesia's ship shot forward. Sure enough, the straits narrowed on either side of them, the shores rocky and steep.

Ahh, the Athenians had chosen their trap well. Unfortunately, the other Persian captains also seemed to recognize the danger, and an all-out race for a tiny patch of open water ahead broke out. As the bigger ships also hoisted full sails and their oars stroked the water faster and faster, the ground Artemesia had gained was eaten up. Inevitably, the larger vessels again bore down on them.

The queen's captain shouted to the pair of approaching vessels to back off, but apparently, they were having none of it. It was every man for himself out here. Whoever got to the neck of the strait first would sail through. Everyone else would chance being crushed.

The ships on either side of them pulled even, then slightly ahead. Tessa winced. They weren't going to make it. Turbulent water before them marked the neck of the strait. She glanced in rising panic at Rustam, whose face was grim with understanding that they were in serious trouble.

"Do something!" she cried to him.

"I can't move an entire ship this size. Not without my gear. I need my crystals or something of equal power to focus my energy on."

Her cuff. It had a time-travel crystal in it. Was that what he was talking about?

The ship on their right banged into them, causing their vessel to rock violently. Tessa was thrown off her feet. Rustam knelt quickly beside her. "Can you swim?" he bit out.

"Yes. You?"

"Yes. When we go in the water, I'll try to stay with you. But if we get separated, try to find something to hang on to, to keep you afloat. This water is deep and cold and you'll tire fast. Head for the Greek shore if you can."

They were in serious trouble if he was talking about what to do when they sank. She said urgently, "I have one calibrated quartz crystal. Is that enough?"

He shook his head and muttered under his breath, "With only one crystal, I'd need a focus object—a substance hardened to withstand unleashed star-navigator energy, and the tearing forces of displacing and reforming."

The Karanovo fragment. Would it work?

She murmured, "There may be a focus object on this ship."

Rustam's eyes widened in surprise. "Impossible!" he exclaimed.

She climbed to her feet, staggering as the ship to the left jostled them. She grabbed his hand and dragged him forward, dodging frantic sailors trying to pad the sides of their vessel with blankets and spare sails. "There!" She pointed at the figurehead. "Her spear tip."

Rustam stared where she indicated. His jaw dropped. "The Karanovo—" He broke off abruptly. "It might work. Give me your crystal."

They were banged hard from both sides this time as the rocky shores funneled the front rank of the Persian fleet mercilessly together. The ship's timbers groaned, punctuated by ominous cracking noises. Behind them, the captain screamed for the crew to prepare to abandon ship.

Tessa tore her belt pouch open and grabbed her arm cuff, thrusting it into his hands.

"Touch me," Rustam yelled over the grinding of wood on wood. "Give me all your power!"

She grasped him from behind, wrapping her arms around his waist and hanging on for all she was worth as the ship began to buckle around them.

Chapter 21

Rustam's energy surged so violently that she could scarcely hang on as it burst out of him. An answering explosion of power from somewhere deep within her stunned her. She felt as if her body were tearing apart, into millions and millions of individual cells connected only loosely by a net of violet energy that grew and grew. The two storms merged, and an indigo tornado built around them, whirling faster and faster as it swelled to encompass the entire ship.

And then, with a great mental gathering of strength, she felt Rustam wrap his mind around the entire vortex and form it into a massive lightning bolt of power that he flung, in its entirety, at the Karanovo fragment.

The ship's deck heaved beneath Tessa's feet as the vessel lifted partially out of the water until its hull seemed to barely skim the surface of the sea. They shot forward like a high-powered motorboat, surging out of the deadly vise created by the other ships, with a grinding, screeching noise of wood scraping wood. And then they were free, shooting forward at twice the speed of the rest of the fleet.

How long they maintained that breakneck pace, she had no idea. Time ceased to have any meaning as raw power surged from her and through her, passing into and through Rustam. It was exhilarating. Beyond exhilarating. It was the same feeling she'd experienced when the two of them made love and leaped to that dark place full of stars, but *more*. So much more. She'd never felt anything like this. This must be what it was like to be a star navigator. And now that she'd experienced it, she instinctively knew that she'd be able to call it forth again. She was *changed*. More alive than she'd ever been before. And she loved it.

She became vaguely aware of something ahead of them, blocking the neck of the strait. More ships. But not moving, not the Persian fleet. Waiting in a solid mass. *The Athenian armada*.

If they didn't slow down, Artemesia's ship was going to slam into that line of vessels like a battering ram.

"Rustam," Tessa urgently called aloud, and sent mentally. "Stop!"

His eyes fluttered open, and he saw the obstacle ahead. All of a sudden, their ship slowed, settling heavily into the water, rocking hard over its own bow wave. Rustam sagged in her arms, supporting himself heavily against the ship's rail before him.

"You okay?" she murmured.

"I'll live. I haven't drained myself like that since my first jump."

She turned to glance behind them. The Persian fleet was well to the rear now in complete chaos as the first rank of ships jammed the strait in a mass of broken wood, tangled canvas and tilting masts, and the rest of the fleet bore down helplessly upon them. It was not a pretty sight. Here and there, the largest vessels were pushing through and pressing forward, but they were only a small fraction of the overall fleet.

"Uh, my lady queen? We have a problem."

That was the ship's captain. Tessa whirled to face where he was pointing. A group of Greek vessels had split away from the others and was approaching fast.

It was too late to run. Their flanks were unprotected. Various military options flew through Tessa's mind, and she discarded each with lightning speed. In an instant, only one truth remained. The best defense was always a good offense.

As she opened her mouth to suggest an attack, Artemesia ordered decisively, "Full speed ahead on the oars. Deploy the battering ram. Let us show these Greeks what we think of their puny navy."

The queen's crew sprang into action, ferocious grins on their faces. Bloodthirsty bunch. But then, Tessa expected no less of any sailors who served this formidable woman, who was such a lioness herself.

The Athenian ships arrayed themselves in a line before the Persian one, daring it to come and get them.

Artemesia's captain bellowed, "Which target, my lady?"

Tessa glanced at the choices. She'd choose the big one in the middle. It appeared as if orders were being shouted from that vessel to the others. Cut the head off the beast and maybe its limbs would cease to function effectively.

Beside her, Artemesia hissed, and Tessa looked over at her. The queen was just pulling a spyglass from her eye. "The middle ship," she snarled. Blindly, Artemesia held the spyglass out, all but punching her in the gut with it. Tessa snatched the piece before it could drop to the deck, then, curious, put it to her eye and focused on the middle ship ahead.

Ahh. No wonder Artemesia was so furious. The Greek general Hippoclides stood wide-legged and arrogant on the deck. The queen's lover had come out to destroy her. Red fury radiated off of Artemesia, infecting the rest of the crew within moments. Tessa was stunned. Was Artemesia a potential star navigator, too? She had the kind of personal energy field that might easily be an indicator. But there was no more time to wonder about it as the enemy ship's oars came out and the two vessels began to charge one another.

It suddenly dawned on Tessa that Rustam was still leaning heavily on the front rail. He'd be thrown out of their vessel when the two collided! Racing forward as the Greek craft loomed, she threw an arm around him.

When she looked down at the water, where he was staring, she saw a wooden flap open just below their feet. Two massive pointed logs armored with metal of some kind emerged. Those must be the battering rams. An interesting innovation. Her studies of military history indicated that ancient sailors merely rammed their ships into one another, and the strongest vessel generally sailed away intact while the other sank. Artemesia, in her zeal to design a better ship, must have come up with this idea of an actual battering ram. Even if those logs shattered on impact, the vessel would still be seaworthy. *Clever.*

Rustam shifted beside her, pulling her attention back to the battle at hand.

"C'mon, you've got to move," she insisted. "We're about to ram the Greek ship and you'll get tossed overboard. You'll never guess who's commanding it."

Rustam didn't answer. He let her wedge herself under his left arm and steer him aft, staggering under his weight until she sat him between the same amphoras of oil she'd slept near last night.

"Hang on," she murmured. "We should slam into the Greeks soon."

Rustam nodded wearily. As she began to stand up, a strange thing happened. All of a sudden, he threw his head up, nostrils flaring sharply. "Who's in command of that vessel?" he demanded.

Surprised, she replied, "Hippoclides. Artemesia's lover."

"The Greek gen—of course." Rustam swore under his

breath in a tongue she'd never heard before, but there was no doubt it was cursing.

"What's wrong?" she asked quickly.

"He's one of us."

Tessa frowned. "Come again?"

"He's exactly like me."

Her jaw dropped. "Are you serious?"

He scowled up at her. "I can feel his aura from here. If I didn't know better, I'd say it was Kentar himself who has possessed Hippoclides's body."

"Who's Kentar?"

"The Centaurian Primus. My supreme commander."

"What in the world would he be doing here?"

"Coming to check up on me, most likely."

"But I thought you crashed here by accident—"

The sentence was interrupted by the captain shouting, "Brace for impact!"

If the ships had looked small to Tessa before, the massive crash as they collided moments later belied the impression. The entire deck heaved and shuddered beneath her, and the sound of cracking, buckling wood was horrendous. Their vessel lurched backward, recoiling from the impact. Coils of hemp line, barrels, spare oars and men rolled over the deck in utter chaos. But then a triumphant shout went up overhead. Tessa looked skyward and saw a sailor tied to the mast shaking his fist gleefully at the Greeks.

She risked a glance forward. Directly in front of them, the Greek ship's prow was split open like a log neatly driven apart by a wedge. A wedge... Ohmigosh, the figurehead!

Tessa jumped up, racing forward to check on the statue's condition. What if her spear had broken off in the impact?

The lady was intact, her bronze spear tip gleaming dully. Thank God! Tessa looked over at the Greek ship and was shocked to see someone staring back at her fixedly. Hippoclides. If he could've stared a hole through her, he would have.

As the Greek ship began to list to starboard beneath his feet, he glared at her. Only at her.

Oh, yes. He knew exactly who—and what—she was. Hatred and a promise of death glittered in his preternaturally intense gaze. He was every bit as forceful as Rustam. However, having had no little experience standing up to her personal Centaurian alpha male, she stared back at Hippoclides, her chin high and her gaze defiant.

That's right, buster. I'm a star navigator, too. Get over it. She let her violet aura flow from within, let it build around her in a whirling display of raw power.

His eyes went wide and he actually staggered back a step in shock.

Or maybe it was just the rapidly sinking ship throwing him off balance. He turned then…and disappeared.

Did he just teleport out? Or maybe he got lost in the chaos of panicked sailors as the deck beneath him slid into the sea.

A voice spoke quietly from behind her. "Everything okay?"

Rustam. What was he doing on his feet again? "You ought to be resting."

"You powered up and were angry."

She answered his unspoken question. "Hippoclides was staring at me. I thought I'd give him something to think about."

"Where is he now?" Rustam asked quickly.

"Gone. He might have teleported out, or I could've just lost sight of him."

Rustam was silent for a moment. "No. He's gone. I can't sense him anymore."

"The Greeks will report him lost at sea and be none the wiser," she commented.

She felt Rustam's wince behind her. "There's going to be hell to pay for your little display when I get home."

She turned quickly to face him. "Really? I'm sorry. I didn't think."

He grinned weakly at her. "No need to apologize, my love. It's good for him to meet women like you and Artemesia, who back down to no man."

Tessa smiled up at him gratefully.

"Go get your piece of the Karanovo stamp. In the bustle to put this ship to rights before the next attack, no one will notice you."

"Next attack?"

He nodded over her shoulder.

Oh, God. The other Greek ships. They might have lost their leader, but they still outnumbered Artemesia four to one. They'd be coming soon.

Tessa turned to have a look at the figurehead. The statue leaned forward, slightly ahead of the prow, as if she were flying. But she appeared sturdy enough. "Block me from view," Tessa murmured to Rustam.

She climbed carefully up onto the rail using a heavy hemp line for balance. She inched forward and put her hand on the lady's back. The wood was warm. Vibrating with energy. *Whoa.* Tessa shifted her other hand and hugged the statue around the waist. She made the mistake of looking down and saw only water churning beneath the prow. A moment of sick nausea washed over her.

"Steady," Rustam murmured. He sent her a wave of reassurance, which she gratefully accepted.

She reached forward with her right arm, running her fingers along the smooth bronze spear. The closer she got to the disk, the warmer the statue got. Finally, she wrapped her hand around the triangular piece. A blast of energy tore through her, so intense it nearly knocked her off her perch. She grasped the wedge and gave it a hard twist, bending it to the side. The solid bronze spear shaft bent but did not break. She repeated the maneuver again. It wobbled, but held on. Thankfully, bronze was a relatively soft and pliable metal. One more hard twist, and the spear tip snapped off in her hand.

"Got it!"

"You'd better get down, darling. We're about to have company."

She looked up and her jaw dropped as all four Greek ships bore down on them at battering speed. *Uh-oh.*

Tessa scrambled backward and into Rustam's waiting arms. He set her down immediately, obviously too weak to support her weight. Wow. He really was wiped out.

"Come about!" Artemesia shouted. "Tell the oarsmen to row for their lives!"

The ship started a ponderous turn, which maybe wasn't so great an idea. In Tessa's estimation, they were going to be broadside to the four attackers right about when they got here.

Tessa helped Rustam make his way aft to their little cubbyhole. Artemesia grabbed his arm on the way past. "Give my ship wings, sorcerer."

"I cannot, my lady."

Artemesia glared at him furiously. "You must."

Tessa snapped, "He didn't say he would not. He said he *could not*. He's wiped out from the last time."

Artemesia turned on her. "Then *you* do it, witch woman. I command it."

The queen didn't need to add that they would all die if they didn't pull some rabbit out of the hat. And soon. Tessa didn't have the first idea how to focus the star navigator power into moving this ship forward. And frankly, she had no idea how much of her own power remained after the first spurt of speed. She'd had enough to put on a pretty show for Hippoclides, but that didn't take much. Nonetheless, the fact remained that they needed to do something.

Tessa thought fast, looking around for what resources were available at hand. The Greek ships were close enough for her to hear their rowing drums, to hear the raucous insults their sailors shouted at the hapless Persian ship they were about to sink.

"Do you have a bow and arrow on board?" Tessa asked urgently.

The terrified captain shook his head, but Artemesia answered, "My hunting bow is below."

"Get it. And several arrows," Tessa ordered. For once, the queen didn't stand on ceremony but nodded and raced below. Tessa turned to the nearest sailors. "Grab these amphoras of oil and pour their contents overboard. All the oil you've got. Hurry!"

In short order, eight giant urns were emptying into the sea. As she'd hoped, the water was generally calm enough for the oil to float in a single slick on the surface.

Artemesia thrust the bow into Tessa's hands. Tessa reached down and tore a long strip of cloth from the hem of her tunic. The Greek ships were getting close now. Close enough to make out individual faces and the fury burning in their eyes.

Frantically, Tessa wrapped the cloth around the end of an arrow and then used it to sop up a puddle of oil that had spilled on the deck. "I need fire."

Everyone looked around, perplexed. Tessa's heart sank to her feet. Surely somebody had a lantern or something lit on this ship. She couldn't believe they all could die for lack of a freaking candle. Her kingdom for a match, dammit!

Rustam stepped forward. He pulled out a small penlike object from his pouch. He muttered an incantation, summoning forth fire, and then he flicked his thumb. The mechanism looked similar to a modern cigarette lighter. A small triangle of blue flame erupted from the end of it.

The sailors around her took a step back, oohing and aahing while she held the cloth-wrapped arrow tip to the flame. It lit instantly. She turned quickly, nocked the arrow and pulled the bowstring to her ear. Murmuring a quick prayer, she loosed the arrow, aiming for the center of the oil slick glistening on the surface of the sea.

The oil caught fire. Not with a spectacular flare, as she'd

hoped, but the blaze spread quickly enough; and in moments, a line of flame stretched across the water between them and the Greek ships. It was only a few feet tall but was growing steadily.

The Greek captains shouted frantically. Their oars reversed direction, digging furiously into the water to slow the ships and turn them away from the now deck-high fire before them.

Slowly, slowly, Artemesia's ship completed its turn and began to creep away. Tessa looked behind them. Smoke rose from the fire, and through the wavering heat waves, the Greek ships ground to a standstill, frustrated in their efforts to destroy Artemesia's craft.

Tessa became aware of their own ship beginning to pick up speed, heading back to the safety of the Persian fleet. They'd made it! Artemesia's crew began to cheer, and the queen basked in their adulation.

"Take me to Xerxes," she ordered. "Let him know that a woman struck the first blow at the Greeks and gained the glory of the day. Let the gods see me and know my name!" she shouted.

As the crew celebrated, Rustam stumbled beside Tessa.

"Let's get you below," she murmured. "You need to lie down."

She guided him into the hold, appropriating Artemesia's bed without hesitation. He stretched out with a sigh and closed his eyes. The crisis past, Tessa became aware of the draped gauze curtains disguising the ship's rough timbers, of the smell of sandalwood incense, the gentle slap of water on the hull.

And then she became aware of something else. Something hard and hot digging into her palm. She looked down. *At long last.* The Karanovo Stamp. Or at least a pie-shaped piece of it. The energy flowing through it was incredible, healing and empowering and strengthening.

In sudden inspiration, she pressed the disk into Rustam's hand. His eyelids fluttered briefly. As she watched, the gray cast to his skin faded, and color returned to his cheeks. His aura turned blue again, then cobalt, then the brilliant royal-blue it usually was. The sunken hollows in his cheeks and below his eyes disappeared, and in a moment, his eyes opened, as alert and aware as usual.

He smiled up at her.

"Welcome back, handsome."

"Thanks. How are you?"

"I've been carrying that thing around for the past few minutes. I'm fine."

He glanced down at the bronze piece in his hand. "Do you know what this is?"

She looked up at him sharply. "Yes, I do. Do you?"

He laughed shortly. "It's one of the main reasons my kind came here. We're under orders to find these pieces—"

He broke off, but she finished quietly for him, "And take them away from mankind. Right?"

He looked up at her bleakly. "Right."

Their gazes met. She'd been sent here to find the medallion, and he'd been sent here to steal it. There was no way both of them could succeed in their missions. One of them had to fail.

She frowned. "You said *one* of the reasons you came here was to find this object. What are the other reasons?"

He actually flinched. She mentally braced herself, but nothing could have prepared her for his next words.

"I was sent here to kill you."

Chapter 22

Rustam watched warily as Tessa leaped to her feet, nearly hitting her head on the ceiling. She subsided back onto the edge of the bed, sick shock written in every line of her face.

He understood the reasons for his federation's standing order to kill humans like her, but in this case, he couldn't possibly obey it. Either way, he owed her an explanation. He sighed and tried to make her understand. "The Centaurian Federation controls star travel throughout the galaxy. We're the only race that consistently produces star navigators, and we need to keep it that way if we're to maintain our position and wealth. When races like yours show a latent talent, we send agents to eliminate those members of the race who carry the star navigator gene. And my dear, without a shadow of a doubt, you have that gene."

Even if he hadn't heard her thoughts, he'd have been able to read them in the expressions crossing her mobile face. *After all we've shared? After all we've been through together? And it comes down to this?*

Aloud, she said, "You made love to me. You made me your consort and gave me your baby. And now you're going to *kill* me?"

He exhaled hard, once again between a rock and a hard place. "My duty is to eliminate you from the human gene pool. But do you really expect me to kill you?" He burst out, "I love you, curse it!"

Some of the rigidity left her shoulders. "I love you, too," she murmured.

He opened his arms and she came to him willingly, plastering herself against him. He loved the feel of her in his arms, loved the tingle of her aura mingling with his. Loved her feistiness, her independence, her intelligence. Hell, he loved everything about her.

If not him, some other Centaurian would most certainly kill her. Especially now that Hippoclides—whom he was sure was Kentar in disguise—knew that she existed.

Desperation coursed through him, the same emotion emanating from Tessa. Why couldn't everyone just leave the two of them alone? They were terrific together, race and politics and military missions aside.

"What are we going to do?" she whispered against his neck.

He didn't want to think about it. Didn't want to hear the words or say the words. He tilted his chin down to kiss her, desperate to stop the inevitable from coming: words of loss and parting.

As always, the moment their lips touched, the magic was there, building between them, larger than either of them, larger than the sum of their individual powers. He plunged his hands into her hair, holding her still for his tongue to plunder her mouth, drinking in her sweetness and tartness and everything that made her special and unique.

"Gods, I can't ever get enough of you," he groaned against her lips.

She laughed ruefully. "I know the feeling." She wiggled

against him, and his body leaped to attention, ready and eager to make love to her. She came to him once more, kissing him voraciously, as if she would devour him whole.

This might be the last time they ever got to do this, and the urgency of it stole his breath away. In response to that thought, she wailed inside his head, echoing his own sentiment exactly. *This can't be the last time!*

But what else could they do? He rolled over, drawing her beneath him, pressing her deep into the soft feather tick, following her down into that place that was theirs alone, a place of darkness and starry skies and a towering passion that dared him to even breathe.

He sucked at her lower lip while she nipped at his. Their tongues wrestled in a wet, slippery swirl that sent his lust surging out of control. Her hands skimmed down his torso, gripping his male flesh and about making him jump out of his skin.

"I want you," she panted hoarsely. "Now."

He didn't hesitate. He followed his instinct to make this woman his completely, to brand her forever his, a part of him for all time. He shoved her clothes up. A quick bunching of his own toga, a hard thrust, and her hot, slick flesh encased him fully. Her gasp of pleasure was a spear straight to his heart.

She was his.

His woman. His partner. His love.

She bucked beneath him, wild in her desperation to take even more of him into her. Their desire galloping away with them, he rode her hard, their bodies straining together, riding a wave of passion that swept them up with its power.

"Look at me," he commanded.

Her feverish eyes opened, and she smiled up at him, every ounce of her love and need for him glowing in shades of violet within her azure gaze. She gripped his shoulders strongly, her nails digging into his flesh. He plowed her harder and deeper, relishing the cries he wrung from her throat, the way she arched as taut as a bow beneath him as ever more intense pleasure built between them.

At the moment of their explosive release, he looked deep into her soul, his own heart completely naked before her. She drank him in, taking everything he was into herself and giving him all she was in return. In that moment, they were one. One spirit. One soul.

And then, as usual, the deep, profound silence of space enshrouded them, as calm and protective as a blanket wrapped gently around them.

Why can't we stay in this place forever? she sent him.

We would die eventually. Our physical bodies need nourishment. It is from those that our power to come to this place springs.

She responded ruefully, *Would that be such a bad way to go?*

He sighed. *There has to be a way for us to be together. I just don't know what it is. But I know this. I cannot harm you. It would be like killing a part of myself.*

A long silence stretched out. *Is it wrong for me to want you to succeed at whatever you do, even if it's bad for me and my people?* she mentally asked at last.

That startled him. *You want me to prevent mankind from gaining star travel?*

No! I want mankind to progress as we're meant to. But I only wish good things for you, too.

Ahh. Yes, I know the feeling. I want you to have success in all you do, as well.

The peace of deep space faded out, and heavy wooden beams wrapped in cloth reappeared around them.

"We've only got one piece of the medallion," she said quietly.

He dug in his pouch and pulled out her arm cuff with its special quartz crystal. "And we've got one travel band."

It was hard to think clearly with his flesh still hot and hard and buried deep inside her, her legs still wrapped around his hips, her bare breasts, freed from the top of her gown, pressing against his chest.

"You take the medallion fragment," he mumbled. "My people will have other chances to find the remaining pieces of it and take one from mankind. I don't need the legendary glory of finding a piece of the Karanovo stamp. I have gained glory enough already in my career." He wrapped her fingers gently around its oblong shape, its otherworldly warmth flaring between their palms. He held out the armband to her, as well. "Here. This is yours, too."

She stared up at it for a long time without taking it. Then she gently pushed the hand cupping the crystal back toward him. "You take it. With that, you can get home, right? You won't be stuck here on Earth anymore."

He flinched. "But if I use it, then you'll be trapped here in ancient times. You won't be able to get back to your own world."

"At least I'm on my home planet. I want you to have the crystal."

"No!" He jumped up out of bed and banged his head—hard—on the ceiling. He swore violently in Centaurian.

Tessa sat up, setting her gown hastily to rights. He already missed the sight of her breasts, the feel of her internal muscles clenching around him. He already wanted her again with every fiber in his being. How in the hell was he going to live without her?

The past two weeks with her flashed before his mind's eye. The night she'd showed up at that feast, wreathed in power. Their kisses. Their arguments. Their lovemaking. Their laughter. He couldn't do it. He couldn't give her up. He wasn't strong enough.

"I insist that you take the crystal." Her voice was low, but hard as steel. She was serious about this.

"Absolutely not."

She opened her mouth to argue, a mulish look in her eyes,

but he cut her off. Although it was tearing his heart in two, he knew what he must do. He reached deep. As deep as when he star-jumped. Maybe deeper. "Kentar knows I'm here. And he knows I've found a powerful star navigator. More of my kind will be arriving here any time now to make sure you don't get away from us. I'll be rescued soon enough."

She stared up at him, appalled as his meaning sunk in.

To reinforce the point, he said forcefully, "You *have* to leave. If you stay in this time and place, you'll *die*."

"But—"

"Don't ask me to go home and leave you here to Centaurian assassins who will do what I cannot. I will not go. If you stay, I stay. And that's all there is to it."

He didn't bother to send her a taste of his determination to do exactly as he'd said. The frustration in her eyes announced clearly that she believed him.

He spoke urgently. "You have to go, my love. The sooner the better. My kind can travel to within a few minutes of a time and place coordinate. Knowing Kentar, he'll pop into this very room with a half-dozen soldiers armed with needle guns and kill you before you even know he's here."

"I can't leave you!" she cried. Anguish swam in her gaze, and the thought that he'd put it there about drove him to his knees. He couldn't bear to hurt her like this. But the alternative was unthinkable.

"You *must,* my darling. It's the only way for you to survive. Kentar doesn't know when you're from. He won't be able to find you if you have all of human history to hide in."

She flung herself, sobbing, into Rustam's arms and he buried his face in her hair. What was that wetness on his cheeks? And his eyes were burning ferociously all of a sudden.

"Will you find me again?" she choked out.

"I promise. If it takes the rest of my days, I'll come to you again. I swear it upon my honor. Upon my life. Upon my heart."

She looked up at him, her beautiful eyes awash in tears. "Early twenty-first century. The United States. Flagstaff, Arizona. Red Rock University. I'll be there. Waiting for you."

Then and there, his heart broke. She had just laid her life in his hands, telling him when and where to find her, and they both knew it.

He kissed her fiercely and she kissed him back just as desperately.

Still kissing her, he slipped the cuff on her left arm.

And pressed the crystal.

Chapter 23

The first thing Tessa became aware of was a swirl of energy building around her. Where had that come from? The energy was white, not her violet, nor Rustam's blue. Was it Kentar? Had he come back for her already?

And then she recognized the building heat across her skin. No!

She became aware of the clasp of cool metal on her left biceps. Rustam must have slipped the cuff on her and activated it! She couldn't leave him! She wasn't ready!

Another disturbance rippled in the air over Rustam's right shoulder. A vortex...but not the one building around her! This one was yellow. And big. Big enough to encompass a half-dozen people.

A humanoid shape began to materialize. *Hippoclides-Kentar.*

And Rustam had his back to him.

And then it hit her. If Kentar knew she was in this time-place and had come back for her, what would he do to Rustam for letting her slip away?

That big, lovable, exasperating jerk! Rustam was planning to sacrifice himself to let her get away safely.

The heat rapidly built to a prickle, and then to a painful electricity zinging across her skin.

Panicked, she reached for her newfound wellspring of power. She didn't have the faintest idea what she was doing, but opened it up all the way, wrapping all her power, all her love, and even her arms as tightly around Rustam as she could. She concentrated with all her might on bringing him with her. Tessa had heard that it was possible for two people to be brought back to the lab if they were holding on to each other. She was leaving nothing to chance, though. She pictured the two of them racing through space and time together, linked in body, spirit and soul. Pictured them materializing back in the professor's lab inside the quartz booth.

Rustam fought her. *No. You go. I must know you're safe.*

Come with me. Be safe with me.

But—

No buts. We'll figure it out later. But first you have to live.

And then it was too late. As the transparent forms of Hippoclides-Kentar and a half-dozen men armed with needle guns solidified behind Rustam, the ship faded out in a nimbus so bright and hot she couldn't bear to look at it. Her body became unnaturally light, and then there was nothing at all.

Her body—if that was the heavy, awkward thing she was suddenly encased in once more—felt as weak as a kitten's. She was so exhausted she didn't think she could open her eyelids. Twin bands of steel supported her entire weight. The tongues of flame licking at her skin faded away, leaving her hypersensitive and achy.

"Brave little fool," a familiar voice murmured into her hair.

Her lips curved faintly. She forced one eye open to peer up at the underside of a square male chin.

"Are we alive?" she mumbled.

"Yes," he answered, amused exasperation lacing his voice.

She became aware of something warm and vibrant in her hand, pulsing energy into her in waves that rolled over her entire body. She was feeling better by the second. "Where are we?"

"I have no idea. Some sort of glass cage. With some very shocked humans outside. Perhaps you'd better take a look."

She lifted her head, and saw the familiar curved walls of the time-travel booth. Beyond it, the stunned faces of Professor Carswell and Beverly Ashton stared back at her.

Tessa murmured, "We made it. We're home."

He grunted. "You're home. Well, that's one thing I managed to get right, in spite of your meddling."

She grinned up at him. "Hey, you're still alive. Don't knock it. Just as we jumped out, Kentar and his pals jumped in."

"I felt them." He sighed, a heavy sound echoing through his chest beneath her ear. "And now I'm a fugitive. You just threw away everything I ever worked for."

She frowned. "Give us a chance to figure something out. The folks here are pretty smart. We can come up with a plan."

Another deep sigh from him with a skeptical edge.

"Welcome home, Captain Marconi," the professor commented, rising up out of her chair and taking off the time-travel headband as she did so. "I see you've brought along a guest."

Tessa opened the booth's door and stepped out. Rustam followed cautiously.

The professor frowned, looking past him into the enclosure. "I felt three spirits. Where's the third one?"

Tessa whirled quickly, terrified that Kentar or one of his men might have managed to hitch a ride on their time jump. There was no one. Only Rustam, smirking. Smugly. At her.

And then it hit her. *The baby.* She was pregnant, just as he'd said she was. His hand came to rest lightly, but possessively, on the small of her back.

From behind her, Athena exclaimed suddenly, "He's Centaurian! Arrest that man!"

Tessa whirled, flinging up her arms in front of him defensively. "He's with me! He's okay!"

Beverly Ashton stepped forward, glaring. "Are you so sure of that? We've been having trouble with his kind."

Rustam, beside her, held his hands carefully away from his sides. "I mean no one here any harm. I did not intend to come to this time-place at all. I'm afraid Tessa took matters into her own hands and decided to include me in her jump, however."

Athena shot a hard glance at her.

Tessa gulped. "It's a long story."

"In there," Athena ordered sharply, pointing at the sound-proof, surveillance-proof briefing room off the main lab. "You, too," she snapped at Rustam.

The two of them followed her and Beverly Ashton into the chamber and took side-by-side seats at the conference table. Tessa reached out her hand, and Rustam grasped it protectively. Their auras swirled and mingled comfortingly.

Athena's gaze narrowed as she studied the two of them, apparently taking in their shared aura, as well. "Start talking, Captain."

Surprisingly, it was Rustam who jumped in to answer, however. "Let's cut to the chase. She can fill in the details later. Tessa is a star navigator."

Athena retorted impatiently, "We know that. Why else would she be involved with this program? It greatly enhances my ability to time-travel a subject if they carry the latent talent."

Rustam snorted. "There's nothing latent about her talent. She's a full-blown navigator now. She's been making deep space jumps for the past two weeks."

Tessa's mouth fell open. *What?* "What are you talking about?"

He turned his gaze on her. "What did you think was happening every time we made love? Those were jumps. Without a ship and without a focus object, and without crystals, as far as I can tell. But I've been a navigator for twenty years, and I know a space jump when I make one."

Tessa peeked over at the professor and the general in chagrin. Nope, they hadn't missed the making-love bit. Thunder rumbled on both their brows. She swung her gaze back to him. "Are you serious?"

He grinned. "Think about it. The darkness of space. The stars all around. The weightlessness. We were out in the middle of the galaxy."

Her? A star navigator? She mumbled under her breath, "Holy cow."

He grumbled, "Now there's an understatement."

"How come we didn't die in the vacuum of space?"

"I created a pressure and oxygen bubble around us. It's an emergency skill all star navigators learn in case something happens to their ship and it doesn't make a jump with them. We can stay in-between like that for a few seconds, normally, but then we have to jump immediately to someplace with an atmosphere. By the third jump, you were creating the bubble yourself, probably without realizing you were doing it."

"But we stayed there for several minutes at a time." As she realized what she'd just said, Tessa's face flamed. She must be beet-red.

He frowned. "I've never heard of anyone being able to stay for extended periods of time like we did. As best I can figure, our combined star power must've been able to sustain the bubble much longer than a single navigator can."

Athena interrupted briskly. "How did you get here, Mr.—"

"His name is Rustam," Tessa interjected quickly.

He said drily, "Lord Commander Rustam Fisoli d'Antonus,

First Navigator of the Fifth Merchant Fleet of the Centaurian Federation, at your service."

Tessa quickly introduced Professor Carswell and General Ashton to him in return, doing her best to hide her trepidation at his rather fancy-sounding title.

Athena said, "I ask again. How did you get here, Lord Commander?"

He shrugged. "Ask her."

Athena's intelligent gaze turned on Tessa, who answered, "Kentar was jumping in just as I started to jump out. Rustam intended to stay behind and sacrifice himself so I'd make it back here safely."

He winced beside her. *You weren't supposed to figure out that part.*

I'm a military officer. The dynamics of the situation were hardly likely to escape me.

Remind me to stop underestimating you, my love.

She continued aloud, "I couldn't leave him there to die. I reached for my power the same way he did when he moved Artemesia's ship, and I wrapped him in the energy field as best I could."

Athena's gaze swiveled to him.

He supplied readily, "Once I realized what she was doing, and that she'd actually generated a powerful enough vortex to move us both, rather than risk her safety I didn't fight the process. And here we are."

"How did you meet him?" Athena shot at her.

Her mouth twitched in humor at the memory. "We met at an orgy. Xerxes was throwing the party. I sensed the disk as soon as I arrived—" She broke off and held out her hand, in which she still clasped the Karanovo medallion. "Here it is, by the way."

Beverly Ashton, who was sitting nearest to her, took the priceless bronze wedge with a faintly shell-shocked look on her face.

"When we met, I abruptly lost my ability to sense anything unless he was with me." She hooked a thumb in Rustam's direction. "The fragment turned out to be mounted on the figurehead of Queen Artemesia's ship. It sailed the day after I arrived, and the two of us chased it south overland. We had to dodge the battle at Thermopylae, and then we headed toward Athens. We hooked up with Artemesia again just before reaching Salamis. Rustam was her court sorcerer, and she was glad to have him back with her."

Tessa glanced up from the tabletop and realized the two women across from her were staring in open shock. She elaborated, "Rustam crashed his spaceship and was stuck in Artemesia's court as her slave. He used bits of his power to convince her he was a wizard and survived that way until we met."

Tessa looked over at him to see his gaze brimming with amusement and veered back to her main story. "Where was I? Oh, yes. Rustam talked us onto Artemesia's ship and told her the Athenians were escaping the city by sea."

"What?" Beverly squawked.

Tessa replied quickly, "It was too late to change the course of history. The Persian fleet was already bearing down on the straits there. We helped Artemesia not get crushed in the logjam while we found the Karanovo fragment. As soon as we had it, we helped her not get sunk by the Greeks. Then we got out of sight so we could make the time jump and arrived back here."

"And you brought the enemy directly into our lab? What were you *thinking?*" Athena growled.

Tessa flinched. "We only had one crystal between the two of us. I figured if I brought him here, we could give him another crystal so he can get back home."

That brought both women to their feet, their expressions furious.

Tessa cut them off hastily. "Look. It was his job to kill me.

But he chose not to. It was his job to steal that fragment from me, too. But he didn't do that, either. In fact, he insisted that I take it and bring it here. He's the one who slipped the cuff on my arm and activated the crystal. Not me. You have this precious piece of the stamp because of him. We owe him. And I owe him my life."

The two women subsided into their chairs. They were definitely not thrilled about this turn of events. They traded grim looks.

"Go outside, the two of you," Athena ordered. "We need a moment to talk. Alone."

Rustam held her chair for her while Tessa stood up. She smiled up at him but feared the expression didn't reach her eyes. They stepped outside and the door popped shut in its soundproof casing behind them.

"They need to kill me," he murmured. "You might have saved me from Kentar, but I believe you did neither of us any favors. You merely prolonged the inevitable."

"Don't say that!" she cried. "I won't let you die! You were willing to sacrifice yourself to save me, and I'll do no less for you!"

He gathered her into his arms. "Ahh, my brave Tessa. I do so love you."

"And I love you, too. That has to count for something." She rested her head against his chest, comforted by the steady thud of his heart. After a while, she murmured, "You have to live."

"Why's that?" he replied quietly.

"I don't want to be a single parent. And any child of yours is going to be a terrible handful to raise. She'll drive me crazy."

A rumble of laughter rose from deep within him. "It's a boy."

"Don't tell me you can control gender, too!"

He grinned down at her. "Actually, it can be done easily in a lab, but when I impregnate a woman by mounting her, nature takes its course in that regard."

"Ha! So it could be a girl!"

"Either way, our child will still be a handful," he remarked, grinning broadly.

"Just think," Tess groused. "With two star navigators for parents, she'll be jumping all over the galaxy by the time she can walk."

The grin faded abruptly from his face and a fierce light came into his eyes. "That's it! You may have found the answer to our problem!"

She blinked up at him. "I did? What answer?"

"Our child. By receiving the recessive navigator gene from each parent, he's guaranteed to be a navigator."

"And?"

"Not since the very first navigators were identified among my people has there been a female navigator to pass along the gene to her offspring."

"Help me out here, Rustam. I'm not following you."

"All of our children will be navigators. One hundred percent of them. The Centaurians are lucky if one in five hundred children is a navigator now. But with you…" His voice trailed off, his eyes thoughtful. With his arm firmly around her shoulders, he dragged her over to the conference room door and knocked firmly on it.

Athena, startled, opened it.

"I have the solution to our mutual problems," he announced.

The professor stepped back from the doorway. "By all means, let's hear it."

Tessa followed him inside once more. She took a chair while he sat on the edge of the table. Ever the alpha male, assuming a position of dominance in a room, she mused.

And you love it, he shot at her.

You can stop picking my thoughts out of my head like that.

Huh. Like you don't do it to me? he retorted.

She stuck her tongue out at him.

"Are you two done?" Athena asked tartly.

Guiltily, Tessa looked over at her boss. "Sorry."

"Were you telepathic before you met him, Tessa? I don't recall that being in your profile."

She answered, "No. I can only do it with him. And only when we're in close proximity."

Athena nodded. "It appears that you've, indeed, blended your powers."

Tessa met Rustam's startled gaze with one of her own. Indeed, neither one of them had done anything with their powers without being within arm's reach of each other for days now.

"Bonded soul mates," he breathed. "Of course."

"Come again?" Tessa asked.

"It's the stuff of legends among my people. I never dreamed it could be real. It's when two star navigators share one set of powers between them. It's reported that a bonded pair's combined abilities are much greater than the sum of their individual powers. But it has been so long since a female star navigator existed who could bond with a male navigator that it has faded to the status of fable."

"You yourself said you find that most legends have a basis in fact," Tessa pointed out.

Rustam nodded, looking thunderstruck. He turned to Professor Carswell and said, "Your race wants to develop star travel, does it not?"

Athena nodded.

He continued, "Having now mastered time travel, more or less, you will need to turn your attention to star travel. My people know how to star-jump."

The three women at the table nodded, following so far.

"My orders are to remove any potential star navigators from the human gene pool. Traditionally, my kind have assumed that meant killing any latent navigators. But what if I take Tessa with me back to Centauri Prime?"

Tessa stopped breathing. She was pretty sure her heart

skipped a beat. A couple of beats, in fact. Go with him? Back to his home world? Travel to another *planet?*

"I can see to it she's fully trained as a star navigator. I don't believe I have any choice in the matter, actually. It does appear that she and I have, indeed, become a bonded pair. I won't be able to travel without her from here on out."

Athena and Beverly looked as stunned as she felt.

He added casually, "And then, of course, there's the baby. He—or she—will need to be trained as a navigator."

The other women's accusing gazes swung in her direction. Athena nodded slowly. "The third spirit I sensed. You're pregnant."

"It appears that way," Tessa said in a small voice.

Beverly burst out, "With an alien child."

"She's half-human," Tessa protested.

"And half *Centaurian.*"

"Well…yes," she conceded.

Rustam interjected, "And fully a star navigator. Humans have no ability to train this child. But my people can. My people *will.* I promise you that."

"We need to talk again," Athena said abruptly. "Out, you two."

Tessa followed Rustam outside yet again, her head spinning with the possibility of being the first human ever to move to another planet, to another civilization. Not to mention the prospect of getting to be with Rustam, after all!

"Do you think they'll go for it?" she asked him anxiously.

He shrugged. "Who knows?" *Do you still have your cuff on? Yes. Why?*

Between the two of us, we can generate enough power to make a break for it.

This lab's shielded. Unless we're in the booth, we couldn't get out of here.

He sent her a word she didn't recognize.

"Is that my first Centaurian language lesson?" she asked wryly.

He chuckled. "Yes. And never repeat it in polite company."

"Duly noted."

The door behind her popped open. The two women stepped out.

Athena announced, "We've made a decision."

Chapter 24

Rustam held his breath. Everything depended on this. His life, his love, his future happiness. He eyed the time-travel booth and calculated the odds of getting there with Tessa before they were seized. Not good, curse it.

"We will let her go…"

His heart surged in his chest until he thought it might explode right out from behind his ribs.

"But we have a few conditions."

He bottled up his exultation to hear their conditions, nodding cautiously. "And those might be?"

Athena held up one finger. "First, I implant a crystal under Tessa's skin where it cannot be removed. She must always have the option of returning here at her discretion."

The professor held up a second finger. "The child must be allowed to return to Earth to learn of his or her human heritage. You must swear not to prejudice the child against humans in any way prior to his or her return."

Tessa swallowed hard beside him, as if it was just starting to hit her what all he was asking her to leave behind.

Athena held up another finger. "Third, Tessa must be fully trained as a star navigator…and she must be allowed to visit Earth to bring that knowledge to us."

His first impulse was to roar in outrage. He couldn't give away his people's monopoly on star travel just like that! It wasn't within his power to give, and even if he could, he wouldn't.

Athena's hard voice intruded upon his anger. "Think before you say no, Lord Commander. Mankind hovers on the brink of discovering it for ourselves, anyway. Your people have failed to erase the star navigator gene from our race. It's too prevalent in human females for you to ever obliterate it completely, shy of eradicating our whole race. And if you were to do that, you know as well as I do that the entire Centaurian race would be annihilated in punishment."

He snapped, "You do not need to quote galactic law at me, madam. I am well aware of the penalty for genocide."

The professor stared him down, as uncowed as Tessa would have been in the same situation. Gods, these human women were something else. Reluctant admiration filled him for all of them.

"Fourth, you will give us your most solemn vow never to reveal the time-place of this lab or any of the nature of our work or scientific progress to anyone outside this room. Tessa will be responsible for enforcing your promise."

"If I give you my word, nobody will need to enforce it," he snapped, aggravated.

"Do you agree to these conditions?" Athena demanded implacably.

He didn't bother to ask what the alternative was. He already knew. He'd be imprisoned and experimented upon until he died because of their ignorance, or illness or else old age claimed him.

"I agree to your conditions. But the real question is, does Tessa agree?"

He turned to face her and said gently, "You will be leaving behind everything and everyone you've ever known. My culture is vastly different from yours and not particularly friendly to women in general. You will be a star navigator, which will grant you a certain special status among my people. But you will be an oddity at best and an outcast at worst."

She turned over his words, obviously weighing them carefully. Out of respect for her, he did not probe her mind to see what she was thinking. Besides, knowing her, she'd tell him soon enough.

She blurted out, "Will you stop sleeping with other women? I don't want to share you."

A crack of laughter escaped him. She never did or said what he expected. But that was part of why he loved her. He replied honestly, "I haven't thought about another woman since I first laid eyes on you, let alone bedded one, and I have no desire to do so. There has never been another female even remotely like you in my life, and I highly doubt there will be another. And besides, with all our children guaranteed to be star navigators, I'm certain my government will give the two of us strict orders to...how does your kind say it...multiply and be fruitful with one another."

A blush climbed her cheeks. "That would be how we say it, yes."

He looked around the room. "Any other conditions any of you would like to set upon this venture?"

Tessa turned to her superiors and surprised him by asking outright, "Do you expect me to spy on the Centaurians for you?"

Beverly Ashton answered frankly, "Anything we can learn of them would be immensely helpful to mankind. We will not ask you to betray your lov—Lord Commander Rustam. But if he will agree to let you report back to us, that would be outstanding."

"My government will want to review any official reports she sends."

He and the general traded knowing looks. The Ashton woman had caught the nuance in his words. He hadn't put a limit on any unofficial reports Tessa might send back.

Beverly Ashton replied with a tight smile, "Understood. Do you think they might be open to some sort of diplomatic communication at some point?"

He turned the idea over in his head, then answered regretfully, "My kind are a long way from accepting the idea of humans in the galactic community. They still subscribe firmly to the theory that all human females with star navigator talent must be eliminated. I am hopeful that Tessa can begin to change their point of view."

She gulped beside him. "I'm not sure I'm up to something like that, Rustam."

"Of course you are. You won me over, did you not?"

"Yes, but I was able to…"

Sleep with me?

You're a bad man—stop making me blush!

That is what you were going to say, isn't it?

Well, yes.

Aloud he said, "I have complete confidence in you, my dear. You'll do fine."

Athena Carswell looked back and forth between them. "Although this lab is shielded, I am not entirely certain that it is proof against your race's mental powers. The two of you should probably leave as soon as possible. Before more of your kind track this place down by tracking you."

He caught the faint frown that passed over Tessa's brow and probed her aura questioningly with his mind. Ahh. Goodbyes. She wanted to say a few before she zoomed off across the galaxy.

He murmured, "Dr. Carswell, I'll need to align the new set of crystals to my vibrational field before we leave. That will take me a little while." He turned to Tessa. "Perhaps you would like to take care of a few last-minute matters while the professor and I see to the crystals?"

Tessa shot him a grateful look. His own heart swelled in response.

"Are you sure you want to make this journey with me?" he asked gently.

She nodded without hesitation. "Absolutely. I just need to make a few phone calls and then I'll be ready to go."

Worried by the wistfulness in her voice, he commented lightly, "If I make you mad enough, you can always activate your crystal and come back home."

She sent back silently, *Must be the baby hormones kicking in. I'm just feeling a little weepy at the idea of leaving behind my friends and family.*

You can still come back to visit.

True.

But not for too long. I'll never let you go, you know. You're mine forever.

I love you, too.

They exchanged affectionate glances that were heating up fast toward him excusing himself and his consort for a few minutes of privacy when Professor Carswell cleared her throat pointedly and shooed Tessa out of the lab.

He spent the next several hours refining the rather crude crystals the humans were using to better fit his specifications. He hated to think of how many years he was advancing their time- and space-travel program by showing them how to align the vibrational frequencies of the crystals more precisely. But he damn well wasn't risking his family's lives with substandard crystals in the first cross-galaxy jump where their bodies came along for the ride.

Tessa announced that she had one last phone call to make from the lab's conference room—to a woman named Alexandra Patton, a friend who, Tessa casually informed him, was also a powerful psychic. He bit back an impulse to ask for more information on how to locate this Alexandra person, who no doubt also carried the star navigator gene, so his kind could find and destroy her. Tessa didn't understand yet how strongly committed the Centaurian Federation was to stopping humans from acquiring space travel. But she'd learn soon enough once they got to Centauri Prime.

The road ahead was going to be hard for both of them. Were it not for the fact that their children were guaranteed to be star navigators, he'd never dream of taking Tessa back to Centauri Prime with him. She would have been dead before she set foot on the Centaurian home world. But with the double protection of being his consort and their ability to turn out lots of little star navigators, they'd be all right. They had to be.

At the end of the day, he believed in the power of their love. He and Tessa were meant to be together, and neither time nor space was enough to keep them apart. Surely a little thing like politics couldn't destroy them.

He waited impatiently while Tessa completed the call to her friend.

And then it was time.

They stepped into the time-travel booth. As the door closed behind them, Athena asked, "Do you two need a power boost from me?"

He laughed. "Are you kidding? Between the two of us, we can leap across the galaxy and back and hardly be fatigued. A single jump to Centauri Prime will be child's play for us."

He wrapped his arms around Tessa, and she did the same, her warm palms caressing his ribs lovingly.

He murmured, "Ahh, my love, this is going to be a grand adventure."

She smiled up at him with all the love in both of their worlds shining in her gaze. "I wouldn't miss it for anything."

And the familiar indigo vortex began to whirl around them, lifting them and their unborn child up and out of themselves and flinging them forward into their future. Together...

* * * * *

*The adventures of the Time Raiders continue in
New York Times bestselling author
P.C. Cast's thrilling, passionate tale of Alexandra Patton's
time jump to 60 AD Britain—to the mystical period
of Queen Boudica, warrior queen of the Celts.
TIME RAIDERS: THE AVENGER
is on its way to readers next month, October 2009, and will
be available wherever you buy books!
Turn the page for a quick peek at this exciting novel.*

60 AD Britain
Camp of Celtic warrior queen, Boudica

"Good morning, my queen." Alex bowed grandly. She was already starting to like Boudica, and it was easy to catch the spirit of excitement that permeated her camp.

"I'm so pleased to see you. Come close beside me. There is someone I know you will be eager to greet." Boudica's smile was filled with genuine warmth.

Alex's gut immediately began to tighten. Someone she'd be eager to greet? *That* was impossible. She didn't *know* anyone in this world!

"Look who has just joined our camp! Another survivor. Our goddess is certainly merciful. She has brought him safely to us, so that now I have a priestess and a druid in my camp. Caradoc, my kinsman, this is Blonwen, the priestess I was telling you about. It is she who the goddess brought to me last night. You said her name was unfamiliar, but you must know her now that you see her."

A tall man stepped out from the group of warriors who stood at Boudica's back and Alex felt dizzy with shock. It was *him!* The left side of the man's face was marked with the sapphire wode in the swirling *S* of her dreams. She could see that the design went down his neck, spread over his broad shoulder and disappeared into his tunic. She looked from that distinctive pattern into eyes that were an unusual amber color. First she saw shock pass over his face, and then he seemed to draw himself up as he silently studied her with a calculating coldness that chilled her blood.

Before he speaks tell him you have a message for him from me and describe what I am wearing. Be certain to mention the spiral circle on my palm. The ghost of the middle-aged woman spoke from her place beside Alex. *Quickly!* she snapped when Alex only stared at her. *Do as I say before he exposes you!*

"I have a message for you from a spirit with a spiral circle on her palm who is wearing a blue tunic embroidered with roses," Alex said, looking from the ghost to the man Boudica had called Caradoc.

She saw his eyes widen and Caradoc said, "What is the message?"

Alex forced herself not to gasp at the sound of his voice. She'd heard this man before! His was the voice from her dreams. He had been the man who begged her to return to him.

Tell my strong, brave son, with these exact words, that his mother would ask him to once more wait—think—and consider, or he may find himself naked and shoeless and dodging from briar patch to briar patch all the way home.

Alex stared at the woman.

Tell him! she commanded.

Alex turned to Caradoc, who was standing beside Boudica.

The queen was watching Alex with an expression of open curiosity.

"Well…" Alex spoke slowly, making sure she got all the words right. "Your mother asks me to tell you to once more wait—think—consider, or you may find yourself naked and shoeless and dodging from briar patch to briar patch all the way home."

Beside him, Boudica threw back her head and laughed. "I had forgotten all about that! How old were you then, Caradoc? Eleven or twelve?"

Caradoc frowned and told his queen, who was still chuckling, "I was twelve." Alex saw his jaw clench and then unclench as he continued to stare at her. Still, he did not speak to her but said to Boudica, "You did not say she was a Soul Speaker."

Eyes sparkling with amusement, Boudica raised her scarlet brows. "Why would I have to tell you that? Her name should have been enough for you to recognize her. Have your wounds affected your mind, Caradoc?"

Alex had been so shocked to see this man whose face and voice were from her dreams that it wasn't until Boudica mentioned it that she noticed Caradoc was injured. There was a gash at his hairline and he had a linen bandage wrapped around his right arm.

"My injuries have done nothing to my memory. Her name is utterly unfamiliar to me," Caradoc said.

Alex braced herself for Caradoc to decry her, and as she did she felt an unexpected wave of disappointment at the thought that she was probably going to have to return to her own time—and that disappointment wasn't just because she hadn't completed her mission. While she waited for Caradoc to expose her as a fraud and call down Boudica's retribution on her for deceiving a queen, she realized that she wasn't ready to return to her modern life.

"My queen, I do not know her as Blonwen," Caradoc said as his gaze met and locked with Alex's. "I only recognize her as a Soul Speaker."

He wasn't going to expose her? Hesitantly Alex let out a long, slow breath of relief.

"Ah, well, Soul Speaker, Priestess, Blonwen. Is it not all one and the same? I am simply pleased you both escaped." The queen smiled warmly at her kinsman and Alex, then all traces of amusement faded from her and she continued in a much more sober voice, "Tell me, Caradoc and Blonwen, is the Isle utterly destroyed?" Boudica said.

Caradoc gave Alex a long, considering look and then said, "I will defer to the Soul Speaker to answer our queen."

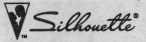

Silhouette®

Romantic
SUSPENSE

> **Sparked by Danger,
> Fueled by Passion.**

The Agent's Secret Baby

by *USA TODAY* bestselling author
Marie Ferrarella

TOP SECRET
DELIVERIES

Dr. Eve Walters suddenly finds herself pregnant
after a regrettable one-night stand and turns to an
online chat room for support. She eventually learns
the true identity of her one-night stand: a DEA agent
with a deadly secret. Adam Serrano does not want
this baby or a relationship, but can fear for Eve's
and the baby's lives convince him that this is what
he has been searching for after all?

Available October wherever books are sold.

**Look for upcoming titles in
the TOP SECRET DELIVERIES miniseries**
The Cowboy's Secret Twins by Carla Cassidy—November
The Soldier's Secret Daughter by Cindy Dees—December

Visit Silhouette Books at www.eHarlequin.com

Touch Me

by *New York Times* bestselling author
JACQUIE D'ALESSANDRO

After spending ten years as a nobleman's mistress,
Genevieve Ralston doesn't have any illusions
about love and sex. So when a gorgeous stranger
suddenly decides to wage a sensual assault on her,
who is she to stop him? Little does she guess he'll
want more than her body....

Available October wherever books are sold.

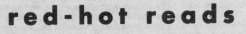

red-hot reads

HB79499

REQUEST YOUR FREE BOOKS!

2 FREE NOVELS PLUS 2 FREE GIFTS!

▼ *Silhouette*®

n o c t u r n e™

Dramatic and Sensual Tales of Paranormal Romance.

YES! Please send me 2 FREE Silhouette® Nocturne™ novels and my 2 FREE gifts (gifts are worth about $10). After receiving them, if I don't wish to receive any more books, I can return the shipping statement marked "cancel." If I don't cancel, I will receive 4 brand-new novels every other month and be billed just $4.47 per book in the U.S. or $4.99 per book in Canada. That's a savings of about 15% off the cover price! It's quite a bargain! Shipping and handling is just 25¢ per book*. I understand that accepting the 2 books and gifts places me under no obligation to buy anything. I can always return a shipment and cancel at any time. Even if I never buy another book from Silhouette, the two free books and gifts are mine to keep forever.

238 SDN ELS4   338 SDN ELXG

Name _____ (PLEASE PRINT) _____

Address _____ Apt. #_____

City _____ State/Prov. _____ Zip/Postal Code _____

Signature (if under 18, a parent or guardian must sign) _____

Mail to the **Silhouette Reader Service:**
IN U.S.A.: P.O. Box 1867, Buffalo, NY 14240-1867
IN CANADA: P.O. Box 609, Fort Erie, Ontario L2A 5X3

Not valid to current subscribers of Silhouette Nocturne books.

Want to try two free books from another line?
Call 1-800-873-8635 or visit www.morefreebooks.com.

* Terms and prices subject to change without notice. Prices do not include applicable taxes. Sales tax applicable in N.Y. Canadian residents will be charged applicable provincial taxes and GST. Offer not valid in Quebec. This offer is limited to one order per household. All orders subject to approval. Credit or debit balances in a customer's account(s) may be offset by any other outstanding balance owed by or to the customer. Please allow 4 to 6 weeks for delivery. Offer available while quantities last.

Your Privacy: Silhouette is committed to protecting your privacy. Our Privacy Policy is available online at www.eHarlequin.com or upon request from the Reader Service. From time to time we make our lists of customers available to reputable third parties who may have a product or service of interest to you. If you would prefer we not share your name and address, please check here. ☐

SN09

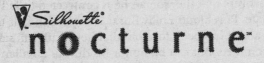

Silhouette®

nocturne™

COMING NEXT MONTH

Available September 29, 2009

#73 TIME RAIDERS: THE AVENGER • P.C. Cast
Time Raiders
For Alexandra Patton, the Time Raider's call sends the reluctant psychic back to 60 AD Briton, a time of brutality and superstition. Armed with only her ability to talk to the dead, Alex must use her feminine charms to entice Caradoc, a savagely sexy Druid warrior, into helping her retrieve the medallion piece crucial to her mission…or risk being stuck in a time not her own.

#74 IMMORTAL WOLF • Bonnie Vanak
As the Kallan, the Draicon werewolves' only executioner, Raphael Robichaux is as ruthless as they come…until he discovers that the woman he is contracted to kill is his mate. Pureblood Emily Burke's very touch kills their kind, and it has been foretold that her death will save the Draicon race. But can he honor his duty as a Kallan by forsaking the woman who is his destiny?

SNCNMBPA0909